I0557457

SHADOW RISING

A LACY MERRICK THRILLER
BOOK 2

ROBIN MAHLE

HARP HOUSE PUBLISHING, LLC.

Published by HARP House Publishing
April, 2017 (1st edition)

Copyright ©2017 by Robin Mahle
All Rights Reserved.

No part of this book may be reproduced, stored in a retrieval system, or transmitted
in any form, by any means, including mechanical, electronic, photocopying,
recording, or otherwise, without the prior written permission of the publisher,
except by a reviewer who wishes to quote brief passages in connection with a
review written for inclusion in a magazine, newspaper, or broadcast. The
characters and events portrayed in this book are fictitious. Any similarity to real
persons, living or dead, is coincidental and not intended by the author.

CHAPTER
ONE

THE DISGRACED FORMER Chinese ambassador stood before his jailer, haggard from weeks of almost total isolation. As he stood in a beam of light that shone inside the minister's office, his hair dangled low on his forehead and an unkempt beard scattered across his face. Lei Jian's recent relocation from the apartment-like accommodations to something akin to a dungeon had been without explanation, until now. Something had changed. And it appeared Beijing had appointed a new minister.

"I'm sure you are wondering why you are here, Jian, and how I came to be standing here now. Firstly, I must apologize for your rather unsuitable lodgings. During the transition of power, there were those who disagreed with your actions against the United States."

Jian looked on, as he knew the previous minister had helped coordinate those actions and this new minister had a different agenda.

"Many threats had been made against your life and, as the newly appointed minister, I could not risk any attempts, successful or otherwise, against one of our former ambassadors. So the premier and I agreed to move you from harm's way. Apparently, you still have his support—for now. Which brings me to the reason you are here today." The minister approached Jian. "The US elections are over and we have met our obligations to them regarding your situation. So you are being released, effective immediately."

Jian studied the new minister. Had they reached some sort of new arrangement with the US? As far as he knew, his sentence was to remain indefinite. This was a cause for concern, one that Jian could not express to this man. A man he didn't know.

"I see no reason why you cannot return to your home." The minister turned from Jian and walked back toward his desk. "With the understanding that you will accept the terms of your release." He pushed forward the papers on his desk and turned to the men who accompanied Jian. "Remove his restraints."

Jian waited until his hands were freed before retrieving the documents and skimming their contents. At this point, it mattered little what they said, so long as he was being released. The rest could be fixed later—after, he would meet with the former minister and gain an understanding of why he was really here. "I will agree to this."

"Then you are free to leave."

"I am grateful, Minister." Jian waited for the guards to open the door and, when they did, for the first time in six months, Jian was free. But there was much to do. He would have to rebuild. The unexpected ousting of the previous minister brought with it a host of new problems. He no longer had the ear of the upper echelons in the ministry. And the ones who had conspired with him were no longer in positions of power. Pressure from the United States had forced Jian into captivity, so who was pulling the strings now, offering freedom?

"Don't forget our agreement, Jian." The minister approached

as Jian stepped through the opening. "The agreement you had with the previous minister is now irrelevant. There will be no contact with your former colleagues." He leaned in to whisper in Jian's ear. "Your negligence has cost us dearly and your release hinges upon your behavior. Should it come to light you have broken any one of your promises, you will be dealt with swiftly and in a most uncomfortable manner." He pulled back and patted Jian on the shoulder. "Now go. Go home to your family. I'm sure they have missed you."

Jian smoothed back his hair before returning the minister's gaze. "*Zàijiàn,* (goodbye.)" And with a curt handshake and smile, Jian departed. However, it had been made clear he was not free, not in the way he had been up until the Americans forced his government's hand.

———

The results had come in and the re-election of the current administration meant the tides had just turned against Lacy Merrick and those who fought with her. She'd been playing the part of the good little soldier at FBI Headquarters for months. Doing her job, finding nuggets of intel that required dissemination in hopes of dousing any potential threats against her country. All the while, knowing the truth about the attack that had ripped her world apart.

She stood alone in her living room, watching the breaking news reports. The same people who had perpetrated the horrific lie would remain in power. The problem did not end with the undersecretary's resignation. And now that months had passed, campaigns had been won, and there were still those who knew the truth, yet kept it hidden, although there had been no guarantees that if the other side won, anything would be changed. Politics were politics and everyone tried to cover their asses. But this was a setback she knew could come and it seemed it had.

Lacy reached for her cell phone and made the call. "Did you see the news?"

"How could I not?"

Agent Will Caison answered in the same tone as she herself must have sounded. "Does this change anything for us?"

"I don't think so. It was going to be an uphill battle regardless. We still have friends, and things are going as planned."

"Does that mean your transfer to Headquarters was approved?"

"Not yet, but it should be any day now. My probationary period here at Louisville is over and Agent Mendez has gone through all the appropriate channels. He knows the importance of what we're doing and he knows this is the only way to continue. We needed to bide our time, but now that the election has passed, we can move forward with less scrutiny."

"You're sure you still want this? I feel like you're the only one making sacrifices."

"Lacy, you've made the greatest sacrifice of all; you lost your husband. What I'm doing? Doesn't compare. And yes, this is what I want."

A knock sounded on her door. "Listen, someone's here. I'd better get going. Talk later?"

"Of course. Bye."

"Bye." Lacy opened the front door. "Hey. This is a surprise. Isn't it a little early for you?"

Aaron Hunter raised the box of doughnuts in his hand. "Brought these. Thought you and the kids might like them. And, I've been up most of the night watching the results come in."

"So you know." She stepped aside to let him in.

"Yep. I suppose it's too early to start drinking." His half-hearted smile faded as he entered. "Guess a sugar rush will have to do."

"I'll get you a coffee." She led the way to the kitchen. "Kids should be down in a minute. Celeste will be taking them to school soon."

Aaron set the box down and grabbed a mug from the cabinet. "I'm glad she's here for you, Lace."

"I'll tell you, she's been an absolute God-send these past few months. And it hasn't been easy for her, I know that." Lacy poured the coffee. "I just got off the phone with Will."

"Oh yeah? How are things going on his end?"

"As planned. He hasn't gotten word yet, but it should be soon."

"I know this is what we wanted, but it doesn't make me any less nervous about what we're doing."

"I'm scared too. I don't know what will happen, or if anything will happen. But we both know that Jay deserved better. All of those who died deserve better."

"They do." He appeared to play down his worries. "It's just that, well, things have settled down. People have been so wrapped up in the election—they've forgotten, or at the very least, want to put it behind them."

"You want to forget too? What they did to Jay? What they did to us?"

"No. I just don't know what more will happen to us—you and the kids, I mean."

"Aaron, I've had nothing but time to think about this. We agreed it couldn't stand. And you know I'll do everything in my power to protect my kids. But I can't live with this. Can you?"

"I wish there was another way."

"We tried—and we made mistakes. We won't make them again. It won't be easy to get to where we need to go. It sounds like you've already written us off and we haven't even started."

"I don't mean to. It's just..."

"Drink your coffee before it gets cold. And I think I'll take this delicious-looking chocolate doughnut." She reached into the box.

"Point taken."

The sound of children's feet padding down the stairs caught Lacy's attention and, a moment later, the kids appeared in the kitchen. "You guys about ready to go to school?"

"Yeah. Can't you take us to school today, Mommy?"

"I have to go to work in a little bit, Jack, but Celeste will take you." She walked toward him and tousled his hair. "Go put on your coat. You too, Olivia."

Celeste was pulling on her own coat when she appeared in the foyer. "Come on, kiddos, let's get going." She continued into the kitchen. "Good morning, Aaron. How are you?"

"Fine, thanks." His words were muffled beneath the mouth full of food. "You kids want a doughnut? I brought them just for you."

"Can we, Mom?" Jackson asked.

"Go ahead, but then you need to get in the car." She turned to Celeste. "Thank you. I shouldn't be late tonight."

"Don't worry if you are. I've got everything under control." Celeste began to usher them through the kitchen and toward the garage side door.

"I know you do. Bye, guys. See you tonight." Lacy returned to her coffee and finished the last of it. "I'd better finish getting ready myself. You don't mind?"

"No. I'll head out. I wanted to stop by to see how you were doing." He stood and grabbed another doughnut. "For the road. I'll show myself out." Aaron kissed Lacy's cheek. "Talk to you later."

———

The promotion that had been dangled before Lacy prior to the attack had been secured shortly after Jay was posthumously cleared of any wrongdoing. A small measure of comfort, save for the fact that the money flowing through from Nova Investments and Argus Solutions had nothing to do with corporate espionage, which it had been ultimately deemed, and everything to do with what was the ultimate goal for the Chinese government. But that was still something she had to prove, that Jian hadn't acted as a rogue agent as the deputy secretary of state had ensured. And in the months that had passed, Lacy had been an exemplary supervisor and it was all by design.

She'd just finished briefing her department head, Michelle Vogel, and was preparing to leave, until Michelle spoke again, turning to another topic Lacy hadn't expected.

"There's going to be a groundbreaking ceremony at the site later this month for the memorial dedication. I've been asked if you might consider speaking."

Lacy halted and locked eyes with Michelle. Words were lost and all she could do was wait for her to continue.

"With everything that happened—I know it's a lot to ask. But the election's over and it seems everyone's eager to put the attack behind them, and moving up the groundbreaking will allow the victims' families to find closure; yourself included. And you're one of us. Frankly, it makes the FBI look good."

Lacy nodded in a way that seemed she was considering her options rather than agreeing to the request. "I'd have to think about it. I can't commit to it right now."

"Of course. Just think about it—please. I wanted to give you a heads-up that this was coming. I know it's been..."

"Right. Thanks for letting me know. I'd better get to work." She could feel Michelle's eyes follow her out the door and the implicit words that trailed. It was a shock to hear that the groundbreaking would be so soon. Lacy hadn't been to the site since her initial visit shortly after the attack. And now, only six months later, they were ready to begin building the memorial that would stand on the perimeter of the mall. Rumors had flown that Nova Investments was going to rebuild on the exact site but took on heavy criticism from the families of victims and survivors. So they instead opted to reconstruct on a nearby property and the site would become a park with the memorial established at the main entrance.

Lacy soon found herself standing in front of her office. An absentminded arrival predicated by troubling reminders, she couldn't recall taking the necessary steps to make it this far. With the flip of a switch, her office lit up and revealed a stark space in desperate need of sentiment. This current version of herself was nothing like the person she was before the attack. She had not felt at home here and therefore did not make it more home-like, with only two exceptions: a picture of her kids and a picture of her family—the very same one that once resided atop Jay's desk and had been the catalyst for her transformation.

Sitting at her desk, Lacy attempted to shift her focus to the job at hand. As the newest civilian regional manager for the FBI's Cyber Division, it was up to her now to meet with her team to discuss the plethora of data from potential terrorist websites, both cyber and radical, that they tried to shut down daily, only to have new ones pop up almost immediately. It was like Whack-a-Mole.

But the arrival of a text message from someone she hadn't spoken with in the past two weeks diverted her attention. Lacy responded and reached for her coat, heading out of her office once again.

She stood under cover of Headquarters' main entrance when rain began to fall from the grey morning skies. The wait, however, was short-lived when she spotted the person from whom the text came. A tender smile appeared on her lips at the sight of the man who'd been responsible for saving not only her life but the lives of her children and her dearest friends.

"Lacy." He offered his hand. "Good to see you."

"A handshake? After all we've been through?" She offered an embrace and he consented. Upon returning to meet him eye to eye, she began, "How are you, Trevor? It's good to see you too."

"Very well, thank you." CIA Agent Trevor Axell pulled her gently toward the edge of the overhang and away from the entrance to avoid eavesdroppers. "I thought it best if we discussed this in person. Sorry to take you away from your office and into the nasty weather."

"It's fine. What's this about? I don't like that look."

"Lacy, I got a call this morning."

"Okay." She swallowed down the lump that had begun to rise in her throat.

"One of our operatives reached out to me. He's in Beijing."

It wasn't the lump in her throat now, but her heart that stopped from fear of what he would say next.

"Lei Jian was set free yesterday."

"How is that possible? I—I thought the Chinese agreed to punish him to keep what he'd done quiet. Does the State Department know about this?"

"I don't know. I haven't made it that far yet, but my assumption is yes. If Beijing wanted to keep open the lines of communication, their ambassador would have made the call. So far as the rest of the department is aware, Jian was a spy and was returned to his government for that reason. So it's not critical to make an objection."

"And so we're just going to agree to this?"

"Oh, I'm sure the deputy secretary will weigh in on the matter. Whether it gets him anywhere, I don't know. Both countries have a lot to lose if Jian speaks out, but I don't think he was released to speak out about it. I came here to tell you directly because my contact thinks he was set free for a reason. They have a new minister in place. He might've let Jian go to finish tying off the loose ends. If that's the case, it's a risky maneuver on their part, one which will require me to gain a full understanding, but what this means is that you, Caison, and possibly Hunter could be targeted. Hell, I could be a target too."

"For God's sake. What are we supposed to do? Will's transfer is imminent. What you're working on with Aaron—everything's been set in motion. We've waited and planned for months. We've laid the groundwork to figure out who knew what and when. Are we just supposed to quit? I can't do that, Trevor, and I think you know that about me by now."

"That I do. This will add an unexpected element we hadn't counted on, Lacy. A very dangerous one. I need time to figure out what Jian's plan is. Why he was freed. I'll have my people keep an eye on him. But in the meantime, keep doing your job, and don't change your routine."

"Are we in immediate danger?"

"He hasn't left the country, and he's not allowed in the US, so no, I don't believe this poses an immediate threat. That being said, I'm doing everything I can to get to the bottom of this and track down his associates to see if there has been any movement from them. We just need to stay alert. I will get answers, Lacy. Very soon."

CHAPTER
TWO

LACY ROLLED out of bed quietly so as not to wake the kids, who were splayed out on her king-sized mattress. She'd agreed to let them sleep with her, at least on the weekends. As if she would ever say no. They all needed each other so much more and while Jackson had shown signs of improvement, Olivia still struggled. More often than not, she wet the bed while in her own room. The girl hadn't had an accident since she was three, but since Jay died, it was happening with much more frequency.

They had been in counseling for months, but Olivia was having the toughest time of all of them, and Lacy was nearly at the end of her rope to find a solution, although the counselor maintained it would just be a matter of time.

Lacy heard Celeste calling up to her from the stairs as she walked out onto the landing. "Yes?" A hushed response.

"I thought I heard you get up. Your phone is ringing. Should I answer it? It's Agent Caison."

"Yes, please. I'm coming." Lacy rushed down the stairs and took the phone from her. "Thank you. Would you mind checking on the kids?" It was her way of asking for some privacy and Celeste was no stranger to that request.

"Morning. Sorry about that. I was upstairs."

"Good morning. This isn't a bad time, is it?" Will asked.

"No. I just got up. Kids and I had a late night. Are you at the office? It's Saturday."

"Yes, actually, I am. But there's a good reason for that."

Lacy peered through the kitchen window and into the yard, recalling that she still needed to rake the leaves because no one else was going to do it. "Care to elaborate?"

"I got the transfer."

She pulled back from the window. "You got it? Today?"

"I got word late last night, actually. It was too late to call you. But that's why I'm here today. Need to start tying up my loose ends, so I thought I'd give you the good news. Also, I talked to Axell. He called me last night. How are you handling everything?"

"I'm not going to lie. I am worried. I wanted to call you, but I knew you had a full plate and..."

"Hey, anytime you want to talk to me, you know you can. And especially about something this big. How's Aaron taking the news?"

"I haven't told him yet. I didn't talk to anyone last night. Just needed some time to process this. With what I've asked from both of you, I wasn't prepared to go down this road. It's another problem and I don't know how we go about handling it."

"I won't be here much longer and we can work through this together. I don't want you to feel as though you're in any danger, or your family. Axell assured me he's got eyes everywhere and if Jian makes a move, he'll know it."

"I hope you're right. It was going to be hard enough getting through this, but now with him back in the mix..." She paused a moment. "When does the transfer take effect?"

"Next week. I'm already looking at apartments."

"Good. And Mendez?"

"We're together on this. One hundred percent. And once I get there, we can do what needs to be done."

———

The border security agent held the passport open, eyeing the picture and the man standing before him to whom the passport belonged.

The dark, slender figure cleared his throat while awaiting the authorization to pass through and enter China from his homeland of the UAE. Ahsan Sajwani hadn't been back here since he was forced to clean up a mess left by his deceased colleagues. And in this moment, it remained unclear if he would be granted entry. However, he had to keep faith that his superior had pulled the appropriate strings to make it happen.

Another glance from the agent, who reached for his stamp. Sajwani held his breath in anticipation of the man's conclusion.

With a push of the stamp, the agent closed the passport book. "*Huānyíng*. Welcome to China." He handed the passport back to Sajwani.

"*Xièxiè* (thank you)." With a polite nod, Sajwani proceeded through to the other side.

A car awaited him and took him to the Ministry on the outskirts of Beijing, near Xiyuan. Upon glancing at the unadorned building, he stepped out of the car and made his way inside, presenting his identification at each step until finally reaching his destination.

He was shown inside by one of Jian's newly appointed security team. "It's good to see you again, sir." Sajwani was only partially versed in Chinese and Jian didn't speak Arabic because most people in Dubai used English.

"It is good to see you too, my old friend." Jian approached him and offered his hand. "Please, come in and sit down. We have much to catch up on." Jian returned to his desk. "Can I get you a drink? You must be ready for one after your flight."

"Thank you, no. I'm fine. I was, however, quite concerned about my entry. How did you manage to pull that one off?"

"Despite what you might think, or what you've been told, I do still have friends in the ministry. There are people out there who feel as we do, which is why I stand here before you today, back in my old office."

"You mentioned on the phone that there were conditions of your release?"

"As you'd expect. I am restricted from traveling outside the country for an indefinite period. I am no longer allowed to act as a consultant with any company outside of China or companies in China who conduct business with the United States."

"And these conditions were imposed by the new minister?"

"Yes, though I believe I will have an opportunity to circumvent his authority and am working on that currently. The premier and I still have a good relationship."

"That is good to hear, sir. I'm not sure we could proceed otherwise. But there was something else, wasn't there?"

"Indeed. It has come to my attention that our friends in America have taken certain measures."

"Our friends?"

"Friends isn't quite the right word. The FBI agent has been transferred to their headquarters."

"I see. To the same location as the woman analyst?"

"Yes."

"You believe they are planning something? Surely they aren't yet aware of your release."

"Their American arrogance would certainly give rise to such an idea. I have people working to get me the details and I am unaware if they have heard of my recent pardon. There are a great many things our friends will need to atone for. My incarceration is but one."

"I suppose then that we will need to put them in their place as our top priority."

"I have friends, but I also have many eyes upon me, and our moves must be planned out carefully." Jian rose. "You should go. Go to your hotel and get some rest. We can meet again tomorrow."

"What should I do in the meantime?"

"Wait for my word. Then we'll reconvene and begin plans to finish what we started."

———

"Hey." A broad-shouldered, stocky blonde stood inside Lacy's doorway.

She turned away from her computer and a wide smile brightened her face. "Will. You're here. I can't believe you're finally here." She met him halfway and threw her arms around his neck. "It's so good to see you. I thought you weren't coming until tomorrow."

"I finished everything that needed to be done and caught an earlier flight. Figured, why not get a jump-start on my new position?"

"Well, I'm thrilled you did. I assume you've already met with your new boss?"

"I have. SSA Kelly."

"What do you think? I don't know much about him."

"Time will tell. Listen, I don't want to keep you. Just thought I'd pop my head in and say hello. And thought maybe we could grab a bite for lunch?"

"How about dinner? I'm slammed right now and it'd be nice not to have to rush. We have a lot to talk about."

"Okay, then. Meet you back here, at say, 6:00?"

"Sure. See you then."

Will began to leave.

"Hey." She stopped him. "I'm glad you're here."

"Me too."

———

Will returned to his office, which was more like a coat closet, but he wasn't going to complain. He wasn't here to ruffle feathers; well, not those feathers. It felt good to be back in Washington. And while he was glad to have been in Louisville for the past two years, he knew he could do some good here. Mendez knew it too and gave the download to his new boss, SSA Sean Kelly, although Will couldn't read Kelly just yet and the two would need to feel each other out for a while. However, time was something he didn't want to squander. There was no telling how long it was going to take to accomplish the goals they'd set forth months ago. And if SSA Kelly wasn't on board, that would add to the growing list of problems.

For now, though, he would take it one day at a time. And the first thing on his list was to get together with Lacy and Aaron. He missed them and didn't realize just how much. They'd become more like a family to him than he'd expected.

He'd found an apartment not far from D.C. proper and was still waiting for the arrival of his furniture, which was supposed to happen this weekend. So, until then, he would be on an air mattress and eating off a cardboard box he'd packed with essentials and brought up with him on the drive. But not tonight. Tonight, he would have dinner with Lacy and he looked forward to it.

———

Noting it was already past six, Lacy started to type a text when the sight of Will caught her attention. "There you are. I was just about to text you. Thought you forgot about dinner."

"Sorry, I'm late. Agent Kelly kept me busy." He walked into her office. "You ready to get out of here?"

"Absolutely." She grabbed her laptop bag and shut down her computer.

"Will Aaron be joining us?"

"Actually, you know I didn't ask him. I should text him. I doubt he has any plans tonight."

"I don't have my car. Took the subway. You mind driving or were you thinking about grabbing something around here?"

"Here's fine. I don't want to drive if I don't have to. Then I can hop on the Metro back here. And just for future reference, that's what we call it around here, the Metro. Not the subway. You don't want to sound like a tourist."

"Duly noted."

———

"I'm glad you could make it on such short notice, Aaron." Lacy opened her menu. "It was a spur-of-the-moment plan. This one over here surprised me by showing up a day early." She looked to Will. "I'm not the only one who has missed having you around."

"Oh? Have you missed me too, Aaron?" His tone was reminiscent of a boy mocking his best friend.

"What? No. I have no idea what she's talking about." His

smirk couldn't be contained. "Just kidding, man. It's really good to see you. We're both glad you're back."

After the waiter brought their drinks, Aaron turned serious. "Lacy told you about Lei Jian?"

"She did and I spoke to Axell." Will tossed back a swig of his beer. "Have either of you talked to him since he brought it to our attention?"

"I haven't," Lacy began. "I wanted to wait until you got here. I've been trying to keep a low profile. Doing my job and all that, like he said."

"Right. Well, this does change things, but as I said, Axell's keeping an eye out. I trust him and I know you guys do too."

"So now that you're here," Aaron said. "What's the plan?"

CHAPTER
THREE

FLAMES BURNED high in the stone fireplace of former Undersecretary Drew Kendrick's den. He peered through the picture window, standing with one hand in his pants pocket and the other holding a glass of scotch whiskey; dueling ice cubes floated inside. All he'd worked for, the relationships he'd garnered, had resulted in what? Becoming powerless and forced into isolation for the "good of the party and the country." The election was over and they'd gotten what they'd wanted, but Kendrick would see no change in his current state. As a result, he'd begun to plan for a different future. The humiliation he'd suffered the day of his arrest and subsequent release; his staff forced to resign with a national security gag order in place so they would not reveal what they had seen that day. Money had begun to dry up and what would he tell his wife when it was finally gone?

His attention was diverted by an incoming call on his cell phone. Upon retrieving it, he noted the caller ID before answering. "Kendrick." He continued to look out onto the grounds of his property, which led to a lake on its southern boundary. "When did this happen?" A sudden shift in his stance as his muscles tensed. "I see. And you're sure there's no cause for alarm?"

While the person on the other end of the line spoke, Kendrick set his drink on the table and began to pace. "Fine. Meet me here in twenty minutes. By the lake." He ended the call and moved again toward the window and the picturesque scene outside that revealed signs of a dying autumn. An ardent desire to reach out to Lei Jian consumed him. He had to know what his former cohort had planned and to ensure retribution was not his goal; at least, not against Kendrick himself. But the risk would be too great. He knew they watched him, monitored him. And now he waited for the only man who would give him options.

Frustrated, he poured another drink and opened the double French doors leading outside to the grassy field blanketed in brown leaves. The fresh, crisp air would help to clear his head. As he saw it, he had two choices: face a government that wanted to bury him or offer himself to a government that might welcome him with open arms.

Kendrick reached the muddy banks of the lake and turned his gaze upon the surface that reflected the bare trees surrounding it. There had to be a way to regain his former influence. The deputy secretary had banished him and the president refused to answer any correspondence. He was alone and Jian was now free.

The sound of leaves crunching underfoot made Kendrick take notice of the man who was now approaching—the man whom he'd spoken to only a short time ago and had given him the unexpected news. "Watch your step. It's a little muddy over here." Kendrick turned to take in the view of the lake once again.

"Thank you for agreeing to meet."

"Did I have a choice?" Kendrick replied.

"Drew, we have reason to believe that Lei Jian will come after you."

"Why the hell was he released? Who authorized that?"

"I wish I knew. Possibly to get him to finish what he started, which he might well do, given the chance. Then they can say they had no part in it. That it was all of Jian's own doing. I can't pretend to know why the MSS would want to start this up again. I don't get involved in that end of things."

"What am I supposed to do?"

"Is there something you want to tell me, Drew? Something that you might be thinking of doing?"

"What are you talking about? I've protected Jian, I've protected our government all along, even after being forced to resign from my position. I never went back on my word." He brushed his fingers through his greying hair. "Thank you for letting me know about this, but Jian must understand that our government did everything possible to keep him from undue punishment. This has nothing to do with me. Not anymore. I have no intention of doing anything except sit here like I have for the past six months." With a final nod, Kendrick continued, "I appreciate the information. Goodbye."

He watched as the man walked away and grew more concerned that they already knew what he'd done. But how the hell could they? He grunted. "Stupid question."

As he turned again, admiring the landscape, the sound of approaching steps once more reached his ears. "Forget something?" Kendrick began to turn when brawny arms wrapped around his neck and his eyes bulged from the pressure. He caught sight of the man causing him harm. "Stop. Please. I didn't say anything. I swear." His airway was closing with little chance for fresh oxygen and his face reddened. He continued to eye the man who was choking the life from him. His fingers worked to pry the powerful forearms from his neck.

Kendrick's head grew light and his vision blurred, but he

continued to struggle, not knowing why this was happening. He'd done everything he said. Kept out of sight, didn't reveal what he'd known. And this was how they were going to repay his loyalty? Thoughts of his wife, Beth, his grown children, and their families. He was about to lose it all. "Why?"

The man pulled back one of his arms and reached for his weapon. He pressed a gun fitted with a silencer into Kendrick's ribs and fired. He released him and Kendrick slumped to the ground. His final question was never to be answered.

———

Inside the CIA headquarters at Langley, Counterterrorism Analyst Trevor Axell reached for the badge that lay on his desk. "You'll need this."

"Thank you." Aaron held his newly minted identification badge between his fingers, examining it with disbelief. "I don't know how you were able to pull this off, but I appreciate it. Lacy appreciates it."

"We all want the same thing here. I won't lie, though; with your sketchy history, I had to call in a lot of favors to get you approved as a contractor. And if I were you, I'd watch your back for a while."

"What do you mean by that?"

"I mean, most of these guys are former staffers coming back as independent contractors because they get paid more. It'll take time for you to gain their trust in there. Be careful what you say and who you say it to."

"Got it." Aaron began to rise.

"You know what we need to do and this will be the best possible place for you to do it. But make no mistake, there will still be risks and I hope you'll be up for the challenge."

"I am. Too much has happened for me to go back to who I was."

"Yeah. The truth has a way of doing that to you." Axell began to show Aaron out. "Monday morning. Don't be late. My ass is on the line here."

"I won't be late." He offered his hand. "Thank you, Agent Axell. We wouldn't have gotten this far without you."

"I know." He smiled. "Go on. Have a good weekend."

———

Beth Kendrick pushed through the doors of her husband's den. "Drew?" She stepped inside and surveyed the room. The fire had dwindled to nothing more than a few glowing embers. Upon spying the French doors, she noticed they were unlocked and began her approach. "Why on earth are you outside without your coat?" She stepped outside and raised a hand to shield her eyes from the glare of the setting sun. "Drew? Honey, are you out here?"

No answer.

She continued farther and shouted again. "Drew? It's time for dinner." Her pulse began to rise with growing concern. It had been three hours since she'd seen him. Beth wrapped her arms around her body for warmth. "Honey, where are you?"

The leaves before her spun from the ground as the breeze kicked up, sending a chill down her already cold body. He wouldn't have left without telling her, so she was confident he was outside somewhere and continued. The house became smaller in the distance as she turned to look back, but Beth pressed on in search of him.

The water lapping against the shores of the lake sounded ahead as she moved in its direction. "If you're out here, ignoring me, you can just forget about dinner." Leaves crunched and twigs snapped beneath each step as she neared the lake. Her eyes squinted again from the glare of the water that made it appear as though something had floated ashore. Another few feet closer and her expression fell.

Beth began to jog until she reached the edge of the lake and saw exactly what was in the water. "Oh God." She ran closer. "Drew? Drew?" Her voice raised to a shout and, upon arrival, she stopped cold. Her hand thrust over her mouth and she shook her head wildly. "No." Her legs became almost too heavy to keep moving forward, but she forced them. "No. No. Drew?"

Finally, she stood over him; her feet were in the freezing water, but she could no longer feel them. Her entire body fell numb. She began to scream. "Drew!" Her hands clamped down on his shoulders and she turned his heavy body upward from the water.

His face was blue, the veins in his eyes burst, and the water around him still flowed red. Beth tried to drag him out by his legs, but he was too heavy, his body caught in the mud. When they fell again from her grip, she stopped.

Her wet hand slipped inside her pocket and grabbed her phone. She tried to steady her fingers enough to dial 911. When they finally did, she answered the operator's question. "My husband is dead."

———

Lacy held two glasses of wine in her hands as she returned to the living room. "Here you go."

"Thanks." Aaron sipped on the mild cabernet. "You want to see it?" He reached into his shirt pocket and withdrew the badge, handing it to Lacy.

She held it between her fingers, eyeing the photo. "Not a bad picture. Hard to believe this is really happening."

"I've been saying that for the past six months. Yet here we are, plotting to go up against very powerful people and now I find myself on the inside."

"That's never been a comfortable place for you." She returned the badge.

"No, it hasn't." Aaron swirled the wine in his glass, appearing captivated by the motion. "But I know this is important and I know history will favor us someday."

Lacy raised her glass. "To making history."

The sound of her doorbell rattled them both.

"Are you expecting someone?" Aaron asked.

"No." She rose from her chair and peeked through the window curtains. "It's Will." Her brow furrowed as she walked to answer the door. "Will? I wasn't expecting you."

"Is this a bad time?"

The look on his face sent a wave of sobriety through her. "No. Come in. What's going on?"

"We need to talk. Is that Aaron's car outside? Is he here?"

"Yes. We're just having a drink in the living room. Can I get you something?"

Will turned his attention to Aaron, who seemed surprised by his arrival. "Whatever you two are drinking."

"Sure. Why don't you go sit down?" Lacy continued into the kitchen while Will made his way to Aaron.

"What's up?" Aaron was never good at playing it cool and his face couldn't hide the anticipation of Will's unexpected arrival.

"Something's happened and it's going to change things for us." He took a seat on the sofa.

"I don't like the sound of that." Lacy returned with a glass for him. "Like we're going to need something stronger than wine." She returned to her chair. "What happened?"

Will downed half the glass before continuing. "Drew Kendrick was found floating in the lake on the edge of his property earlier this evening. Shot dead."

Lacy's face deadpanned as she carefully placed her glass on the side table. "Murdered."

Will could only nod his confirmation.

"How do you know this? Who told you?" Aaron asked.

"Alexandria police were dispatched to Kendrick's home after receiving a 911 call from his wife. After they arrived on the scene and realized who it was, they called Headquarters." He finished off the glass. "From there, word spread pretty quickly and it reached our department. My new boss called us in, believing it could be a terrorist-related event."

"Because since the attack, everything is being treated like terrorism," Lacy added.

"Pretty much."

"What does this mean for us?" Aaron asked. "Who do you think killed him? Jian? I thought Axell had eyes on him."

"Might not have been him, but it makes the most sense that he would've ordered it," Lacy began. "He and Kendrick had an agreement. Why wouldn't he take matters into his own hands and silence the only one who knew the whole story behind the attack and had direct involvement? Maybe as a way to regain favor in his own government. What's the Bureau's plan?"

"It'll be a murder investigation of a retired government official, handled by the Washington Field Office, with our department receiving updates as necessary."

"You haven't answered my question. How does this change *our* plans?" Aaron asked.

"Depends on who's responsible. In my opinion, Jian had the

most to lose with Kendrick around. Could've been retaliation or simply tying up loose ends. What I think it means for us is that we don't have as much time as we thought we had. Whoever killed him wanted him out of the way for their own gains."

"This isn't loose ends. This is retaliation for him being locked up and Kendrick having faced zero punishment. And I doubt he'll stop there. He knows who we are," Lacy replied.

Aaron regarded her with a growing concern. "And where."

———

Inside CIA headquarters wasn't a place Aaron Hunter had ever expected to find himself. Nevertheless, he stood in the lobby of the old building, staring at the wall of unnamed fallen agents, and was humbled.

"Mr. Hunter?" A young woman in a pencil skirt and buttoned-down blouse approached.

"Yes. I'm Aaron Hunter." He fumbled for his badge.

"You'll want to put that on. Please, follow me. I'll show you to your workstation." She began to head back into the building. "So, where did they find you?"

"Sorry?"

"Most of the contractors we use come from a firm or were former employees or something like that. So, where are you from?"

"Oh, one of the firms."

"Okay. You don't have to tell me. Just making conversation. I'm Renee Childs. I'm responsible for your training, getting you access, and helping you get settled in."

"Nice to meet you, Renee. You'll have to forgive me. I'm not used to working around a lot of people. I can be a little anti-social."

"So are most of the people working here. Don't worry about it.

You'll have your own space. We're very segmented here. And it's that way on purpose."

"If I told you, I'd have to kill you sort of thing?" Aaron chuckled.

"Something like that."

Aaron seemed concerned when she didn't laugh in return. He thrust his hands in his pockets and continued to follow her, dispensing with any further small talk.

"This is it. This is your workstation."

Aaron surveyed the less-than-ideal workspace. "You weren't kidding about seclusion."

"Oh, we don't joke around here." At this, she finally smiled.

An awkward laugh escaped him as he reconsidered what he'd gotten himself into.

"I'll get you logged in. Show you how to navigate the programs and, within a few days, you should be up and running on your own. I'll be available to answer any questions, though. I don't want you to feel abandoned. Should we get started?"

"Ready when you are."

Aaron had always been a quick learner, which was what made him one of the best white hats around. Those were the good guys, in hacker terms. They helped to find loopholes in programs and weak security so that they could fix them for companies who hired him. Technology changed faster than any other industry and it was his job to keep up on the latest in cyber security, the dark web, and keep his clients safe. But this was different. The programs the CIA used were unlike anything he'd ever seen. The sheer magnitude of their reach was both beautiful and terrifying. And all in the name of national security.

"Why don't you take a look at a few of the reports I've put together for you? It'll give you a sense of what we're looking for from an analysis standpoint. I have a briefing to attend, but I'll be back in about an hour. Should give you enough time to get familiar with things."

"Sure. Thank you." Aaron waited for her to leave the small space that could scarcely pass for a cubicle. There were five others in his quadrant, each confined to similar spaces. He assumed each worked on similar but different aspects because as Renee indicated, segmentation was key.

It almost seemed counterintuitive to Aaron, though. Too great an opportunity to miss something when everyone worked on separate tasks. Perhaps there was an overseer who would piece everything together and the lowly data miners merely input their findings.

However, the opportunity for some alone time was exactly what Aaron needed right now. Perusing the reports, deciphering the data and how it was gathered was his best chance at getting to the information he needed.

As he began to understand the inner workings of this part of the clandestine agency, interpreting the materials and sources from which they were derived, a pattern formed. It was this pattern that he would need to fully understand because what he was looking for would not simply present itself. It would be buried deep inside the code, the data mined, and the capabilities of the programs themselves. Once he was armed with that information, he could use it to find out the depth of the conspiracy. Something they had been working on for a long while, only making little progress. And with Agent Axell's help, that conspiracy could be exposed, and finally, the truth would be revealed.

CHAPTER
FOUR

THE SCHOOL BELL rang and children poured out of the building, scattering in every direction. Lacy waited by the main entrance. "Do you see your sister yet?"

"No. Not yet." Jackson held his mother's hand and peered into the yard.

"There she is. Up ahead." She tugged at her son's hand as they walked to meet Olivia halfway.

Olivia searched for them through wisps of hair that swathed her face in the wind. Lacy raised her hand and caught the young girl's attention. But something else caught hers at that moment. From the corner of her eye, she spotted a man in an overcoat and hat in the distance. His motionless presence was a stark cry from the hordes of children and parents who collected them.

The man stood at the far end of the entrance, hands in his coat pockets and appearing to stare directly at Lacy through his thick-rimmed, shaded lens. Her hackles raised immediately in response. It was the same wary feeling that she was being watched. For weeks after Jian's capture, Lacy constantly peered over her shoulder, fearing he would send more people after her, or Aaron, or all of them. But nothing ever came of it and, after a time, the feeling passed. Now it was back. Months later and knowing Jian was again free, she began to fear for the safety of her family, despite Axell's best efforts to reassure her otherwise.

"Come on, sweetheart." They reached Olivia and she pulled both children along with haste to her car. While opening the rear door, she cast her sights in the direction of the man in the overcoat. "Get in, guys—quickly."

Lacy jumped into the driver's seat and started the engine. A final glance outside the school and the man had disappeared. In the rearview, she checked the kids were buckled in and began to pull out of the parking lot, still in search of the mystery man, but he was nowhere to be found. Her pulse still raced as the memories of past fears resurfaced.

"Are you okay, Mom?" Olivia asked.

"Yes. I'm fine, baby. Let's just go home. We're all fine." Her attempts to convince even herself of this fact had failed.

They returned home in what seemed to be record time and Lacy ushered the kids inside.

"Hi, kiddos." Celeste offered them a warm greeting.

"Would you mind getting them a snack? I have to make a call." Without waiting for a response, Lacy stepped out through the rear door and onto the deck that overlooked the lush back garden. With her phone pressed against her ear, she began, "Hey, it's me. Can you talk?"

"Hang on," Will replied.

Lacy paced the deck, her heels sinking a little into the wooden slats that were soft from recent rains. She eyed the large back garden as though someone might appear from behind a tree.

"Okay, I can talk now. What's going on?"

"I was at the school, picking up Olivia, and I saw someone."

"Who?"

"I didn't recognize him, but Will, I felt like he was watching me or Olivia, maybe both of us."

"Wait, now just hold on a second. Are you sure about this? You remember what it was like for you a few months ago? Are you sure you're not just having a little bit of a setback, given everything that's happened recently?"

"No. I'm not paranoid, okay? A man in an overcoat, wearing dark sunglasses was watching us. I'm certain of it."

"Did he follow you?"

"No. I started to pull out of the parking lot and he was gone. Just disappeared." She gripped the deck railing. "Will, I think it was one of Jian's people. I think he's going to come after us."

"Okay, Lacy, I need you to take a breath. Calm down a minute and think about what you're saying."

"Please don't. I know what I saw. Drew Kendrick was murdered and now I see someone lurking at my kid's school? No way is that a coincidence. What are we going to do?"

"I'll come by after work and we can talk more about it, okay? For the time being, just stay at home. Don't go to the store, don't send Celeste out; just hang tight. I'll be there in a couple of hours."

"Yeah, okay. Thank you, Will." Lacy ended the call and turned toward the doors, peering inside the kitchen.

The kids were eating a snack while Celeste drank a cup of coffee. Lacy was torn, once again, between fighting for the truth and fighting for the safety of her family. They had to come first and that could mean leaving the only home they'd ever known. Jian had proven once before that he could get to her family. Had he just done it again?

———

Lacy closed the refrigerator door and handed a bottle of beer to Will while she popped open a can of Diet Coke. "Thanks for coming over. I'm sure it's been a long day for you."

"I won't dismiss what you felt today and I think it's good we hash it out and see if we're dealing with a real problem here." Will wrapped his hand around the cap and twisted it off the bottle. "Thanks for the brew."

"I'm not being paranoid. I know what I saw. I know the parents who pick up their kids and this guy stood out like a sore thumb. And if it turns out he's one of Jian's men, then there's no way we're safe here."

"We should talk to Axell. If Jian or his people are on the move, he'll know it."

"And in the meantime?"

"In the meantime, maybe you should consider taking Olivia out of school."

Lacy peered into the darkened street outside, flicking the ring on the can of Diet Coke. "I've tried so hard to return them to normal." She turned back to Will. "You know how long it took for them to stop sleeping in my bed? They haven't. They aren't over this and neither am I."

"Of course you're not. This was never going to be easy on any of you and I'm so very sorry about that. But you do still have a choice, Lacy."

"Do I?"

"With Jian free, the Bureau can protect you. Send you some-place safe."

"No—they can't. No one knows what really happened. Not at our level. Mobley made a deal with the deputy secretary. Kendrick retired, and Jian was sent back to Beijing with the promise that they would handle him." She took a drink of soda. "And look how that turned out. It was all so neatly swept under the rug. The only one in power who can help us is Director Mobley, and we both know what happened the last time he tried."

———

Aaron unlocked the door to his apartment and entered the cold one-bedroom unit. He made his way to the thermostat, noting it showed 57 degrees. "Damn it." He tapped on it several times and soon realized the heat had once again cut out. The hour was late and no after-hours maintenance was offered in his budget-friendly, slightly down-market building. He walked toward the coat closet and retrieved the space heater employed for such occasions, as they happened more often than not. Now that he was getting a steady paycheck from the CIA, he just might be able to afford to leave this shithole and get something decent. However, that could just be a pipe dream. What he had been tasked with, if caught, could find him in prison for the rest of his life. Still, he could hold out hope.

Aaron smiled at the absurdity while he warmed his feet by the heater and rested on his couch. His thoughts turned to Lacy. He'd expected to hear from her and considered reaching out. It was late and what did he have to say anyway that would be at all comforting?

He hadn't seen much of her in recent days, while he was being screened by the CIA. Whatever Agent Axell had done, whatever strings he'd pulled, he'd done well because Aaron had no business being allowed to handle classified information. While he'd never been convicted of any wrongdoing, there had been a time when he would offer advice to novices in the industry via his blog. And well, once something was on the internet, it never really went away. But there was something larger at stake now, a cause that Axell believed in too and so he did what he did for it—

and for Lacy, a woman for whom he cared deeply, perhaps too deeply.

The two had spent much time together in the months after the attack. Sometimes it was only to keep each other sane in this madness, but sometimes it was for her to lean on him; have his shoulder to cry on when she needed it. Not that it happened often. Her strength was admirable. But he was there for her and now so was Caison. He admired Will too. All he'd done to help them both through this. Hell, he saved their lives. But it didn't change the jealousy he'd begun to feel since his arrival. Now she had both of them to offer comfort. In the back of his mind, Aaron believed Lacy could have feelings for Will. She never alluded to it, of course. She still loved Jay, no doubt about that, but he was gone and, at some point, she would find another.

———

Ahsan Sajwani waited in line at airport security in Beijing. He approached the officer and handed over his UAE passport.

"Headed home?" the officer asked.

"Yes." He remained expressionless as the man perused the pages of his document and scrutinized the photo.

The officer stamped the passport and handed it back to Sajwani. "Have a pleasant flight, sir."

With a nod, Sajwani made his way to the gate and boarded the plane, traveling first class. He pressed the call button for a flight attendant.

"Yes sir?"

"May I get a cocktail, please?"

"Certainly, sir. What can I get you?"

He placed his order, knowing that once he arrived back in Dubai because he was Muslim, alcohol was generally not allowed.

Sajwani was hardly a devout Muslim, though. If he had been, his god would certainly punish him for the atrocities he had already committed. But in the eyes of the UAE, he was. It was easier for him to obtain the information he needed and garner the help he required if he appeared devout. So he played whatever role was necessary to achieve his goals and the goals of the man who paid his bills.

The plane soared into the skies and, shortly after leveling off, his drink arrived.

"Thank you." While sipping on his cocktail, Sajwani retrieved his laptop and began to work. The task set forth by Lei Jian would not be an easy one, but the ball was already rolling, as they say, and it was up to him to put in place the necessary arrangements to move forward.

Several hours later, Sajwani awoke to the captain's announcement that the plane was descending into Dubai airport. The nine-hour flight was almost over, but Sajwani's day had just begun.

On arrival, he hailed a cab. "The Excelsior Hotel, please." He turned on his cell phone and made the call. "I'm here. Yes, sir, I understand what needs to happen. I'll be in touch when it's done."

The hotel room he'd booked was on the top floor and, upon his arrival, a package awaited him. Sajwani opened the large box and unlocked the case inside it with a key from his pocket. He raised the lid and examined the contents before retrieving it.

The slender barrel of the M82 military-grade weapon brought a smile to his face as he caressed it with every bit of the passion of a man caressing a woman. The .50 caliber sniper rifle was the perfect tool for his current needs and was a gift from Jian to get the job done.

Sajwani secured the scope and held it to his eye, aiming it toward the window of his room. He carefully placed the rifle back in its case and prepared for the next morning. The planning involved had been extensive and the time had come for him to execute the first part of the task Jian had sent forth.

––––––––

Construction in Dubai was ongoing and Sajwani used that to his advantage. He was situated on the fifth floor of a building adjacent to the target. Interior construction was almost complete, but work would not commence today. A call to the project managers confirmed it would remain empty until the afternoon, at which time the job would already have been completed.

The precision required meant any changes would result in the calling off of the mission. With his phone to his ear, he began, "Is he on time?" He waited for an answer. "Good. I'm here." Sajwani placed his phone on the ground began to set up the tripod and cut the opening into the window. The winds whistled through the newly breached glass, although he was on a lower floor and the enormous structures surrounding the building shielded much of it. He leaned down and peered through the scope to set up his aim.

The building across the street was in his sights. The sixth-floor boardroom with a large conference table occupied much of the space. Many factors had been taken into consideration in order to make the shot count. The wind, the height, the trajectory, and, finally, the window on the other building. But the .50 caliber weapon was chosen specifically for this task and could easily penetrate the standard level 4 glass that surrounded the building, and take his target down with accuracy.

––––––––

Mr. Marquez, president of the Bank of Panama, entered the conference room of the Dubai developer his bank was attempting to woo. Surrounded by his usual entourage, he approached the table where others in attendance had already gathered. "Mr. Salim, it is an honor to finally meet you in person. Thank you for the kind invitation to your beautiful city."

"It is a pleasure to meet you as well. Please take a seat and we can begin."

———

Sajwani tensed as he spotted his target. Through the lens, he watched the man shake hands with the others in the room and move toward his chair. This was the moment he waited for. Pressure from his index finger was applied slowly to the trigger and, in a split second, the bullet struck a hole through the glass and pierced the man in the back. Mr. Marquez crumpled to the ground while those around him scattered.

Sajwani raised with confidence, lowered the rifle, and made his departure.

CHAPTER
FIVE

VISIONS of the charred remains of the mall hovered in the back of Lacy's mind, sometimes drifting to the forefront at night while she slept. Sometimes they appeared while she was in the middle of a conversation, and for no other reason than to remind her of what she'd lost. And now here they were again, distracting her from noticing Celeste had knocked on her bedroom door.

"Lacy? May I come in?" Her voice sounded on the other side.

Lacy pulled herself from the bed and reached for her robe, which rested on the bench at its foot. "Hang on a second." As she secured the belt around her slight waist, she continued, "Come in."

"I didn't mean to wake you; it's just that Mr. Axell is here to see you."

"He is?" She began to smooth her hair. "I'll be right down. Please offer him a coffee, if you would."

"Certainly." Celeste closed the door.

As her footfalls faded in the distance, Lacy's thoughts quickly turned to why Agent Axell had arrived unannounced. She reached for her cell on her nightstand. No messages. She approached her bedroom window and peered through, noticing that his car was parked alongside the front of her home. Lacy dropped the curtain and quickly changed into clothes and pushed her hair back with a headband.

Moments later, she reached the top of the landing where Agent Axell waited at the bottom. "Good morning." Lacy stepped cautiously after noting his blank expression. "What happened?"

He waited for her to reach the bottom of the stairs. "I'll take that coffee now."

Lacy walked into the kitchen. "Thank you, Celeste. I'll take it from here." She poured two mugs full of fresh brew and placed one in front of Axell while he pulled out a stool to sit down. "Here you go." She waited for him to begin, but instead, he sipped on the coffee.

"We've got a problem, Lacy."

"Forgive me, but that seems obvious. What's happened, Trevor? Are Will and Aaron okay?"

"Yes. They're fine. Sorry. I should've started with that."

Her shoulders dropped with relief. "Thank God."

"You know I've got people watching Jian?"

She nodded.

"He's got someone working for him again, which I suspect is Ahsan Sajwani, but I don't have confirmation of that yet. And I just received intel that the president of the bank in Panama, the one used to transfer the money..."

"Yes, I know." Lacy was growing impatient, partly due to a lack of caffeine and partly due to Axell's dance around the problem, a tactic he was not prone to using.

"He was in Dubai for a meeting with a developer and was assassinated yesterday morning."

Lacy leaned against the back row of cabinets. "Kendrick's dead and now Marquez." Her lips pursed, turning them white as she cast her stare through the kitchen window. "I saw someone at my kids' school last week." She returned her attention. "Jian's coming after me, isn't he? He's killing everyone who was involved with the cover-up. And now it's my turn."

"I don't want to jump to conclusions, but I'm starting to think that's a possibility."

"Come on, Trevor." Her lips raised into an ironic smile. "You don't *think* so. You wouldn't be here if that were the case. You *know* so—don't you?"

"I can't say with absolute certainty, Lacy. But it's time to start taking extra precautions."

"I'll protect my children at any cost; you know that. But if I'm not safe, then neither is Aaron or Will, and neither are you or Agent Colburn."

"Don't worry about us. We can handle ourselves."

"You don't think I can handle myself?"

"That's not what I said. You have your kids to think about and I understand that."

"Do you have children, Trevor?"

He nodded. "Two of them. Senior in high school and a junior in college."

"And a wife? I've never asked you about your family in all this time."

"She passed a few years ago."

"I'm sorry. I didn't know."

"I know you didn't. So you see, you're the one in the precarious position here. Your children can't afford to lose you too."

"What are our options? What extra precautions can we take?"

"Like you, I believe your children are the most important consideration in this. At the very least, if you want to continue, then you need to take them someplace safe. Someplace where they can't be touched."

"For how long?"

"As long as it takes."

Lacy began to consider the idea of leaving them after promising never to put them through that again. Jackson was still young enough to forgive her, but Olivia—her maturity reached far beyond that of a seven-year-old, especially since Jay died. The older sister had taken it upon herself to care for Jackson in a way Lacy had never seen before. She'd become a mother to him, almost.

And where could Lacy send them this time where they would not be found? Jian had already proven his ability to reach them once before. Perhaps that was the fault of the man sitting before her now, warning her of the need to separate from her family once again. She studied Axell. He was a man who showed little emotion. A man who did not mince words. What he was telling her was the truth. "I know where they'll be safe."

"Then don't tell anyone. Not me, not Caison, and not Hunter." Axell began to rise. "And Lacy, you won't be able to stay here. It's too risky. Neither will Celeste."

Lacy followed him to the front door.

"Don't do anything from here." Axell surveyed the foyer and living areas in his view. "You understand?"

She nodded. "Thank you for coming by." Lacy pulled open the door. "You'll let me know if anything else turns up?"

"I will. Goodbye, Lacy, and—I'm sorry."

Upon closing the door, she turned to glance up at the staircase. The kids were still asleep. There was only one place Lacy knew would be far from Lei Jian's reach. A place her children had never once visited. A place where they would know no one, not even the ones with whom they would be living.

Her still-wounded heart broke again under the weight of this decision. She wasn't even sure they would take her kids, but she would have to try. There was no other place.

Lacy walked to the foyer table and pulled open a drawer. She retrieved a disposable cell phone that was tucked inside and reached for her keys. "Celeste?" She walked into the family room. "I'm going for a run."

"Everything all right?"

"Yes. Everything's fine. I won't be long."

"It's cold outside. You should take your fleece."

"Thank you. I will." She reached for her hoodie that hung on the coat rack and opened the door. The air hit her skin like a quick blast of icy air from a freezer.

She pulled a deep breath into her lungs and began to jog down the path to the sidewalk and away from the cul-de-sac. Behind the homes was a trail that carried alongside the untouched government lands dense with trees and streams flowing through to an inlet a few miles away. This was not a run to clear her head or consider her options; this was a way to gain distance, to get to a place where she could make the call no mother would ever want to make.

Upon reaching a safe distance away from her home, fearing she might already be under the watchful eye of the enemy, Lacy retrieved the burner phone and made the call. She waited for an answer, hoping there would be one because leaving a message of this sort was out of the question. She hadn't spoken to her since the funeral and the two were never close, which she regretted, especially now.

"Megan? It's Lacy."

"Lacy? I didn't recognize your number. How are you? How are the kids?"

"Fine. We're all fine. Hanging in there, you know."

"Sure."

"I'm sorry we haven't spoken in a while. Not since the funeral, but..." Lacy inhaled deeply and shut her eyes to stop the stinging.

"Is everything okay?"

"Megan, there's something I have to ask you." Her words struggled to free themselves as she was forced to come to grips with this new reality. "I need to know if you can take care of the kids for a while."

"Take care of them? You mean, have them stay with us? Here in Long Island?"

"Yes."

"What's going on, Lacy? What happened? Why are you asking me this?"

"I can't say, not yet and maybe not ever. I need to know if you and Eric can do me this favor I never thought I'd have to ask. Can they come and live with your family for a time until I know it's safe for me to bring them home?"

"Safe? Okay, now you're scaring me. Lacy, you need to tell me what's going on. If you're asking me something like this, I deserve to be told why."

"I can't. No one can know. No one. Please—Megan, I wouldn't ask if..."

"I know you wouldn't."

Lacy waited for her to continue. Instead, there was silence and she feared what the answer would be. "I know you and Eric would take good care of them. That would never be a question in my mind. And the kids, well, the cousins should get to know each other. That's something we should've done a long time ago." She paused again. "If it's a question of money, I have enough. I wouldn't put that financial burden on you."

"It's not that, Lacy."

"I'm asking more than anyone should. I get that. This is something I have to do for them. It's the only way we'll get through to the other side."

"Jesus, Lacy. You sound like you're going on some dangerous journey."

She didn't respond, because that was exactly what this was—a dangerous journey that she couldn't be sure of surviving.

"I'll have to talk to Eric."

"Of course. I would expect that. I know what I'm asking, Megan. And I think you know me well enough to know that this is my last resort."

"How long can you give me?"

"As long as it takes, I suppose, but for the kids—the sooner the better." She couldn't burden her with the knowledge that there was no time to consider the request and that the longer it took for them to reach a conclusion, the riskier it would get for the children's safety.

"Eric's taken Jake to soccer practice. He'll be home in an hour. I'll talk to him then and will get you an answer by the end of today. Will that be okay?"

A measured sigh of relief escaped her. "Yes. Thank you, Megan."

"Don't thank me yet. I have to consider my husband and my own kids in this."

"I understand. Please use this number when you've decided one way or the other. Goodbye, Megan. And thank you." Lacy ended the call and peered upward toward the cloudy skies. "What more do you want from me? What more do I have to give?"

———

Lacy knocked on Olivia's bedroom door. "Honey, Celeste has come to say goodbye. Will you open the door, please?" When there was no answer, she tried the handle and regarded Celeste. "It's locked."

"Let me try." She moved in closer. "Liv? Sweetheart, will you let me give you a great big hug before I go? I'd be very sad to leave without that."

A moment later, the door opened slowly and the small girl with strands of hair clinging to her tear-stained cheeks looked up. "I don't want you to go." She rushed to Celeste and threw her arms around her. "You can't leave. You have to come with us, just like before, remember?" She looked up with a small sliver of hope gleaming in her eyes.

"Not this time, sweetheart. You're going to visit your aunt and uncle and cousins. Won't that be a wonderful adventure?"

"No! I don't know them. I don't want to stay with them. She's making us go and she's making you go too."

Lacy's lips began to quiver as she tried to hide the pain of her daughter's scathing words.

"Oh, it won't be forever. You'll be home before you know it. And I'll be back too. But for now, we must say goodbye." Celeste kissed the top of her head and slowly crouched down on crackling knees. "I love you with all my heart and I will think about you every single day."

The two embraced and Lacy looked away, wiping the tears that pooled in her eyes. Jackson came out of his room and approached them. "Can I have a hug too?"

"Oh, sweetheart, of course you can." Celeste pulled the boy in and hugged both children tightly. "We'll all be back here before we know it and everything will be just fine."

Lacy couldn't offer such a guarantee but prayed Celeste was right.

"Okay, I have to go now." She raised upright again with a little help from Lacy. "I have a plane to catch."

Lacy followed Celeste down the steps where her bags sat by the door. Outside, a cab waited to take her someplace safe—a place Lacy did not know and asked that she keep to herself. "Wait."

Celeste stopped in the doorway.

Lacy wrapped her arms around the older woman who'd been like a mother to her and a grandmother to her children. "I'm so sorry. You've done so much for the kids and me. I love you and I'll miss you."

"Just promise you'll call me whenever this is done. Finally done."

"I will. I promise."

"Goodbye, Lacy." Celeste took hold of her luggage and pulled it along on its wheels down the steps and along the path to the curb where the cab driver waited. She turned back to see the kids standing next to their mother. "Goodbye, my loves."

When the cab pulled away, Lacy closed the door and turned to the kids with a tender smile.

"I hate you." Olivia clenched her fists. "I hate you and I'm not going to live with Aunt Megan and Uncle Eric." She ran up the stairs, wailing with sorrow. "I hate you! I hate you!"

Olivia's bedroom door slammed and Lacy flinched. She placed her hand over her mouth and closed her eyes while tears streamed down her face.

"It's okay, Mommy. She's just mad. I don't hate you."

Lacy knelt and pulled Jackson close and began to cry.

———

Aaron spotted Lacy walking down the stairs and as she reached the bottom, he asked, "Are you sure you don't want me to come with you?"

"No. I need to do this on my own. The fewer people who know, the better."

"Did Caison tell you that?"

"No. Trevor did. And he's right."

"And you're not second-guessing your decision?"

"Of course I am. And I have been every second of every day for the past three days. But until this is resolved, I can't be sure we'll ever be safe and I can't risk that. I can't risk their lives—not again."

Aaron reached for the suitcases. "Let me at least get these loaded up for you." He walked outside to the cab.

Lacy called out. "Kids, we need to go now." She held the banister for support. Her energy was drained. She hadn't slept and it had taken everything she had to make this happen in such a short amount of time. Once Megan called with the okay, the arrangements had to be made quickly. And Lacy wondered how much energy she had for the flight ahead. If Jian wanted to destroy her, he'd already done that by forcing her to send her children away. But no one would find them with Jay's sister. When he was alive, they rarely saw each other, hardly spoke to one another, and only sent the occasional Christmas and birthday cards. Not that they didn't love each other; they just weren't close. Megan had her family and Jay had his and they were miles apart.

Now Lacy needed her more than ever and, in the end, Megan had come through. She'd convinced her husband to allow the kids to stay for an indefinite amount of time, perhaps even forever if Lacy didn't make it. Of course, she'd not said as much to Megan and hoped not to have to cross that bridge. Although unspoken, it seemed Megan understood what was at stake.

The kids appeared on the landing, their backpacks slung over their shoulders, wearing expressions not much different from those they wore on the day of their father's funeral.

"Come on, guys. The cab driver's waiting for us. Our flight leaves soon."

They made their way outside where Aaron stood, holding the rear passenger door open. He smiled at the kids, but they didn't return one. He turned to Lacy. "You have everything?"

"Yes."

"And you're coming back tomorrow?"

She nodded. "I need to get them settled in. I owe them that much."

———

The modest Long Island home stood in the distance as the cab approached and rolled to a stop.

"Thank you." Lacy handed the driver the money and stepped out. "Come on, guys. We're here."

Neither said a word but did as she asked.

Lacy grabbed the suitcases the driver placed on the sidewalk. "Let's go see your cousins."

The kids followed with their backpacks in tow and the front door opened to the clear late afternoon skies.

Megan stepped outside to greet them. "You're here! Wow. You two have grown. Haven't seen you since..." She trailed off.

"Since my dad's funeral," Olivia finished with a tinge of anger in her voice.

"Yes, that's right. Please, come in. Your cousins can't wait to meet you." She eyed Lacy. "How was your flight?"

"Good. Thanks. The kids are pretty tired, though."

"I'm sure you all are." She closed the door behind Lacy. "Just leave the bags. I'll get Eric to take them up to your room."

"You have a beautiful home, Megan. I wish we'd all come to see it sooner."

"It's not much. Nothing like what you guys have, but we like it."

A wave of shame washed over Lacy. For what, she didn't know. Perhaps guilt that she and Jay had been much better off financially. But a lot had changed now that he was gone.

———

Olivia and Jackson stood in the entryway as Lacy said her goodbyes to her in-laws. "What you two are doing for me—I'll never forget it."

"I know you would do the same for us," Megan replied.

And she would have, no questions asked. Just exactly as they'd done for her now.

"Guys, your mom's leaving. Give her hugs."

Jackson didn't hesitate and rushed to Lacy's side. "Bye, Mommy. I love you. Don't be gone too long, okay? Promise?"

"I promise." Her voice cracked as she looked at Olivia. But Olivia didn't budge. "Come on, sweetheart." She opened her arms. "Please. I'll miss you so much."

Olivia stared her mother in the eyes and held that stare. Lacy saw the anger seething beneath them. "I'll be back before you know it and we'll all go home again."

"That's what you said the last time." Olivia turned and marched up the stairs.

"She just needs some time. She'll be okay," Megan seemed to try to soothe the tension.

"I hope she'll forgive me one day." Lacy held Jackson a final time and turned to Megan. "I'll call as often as I can. But if you don't hear from me, please don't try to reach out, unless it's urgent. I'll have someone else call you if I can't. And, in the event, well, like we talked about."

"I know. This will all work out and you'll be back with your kids as soon as you can. We all know that, Lacy." She turned to her husband.

"It'll be okay," Eric replied. "You have a safe flight home, Lacy." He offered a distant and brief embrace.

Lacy looked up the stairs a final time and spotted Olivia peeking around the corner. "I love you, baby, and I'll miss you more than you'll ever know." She watched as her daughter disappeared again.

CHAPTER
SIX

HEADLIGHTS TRAVELED past the living room window and pulled Lacy's attention from the persistent visions of her daughter's face. A face full of anger and perceived betrayal. The flight home offered no respite, and now curled up on her sofa, still her thoughts swirled. But the shining headlights outside belonged to someone she had predicted would arrive at this moment.

The doorbell chimed and it was all she could do to heave her body from the static position and answer the bell. "Come in." Lacy stepped aside.

"I'd ask how you're doing, but I already have my answer." Will entered and stood before her, taking hold of her hand. "I won't pretend to understand what you're going through. All I can say is how sorry I am."

She closed the door and led the way into the kitchen. "You want a drink?" Something she'd found herself reaching for more often as of late.

"Sure."

"I know why you're here." Lacy placed a glass of wine in front of him. "I have no other place to go."

"You can't stay here, Lacy, but you already knew that. Aaron can't stay in his place either. Lei Jian knows where you both live and until we know his exact location or that of his associates, this is a no-brainer."

"You're right. I do know that, which is why I had to send my kids away—again. And for the same reason." She sipped on her wine. "I won't let him get away this time. If we don't put an end to this, my family will never be safe. I see that now."

"I spoke with Axell about it and we both think you two would be safer with me. Jian might know I'm here, but he doesn't know where I live."

"And how long do you think that will last? A day? A week? How long before he finds all of us again?" She looked away as her eyes reddened. "No. I won't leave my home. He's taken everything away from me and I won't let him take the only thing I have left of Jay. This house. *Our* house."

"Lacy, I need you to be objective about this. Look at the big picture."

"I won't run away again, Will. If he wants me, he can come and get me. But as for Aaron, he should stay with you. I love him dearly, but he isn't cut out for this."

"You're a stubborn woman." Will regarded her tenacity. "If you won't leave here, then we'll have to make arrangements to keep our guard up. Aaron should stay here and Axell and I will organize a detail."

"You can't do that. No one can know what's happening. We can't trust anyone in either agency. We have no idea who Jian has in his pocket now. Someone had to reveal Kendrick's location. Someone else is helping him take out those of us who knew his plan."

"I'm starting to think it's possible that it was the deputy secretary. He stands to lose the most."

"I don't know about that. It wouldn't serve him any purpose. In fact, just the opposite. He has to be fuming knowing that Jian's been freed. It puts his department at risk. The secretary, maybe even the president. The problem is, we still don't know how far Jian's reach extends."

"Or if it stops with him. He could have other collaborators on his side—in the ministry itself." Will tossed back the rest of his wine. "I suppose it's Axell's job to figure that out."

"Which is exactly the reason why Aaron is in place at Langley. To help him figure that out. Something we thought we had time to do."

"I'll leave it to you to speak to Aaron, then. I don't think he'll have any qualms about staying here. In fact, I think he'll be glad to."

Lacy detected a chary tone in his voice and noted a shift in his gaze. "Why do you say it like that?"

Will raised his eyes to meet hers. "You don't see it?" When she didn't respond, he continued, "For the past several months, he's had you all to himself. I was in Louisville, trying to get my transfer. Axell was doing what he needed to do to get Aaron on board and you were biding your time until everything came together." He ran his index finger along the rim of the empty wine glass. "Lacy, there is no doubt in my mind that he has feelings for you. You've both risked your lives and come through it. You knew each other before all of this. Both of you loved Jay. It makes perfect sense, except that his feelings for you could get in the way and be a distraction from what he needs to do."

"You're wrong. He feels responsible for what happened to Jay and has told me so. If he'd known the information he'd given Jay that day—the day of the attack—he'd have done things differently. I know he loves me, but not in the way you think he does."

Although she believed the words she spoke were true, there was a hint of uncertainty behind them.

"Okay. If you say so. You know him better than I do. I'd better be going."

"You don't want to stay and have something to eat?"

He paused to consider her invitation. "No—thank you. I should go home. Seems strange to say that and not be headed on a plane to Kentucky." He chuckled before standing from the stool. "From this point forward, there's no turning back. Concerns about Jian weren't in our initial plans, but we'll have to adapt. I'll do my best to find a solution to keep you here as long as possible, but if we get intel on movement..."

"I understand." Lacy followed him as he made his way to the door. "Thank you for checking in on me. It means a lot." She unveiled a thin smile before wrapping her arms around his neck. "This is the beginning of the end, Will, and I'm doing my best to remember what's at stake."

"I hope so. Good night and we'll talk more tomorrow after I've had a chance to get with Axell." With a final nod, Will stepped out into the darkness.

Lacy watched him pull away until the red glow of his taillights was no longer visible. She closed the door and turned in, realizing she was alone in a cavernous space that used to be filled with love and laughter, all of which were gone, but she was determined not to leave this home. No one, not even Lei Jian, was going to make that happen.

———

The attractive presentation of food on her plate did nothing to stimulate Lacy's appetite. The restaurant was too loud and too busy and while those attributes didn't usually bother her, they did today.

"You're not hungry?" Aaron asked.

"Not really. I'm sorry we didn't get to catch up this weekend, but you know..."

"I know. It's okay." With his napkin, Aaron wiped the corners of his mouth and placed his hands against his thighs. "I'll be on my own from here on out. No one looking over my shoulder. Well, not directly, anyway."

"What's it like there?"

"I don't have anything to compare it to, I suppose, but it's okay. People are nice enough, although I'm pretty sure they don't like me."

"What makes you say that?"

"Something Axell said about contractors being former employees. It seems like a pretty tight network."

"Still hard to imagine you holding down a 9 to 5." She smiled. "I'm glad you stuck with me, though. I don't know what I'd do..."

"I wanted to do this. No matter what happens in the end, this was my choice." He inhaled a deep breath. "And, now that I'll have some autonomy, I should be able to do what needs to be done."

Lacy peered through the window at the sea of people passing by. "Have you talked to Trevor or Will about—um—security?"

"I understand I'll have to take up residence elsewhere."

"And are you okay with that? In the short-term?"

"Yes. The thought of you alone in that house." He shook his head. "You shouldn't be alone there and if I can offer a shoulder or anything like that, you know I will, without hesitation."

"Thank you. It'll be good to have you near. I don't know if Trevor and Will can protect us as much as they would like, but this was my decision and I'm sticking with it."

"They'll do everything in their power, Lacy."

"How soon can you get your things?"

"Tonight. But for now, I'm afraid I need to get back to the office." He reached for his wallet.

"You don't need to pay for my lunch."

"I've got a steady job now. I can afford it." He dropped two twenties on the table. "I'll call you when I'm on my way this evening." Aaron left the restaurant and passed by the window while Lacy looked on. He raised his fingers in a slight wave and continued toward his car.

On the drive back, he considered what staying with Lacy would mean for him. He cared for her deeply, maybe even loved her, but he was torn because she was Jay's wife after all. A sense of betrayal crept up inside him. But they needed each other if both were to survive the coming days and weeks ahead.

He'd felt a small glimmer of hope that Lacy had refused Will's invitation to stay with him. While it made infinitely more sense for her to stay at her home, Aaron couldn't help but think that perhaps she didn't have feelings for Will, as he'd suspected.

But in the end, he supposed none of that mattered right now. Feelings couldn't be allowed to get in the way of his goals. And on his return, his task awaited him. Agent Axell had given him new information on Ahsan Sajwani. It seemed he was back in Jian's employ. It would be up to Aaron to do what he did best, and that was to work around the security measures and protocols in place in the many CIA databases to garner a location and any other pertinent information on the man.

He shared close quarters with other analysts who were also contractors. His mentor, Renee, had finished her training and he was now assigned specific duties as it related to the filtering of data acquired through the NSA and a multitude of other government agencies.

But getting to the information he now needed would be no simple assignment. Access was monitored and that would be the first thing to circumvent, although Axell was able to offer assistance in that area. He and whoever worked with him had given Aaron a sign-in to a database that he would not normally have access to. This was a workaround for the first item on the list —find out where Sajwani was and if he had already made other travel plans; particularly US travel plans. He needed to find out if Sajwani was traveling under an alias, and if he'd left Dubai, which was where they were sure he was, considering the death of the Panama bank president.

Aaron snuck a glance at his counterparts who were busy with their own assignments, legitimate ones that he'd been hired to complete and would do so, but not yet. Not until he got what he needed. He attempted to log in using Axell's bogus information. And it worked. A knowing smile briefly masked his face. He continued to probe inside the unfamiliar territory. This system was like nothing he'd ever come across before. It was thrilling and terrifying at the same time. Aaron had always considered himself an expert, but in looking at the sheer complexity of this system, he found he was sorely mistaken. An expert, perhaps, in the world of weak corporate security and downright pathetic security of such important institutions as banking and online retailers. But this was the CIA.

He marveled at the ease of use, and the power it contained. And with some additional keystrokes, Aaron gained access to Sajwani's passport information. He, in fact, had traveled under his own name to both Beijing and Dubai, which seemed, at first glance, a careless move. However, upon further inspection, there was nothing of note in his documents. No refusals of entry; he wasn't on any "no-fly" lists. By all accounts, Sajwani would no more gain the attention of security agents than Aaron himself would. That was where the danger lay. Sajwani was free to travel anywhere and by any means. But would he do so here in this country?

Aaron tracked down the residency status of Sajwani and noted he was still a legal resident of Dubai, though he'd spent a fair bit of time in Beijing and, prior to that, had of course, been to the US for a brief period of time. At which time, he'd murdered several people on Jian's behalf, though only Aaron and a handful of others were privy to that information. It was information that could come back to haunt him. What he needed to know now, however, was Sajwani's future travel plans.

"Hey. Whatcha working on?" Renee Childs now stood behind him.

Aaron clicked off the screen before she could get a better look, but as he turned toward her, he noticed a suspicious eye cast in his direction. "Just processing the records request from Ops."

"Oh, okay." Her downturned mouth and folded arms suggested she was not okay at all. "You're a technical analyst, Aaron. You'd do well to remember that as a contracted member of our team, it is critical that you follow our protocols."

"Of course. I understand." His pulse raced and he worked to steady the nervous twitch in his leg, something that always happened when he was about to get caught, which happened more frequently than he'd let on in the past. That was the reason why Agent Axell had to work so hard to get him here in the first place. Cleaning up his past wasn't an easy thing to do.

"Good. Then I'll let you get back to work."

As she turned to leave, Aaron's colleagues glared at him before finally turning away themselves. This wasn't the way to start his burgeoning career in the CIA, even if he knew it would never last. The goal wasn't to gain a lifelong job, but to get in and get out because when they got what they needed and got it out for all to see, everything would change.

———

Amid the dimming skies, Aaron walked out of the CIA headquarters building. Near the southwest entrance was a piece of the Berlin Wall and as he passed the monument, situated exactly as it had been in Berlin, the importance of what he was doing struck him in a most severe manner. Nothing in his life to date had been as important as this. Everything he'd gone through to help Jay and Lacy had been in search of justice for those killed in the attack. Those who no longer had a voice. And while Aaron never believed he would ever make such a contribution to society, staring at that wall reminded him of the power of the people. All people.

He continued toward the parking lot and pressed the remote to open the driver's side door. As he slid inside, a burst of fear surged through him at the sight of a head popping up over the rear passenger seat. "Shit! What the hell, Axell? You scared the shit out of me."

"Sorry about that. Just drive. Can't take the chance of being seen with you here."

"How am I supposed to get through security with you back there? You're not invisible, you know."

"I got it covered. Just drive."

When Aaron reached the guard gate, he flashed his badge and the guard didn't bother checking the back seat. He only glanced at Aaron's carrier bag lying next to him in the passenger seat, which had already gone through intense inspection before he'd been allowed to leave. Ever since Snowden, they didn't chance anything being smuggled out of Langley.

"Okay. We're in the clear." Axell raised his head once again. "What'd you find out?"

"Is this how it's going to be now? You're going to sneak up on me?" Aaron was still pissed at the intrusion.

"There's no way I can risk association with you any more than I already have. Getting you here was one thing, but meeting up with you on a regular basis? That would raise some flags."

"Fine. Sajwani's using his real name to travel. So far as I can tell, he's still in Dubai."

"Good. I can work with that. Has he made any purchases that would indicate travel here to the US?"

"Not that I could find. I'd just gotten into the information when my supervisor dropped in. I can't be sure if she knew what I was looking at."

"Son of a bitch. I knew it was too soon to have you move on anything. But with Jian upping his own timeline, I didn't have a choice. You'll have to be more discreet next time."

"How the hell am I supposed to do that?"

"Wait until there's a meeting or, I don't know, use your brain. You're the hacker, not me."

"Okay, okay. I get it. I was careless. I'll take better precautions next time."

"Let's just hope there is a next time. You talk to Lacy yet?"

"I had lunch with her today. I'm going to grab my stuff now and head over to her place. Now it's your turn to do your job."

Axell eyed Aaron. "Yes, it is. And don't you worry about it. I got it covered."

CHAPTER
SEVEN

THIS WAS A MISTAKE. In her heart, Lacy knew she should leave this place and now Aaron would be here with her. Both like fish in a barrel, waiting to be picked off by Lei Jian's men. Will was right and so was Trevor, but she refused out of a sense of duty to Jay. And now Aaron was walking up the steps to the front door. When he spotted her peering through the kitchen window, he shrugged his shoulders as if to say "What now?"

Lacy dropped the curtain and made her way toward the door. Upon opening it, she spotted Aaron's sparse belongings. "That's everything?"

"I don't plan on staying long." He leaned in to kiss her on the cheek. "Thanks for letting me hang out here with you."

"You can thank me when we both get out of this alive." Will had pulled up in his car as she was ready to close the door. "I didn't know Will was coming over too."

"He said he wanted to make sure we were on the same page and that Axell requested the three of us talk before continuing."

"It's a little late for that, isn't it?" Lacy said, waiting for Will to approach the entry.

"Maybe it is. I think Jian's got him on edge."

"He's got all of us on edge." She smiled as Will drew near. "I wasn't expecting you. Come on in. Join the party."

"Thanks. Axell asked…"

"I know." She closed the door. "Well, here we all are once again. Can I get anyone anything?"

"Just water for me, thanks. I'm still on the clock," Will replied.

The three made their way into the kitchen.

"It's quiet without the kids around." Aaron appeared to regret the comment as soon as it left his lips. "I'm sorry. I didn't mean…"

"Don't worry about it. It is quiet. I thought I'd appreciate the silence, but no. The emptiness just widens the hole in my heart." Lacy handed Aaron a beer. "And a water for you. So, what is it that Trevor wanted us to talk about?"

"I was able to get some information today before I was cut short, and I relayed that to Axell. As of right now, Sajwani is still in Dubai with no immediate travel plans," Aaron said.

"Good. That buys us enough time to get set up here," Will replied.

Lacy's brow furrowed. "What do you mean—set up?"

"I've got a team heading over now. They're going to set up surveillance: audio and video. We're going to monitor your landline as well as your personal cell. Your work cell may already be monitored. I'm working on an answer to that."

"That's information I could've used earlier."

"Why? Did something happen?" Will asked.

"No. Just would've been nice to know that Big Brother is listening."

"It isn't so much Big Brother as us. Our team. Axell's people. We can't take anything for granted right now. The pace with which Jian is moving leaves us no room for uncertainty."

"Where is all of this surveillance going to be sent? To Trevor?" Lacy asked.

"He and Agent Colburn will be monitoring it directly."

"And what happens if Jian's people come here?" Aaron asked.

"I've kept a few people in my confidence. Agent Porter, for one. SSA Mendez has someone he trusts here as well. We've told them enough, but not too much."

"Sounds like our little circle has widened substantially. Are you sure that's a good idea?"

"So far as they know, it's just another operation. Lacy, we have no choice but to put our trust in more people. There's no way we can approach this in the same manner as before."

"You mean running to a different place every day?" Aaron said.

"Yes. We were in a regrettable situation then and Axell and I agree we can't let that happen a second time. We have to be the ones in control. We have to set the rules this time. Jian won't have his government to hide behind."

"Really? Then why was he released?" Lacy asked.

"That's a very good question. Maybe it was to show our government that the MSS still controls its own people. Maybe the previous minister had enough pull to have him released. Axell's working on the details of why. I'm just trying to figure out how."

"What about the FBI director? Has anyone talked to him?" Aaron asked.

"What good would that do?" Lacy turned to him. "They refused to believe, or rather, acknowledge the truth and what we went through to get to the truth. Director Mobley can't help us. He already tried."

"She's right. We're on our own from a senior-level standpoint. But we're ready this time. And we have good people helping us."

The doorbell rang.

"Speaking of good people, here they are now. That's the surveillance crew."

———

Deputy Secretary Wendell Turner sat at his desk, head in his hands. Upon raising again, his eyes met with the ambassador's. "What are we going to do about this?"

"I've put pressure on the ministry to take him back into custody, but they're refusing. They say it won't affect the US because his passport is still revoked. They believe they've resolved the matter of Lei Jian." The US Ambassador to China stood almost at attention.

"Of course they do. Pardon me, but I'm having a hard time believing this wasn't timed perfectly. Right after the election, release one of their spies? What about Kendrick's death? Does the Washington Field Office have any indications as to who's responsible?"

"Not that I've been told, but then, I assume you would know before I would."

"Right. I'll meet with the agent-in-charge for an update." Turner stood from his chair. "Damn it. Does their new minister really believe Jian will just sit back and do nothing? Do they not understand that he must still have friends?"

"At this point, sir, I'm not sure he cares. I get the impression that they've washed their hands of him. Deputy Turner, Lei Jian is a powerful man with support from at least some in his government. While we can't confirm he was responsible, in some manner, for the former undersecretary's death, it's highly likely he was."

"Of course he was." Anger still seethed inside him. "Kendrick blew the whistle on him, and he won't be the last on his list. He wants revenge for losing six months of his life, for losing the power he once had. It doesn't seem to matter to him that we kept our end of the bargain in order to continue on the path to diplomacy." Turner paused to gather himself. "We need to find him and put an end to this ourselves. We will not be held hostage by the new minister or by Lei Jian."

"I'll keep you up to speed on any new developments." The ambassador took his leave.

The tale Turner had spun in order to keep the truth hidden had been successful. However, with Jian's release, he stood to lose his credibility, and probably a hell of a lot more than that. Kendrick's death was a major thorn in his side that had to be dealt with and he already realized he couldn't buy the FBI agent's loyalty. He'd put his toe in those waters and it was clearly icy. He knew damn well it had to be Lei Jian's people, but he had to hope that the Bureau wouldn't uncover the reason why.

———

Lacy closed the door as the final crewmember parted. "I guess that's it. My every move inside my own home will be monitored."

"It's for your safety and Aaron's," Will began. "Jian has forced our hand. If his people come here, we'll know. If they enter your community, we'll know. You two will be safe here, and he knows it would be suicide for him to make any attempts at contact either at FBI Headquarters or Langley. Jian is brash, but he isn't stupid."

"It's just when we're here," Lacy added.

"Yes. This is where he'll think you're the most vulnerable. But you're not. Not anymore. Look, it's getting late. I'd better be going." He opened the door. "I'll see you tomorrow. Aaron, Axell says you're doing a great job. Thank you for your help." He continued outside and rubbed his hands together for warmth as he walked toward his car.

Lacy closed the door when he pulled away and turned to Aaron. "Guess we're roomies now." She moved toward him. "I'm glad you're here, though. I really am. It was my decision to stay here and I hope, for our sake, it wasn't the wrong one. I'm going to head up to bed now. You know where your room is." Lacy grabbed her cell from the side table and walked past him to the stairs. "Good night, Aaron."

"Good night."

Upon entering her room, Lacy was now particularly cautious about being watched. They hadn't put a camera in her bedroom or bathrooms, but there were two mounted outside her window on the second floor in the event someone attempted to enter through her bedroom. But if they got that close, it would probably be too late anyway. A thought on which she didn't care to dwell. Still, a creeping feeling crawled along her skin as she undressed.

Climbing into bed, the loneliness weighed down her already heavy heart. She thought she'd made it through the worst of it. That her sacrifices were over. They were not. Not by a long shot. At least her children were safe. No one would connect the dots to her sister-in-law. That offered a great measure of comfort because, in the end, this was for them. For their future.

As her thoughts turned to the friend she'd nearly forsaken, her gratitude extended to him as well. How much better off he would have been had Jay never reached out to him? But how much worse off she would be if that had been the case. Aaron was a blessing in disguise and it would be up to her to ensure his safety too. He was not cut out for covert espionage, but he was doing it for her. Perhaps Will had been right. Certain feelings had been directed toward her in recent weeks and she had chosen to ignore them. It was too much too soon and acknowledging them would be tantamount to betrayal in her mind, even if she had no intention of reciprocation. But she needed him; his friendship and his shoulder. It was selfish to think that way, but there it was. Maybe someday, when this was all over, maybe then she could consider an alternate future. That time, however, was not now.

———

Will Caison knocked on the door of the apartment. He nodded as Agent Colburn opened it and let him in. "Are you uplinked?"

"We are. You want to have a look? It's dark. Looks like they've gone to sleep."

Will approached the monitors that sat atop the folding tables inside the otherwise empty space, save for a futon against the back wall. He observed the exterior angles, including the camera mounted inside the emergency entrance relay at the community gate. "Looks like we've got everything covered. I told you my guys were good. And we're only minutes away. Good call on securing a location. I've also got people parked near the entrance and stationed at the trail behind the home."

"How'd you get authorization?"

"Suspected home-grown terrorists gathering in the suburbs. Nothing new there. Got SSA Kelly to sign off on it. I don't know for how long, but I'll take what I can get." He moved toward the small kitchen. "I'll take the first shift. You should go home, and get some rest."

Colburn pointed his index finger at one of the screens. "You'll get a warning if the system picks up movement, in the event you fall asleep, so don't feel like you need to stay up all night."

"I'm not tired. I'd like to just make sure everything's working as it should tonight. We're at our most vulnerable right now. We don't know who's working for Jian or where they might be."

"Whatever you say, Caison." Colburn pulled his coat off the chair. "I'll stop by in the morning and keep an eye on the place during the day. I've got a guy who can sub in if I can't make it."

"Sounds good. Night." Will took a seat in the chair and studied the monitors. He heard the door close behind him and the dead-bolt lock from Colburn's key outside.

The cameras offered an infrared view of both the interior and exterior areas, which allowed him to see even though it was dark. He gazed at the screen, which displayed the upstairs landing and the hall leading to Lacy's bedroom. He wondered if she was asleep but figured it wasn't likely. Who would be? He admired her for what she had done and what she was doing now. Continuing to pursue the truth no matter what the cost. Admiration, however, wasn't enough. Will would see to it that she remained safe, and her friend, Hunter. Regardless of how he felt about him; that Hunter was too reliant upon Lacy; that it could become a problem when the time came to act once again. But he had to give credit where it was due. Hunter had overcome much of his fears and insecurities to successfully assimilate in a place Will considered the most dangerous of all. The inner workings of the CIA. Getting caught doing what he was doing there would mean treason. It would take a strong constitution to accomplish what needed to be done and, so far, Aaron Hunter was doing an impeccable job.

———

The former minister ended the call and turned to his friend. "They're refusing to reinstate your passport. You are to stay here in Beijing until such time as the FBI determines who was responsible for killing the American diplomat."

Jian regarded the only one inside the MSS who still believed in him. "You couldn't convince the new minister that I would pose no threat to the agreement set forth between the US State Department and our government? I have fully honored the terms."

"Have you? Then where is your Arabic friend? Ahsan Sajwani?"

"As I understand it, he is home, in Dubai."

"You have put everything at risk, once again. This was not *our* agreement."

"*Our* agreement was to ensure loose ends had been tied so that we may offer evidence of our usefulness. And that is exactly what I have been doing."

"The undersecretary was not part of that agreement, Jian."

"The Americans stood to lose the most if he talked. And as I told you, I am not responsible for his death. It was probably one of his own people. Now that their elections are over, perhaps they had their own liquidation orders."

"You've put me in an undesirable position. Now I must defend you once again and the premier is tired of seeing my face, especially when I have nothing new to offer him."

"That's where you are wrong. You have everything to offer him."

"And how's that?"

"You offer assurances that he will get the cooperation of the US government. The President of the People's Republic of China will get the trade agreements he desires. But only if the United States understands that we will finish their dirty work for them."

"Are you admitting culpability in the death of their undersecretary?"

"As I said, that was not done under my direction. And the others? The FBI agent and the civilian worker? They will be dealt with. This will all go away and the premier and our new minister can continue to keep their hands clean."

"And where will that leave us, Jian?"

"Isn't it obvious? You want to be returned to power, as do I. Your desire to serve as the premier's adviser will come to fruition if we are successful. The president will see what we've done for him. And what we can continue to do. This is just the beginning, Minister."

CHAPTER
EIGHT

IT WAS AN UNSHAKABLE FEELING. An itch that couldn't be scratched. The feeling of being followed, being watched. And now as she walked into the J. Edgar Hoover building, the sensation burrowed deeper. She'd been hunted before, and for the same reason, but this was different. And all she could do was wade through this river of fear and do her best to keep her head above water. Upon arriving at her desk, Michelle Vogel approached.

"Can I talk to you for a moment?"

Without a word in reply, Lacy immediately followed Michelle back to her office. This must have been important because she closed the door as Lacy took her seat. Yet another wave of uncertainty in this current crashed against her.

"I received a call early this morning." Michelle returned to her desk and lowered herself in a calculated manner. "I thought it best to wait to speak to you about it in person, rather than call you."

"Okay. Why do I get a bad feeling about this?"

"A request has been made on behalf of the Washington Field Office." She eyed Lacy. "They want to look into your association with Undersecretary Kendrick in connection with his death."

"My association? I had no association with him. This came from the WFO?"

"The office has formed a special task force to investigate Kendrick's murder. He was, after all, a high-ranking government official. This is standard protocol."

"They aren't going to find any connection because there was none."

"I understand. However, what has been discovered was Jay's alleged involvement with Nova Investments, which, of course, ties in with the attack."

"Which was later debunked."

"Nevertheless, in the search conducted at the Kendrick home, evidence was discovered."

"Of what?"

"They found Jay's name scrawled on a pad of paper."

"What? That's not possible. The only way Kendrick would've known about Jay is if..." She paused and soon reached the logical conclusion. "If it was planted there either by Jian's man who killed him, or someone at the State Department, both of whom are equally interested in keeping me quiet."

"Lacy, I think something larger is at play here." Michelle eyed the corridor through her window, confirming she would not be interrupted. "You and I both know Kendrick's death is part of a much larger problem for the State Department. A problem that, if unleashed, would bring the entire department down and possibly even the presidency. That will never be allowed to happen."

"So, while the true enemy of the state, Lei Jian, remains free, my own government is after me?"

"In my opinion, I think the sole purpose of the request is to remind you of what's at stake."

"You mean, it's a threat?"

Michelle nodded. "Issued by someone of much higher authority than anyone at the WFO. However, I will still have to comply and your personnel files, including the information you brought forward to me regarding Argus Solutions and Nova Investments—and Jay, will need to be turned over."

"So they can hold it over my head for the rest of my life. Say something, and I risk destroying not only my career but smearing my husband's name. Say nothing, and things will go on as usual." Lacy had already come to the conclusion that continuing to pursue this would almost certainly destroy her career. She was prepared for that. But to destroy Jay's legacy, for word ever to reach her children's ears that their father was a traitor to his country, she couldn't allow that to happen. "Give them what they want. They want my head on a platter, give them that too." Lacy stood. "Right now, I've got work to do."

———

"Did you hear?" Lacy poked her head around Will's opened door.

Her unexpected arrival startled him. "Lacy, what are you doing here? And did I hear what?"

She tossed her head as a summons and began walking away. He quickly followed as she marched through the halls with purpose.

"Hey, what's going on?"

"Wait." She continued to the elevators and remained silent as they made their way to the lobby. Upon exiting, she added, "Outside."

A rear exit led them to the gardens adjacent to the north entrance.

"Okay. Now can you tell me what's going on?" Will folded his arms.

"We're going to have to work quickly. I don't know how much longer I'll be here."

"What are you talking about? What happened?"

"They want me gone. They've asked my boss to turn over my records."

"Who wants you gone?"

"The State Department. Well, the request came from the WFO, but it's State pushing for it. I know it is. They know what we're planning."

"Just take a breath for a second. There's no way anyone knows anything. We haven't done anything, not really."

"Then why now? It's been six months. Why come after me now?" She didn't wait for him to answer. "I'll tell you why. It's Kendrick. He's dead and they're trying to keep a lid on things. They know Jian is behind it and they're afraid of what he'll do. What he'll say." She paused, but only for a breath. "Do you know what it would do if he came out and said that the FBI and CIA knew what he'd done along with the State Department?"

"You think Jian's goal in all this is to expose the fact that China was responsible for the attack? That he himself was responsible?" Will began to shake his head. "That would be cutting off his nose to spite his face. I can't see that happening."

"We know what he's capable of doing. Kendrick did too and look where that got him. The State Department? They don't know. They think they do, but they don't. Kendrick was operating right under their noses and they knew nothing about it."

"That's what we've been led to believe," Will added.

Lacy eyed him carefully. "You don't think that's the case? We didn't find any evidence of collusion from others in the department in our surveillance of Kendrick."

"I can't say for sure, but the way it was so quickly shoved under the rug, just seems—well, more than just political CYA prior to an election. But what matters is that we work quickly in the event you're again placed on leave."

"They won't bother with that formality. We just keep moving forward. Only now, I have to watch out not only for Jian's people but my own government as well."

Will gently clasped her shoulder. "You're not alone, Lacy. You have a very capable and loyal team behind you. You think I would've moved 600-odd miles away if this wasn't important to me? If this didn't mean everything to me? It makes me sick what happened. And I can't let it rest. Just like you can't." He surveyed the grounds. "Listen, I'll talk to Axell and Colburn. They might already know, but in the event they don't; they should. If you're being ousted, it won't be long before the same thing happens to me and then probably Hunter too."

"We'll be dead in the water if that happens. Aaron needs access. We all do. Otherwise, what do we have?" she continued.

"Let's just take this one step at a time. You should go back inside ahead of me. I'm going to make a few calls, then I'll go back too. Just do what you came to do, Lacy. I'll stop by tonight to see how things are going."

"Who's monitoring the house right now?"

"Someone Colburn sent. I met him briefly this morning before I left. Don't worry. Eyes will be on your house and the surrounding area 24/7."

She nodded. "I'll see you later, then."

He waited for her to leave and continued into the lush, manicured grounds. With a suspicious glance in every direction, he made the call. "Axell, we've got a problem."

Lacy returned to her desk, certain now that they were after her, even if she couldn't define exactly who "they" were. That river was getting deeper, and the itch was almost impossible to scratch. But she pressed on, desperate for some evidence to cling to before they pulled the rug out from beneath her.

She logged into the US Office of Personnel Management, the same agency China hacked into a few years ago, and obtained social security numbers, addresses, and the like on more than 1500 government workers. But what Lacy needed now was Kendrick's records. Not only his but the deputy secretary's as well, in an effort to cover all her bases. She didn't have the security clearance to access such information, so Aaron did his part by penetrating the OPM database from Langley and raising her clearance level from Confidential to Top Secret. There was only one level higher and that was Sensitive Compartmented Information. That was what the deputy secretary and others in his charge would have.

With a watchful eye in every direction, Lacy retrieved the files. Her goal was to discover any dealings with foreign governments unrelated to their positions. In other words, this was the first step in discovering if either had financial or social ties to China or Chinese-owned corporations in the U.S.

Not only that, but Lacy would get the addresses of both Kendrick and Deputy Turner, including all properties they owned and if any such properties were acquired with dubious funds. That part, Aaron would have to help her with as that information wasn't accessible through this system.

Finally, she would access her own files to determine who else might have requested her information besides the WFO. She needed to know who was on the inside looking at her.

As far as Jian, Ahsan Sajwani, and anyone else under Jian's employ; that would be left up to Aaron and her friends at the CIA.

But this was a step in the right direction. One she wished hadn't taken so long to make, in light of recent developments.

Part of their initial plan was for Lacy to buy time. Time to get Will here. Time to lay low. Time for those who might be concerned about her to confirm that she posed no threat. That time had passed. She was now a direct threat to all those involved in the death of her husband.

———

Lacy waited at the entrance of the train station for Aaron to arrive. Her camel-colored wool coat flapped around her calves while leaves swirled at her feet. In her pocket, her fingers twirled the storage device. A micro SD card she'd hidden in the slot inside her cell phone, which had remained undetected as she exited FBI Headquarters.

She hoped Aaron was able to retrieve the necessary information, though getting it out of Langley would prove difficult. However, she stopped underestimating Aaron's abilities long ago; from the moment he'd hacked into her computer at Cornell in order to send a message. She recalled that message even now. A Tetris-style game, that at the end of it, created a heart on her screen. There was a time, albeit brief in their history, when Aaron attempted to woo her. Instead, her affections were directed to Jay and only Jay.

As she spotted Aaron in the distance, his eyes meeting hers, she pushed away the enduring thoughts of the girl and boy they used to be. There was no innocence left in either of them. But she would trust Aaron with her life, as would he. And as far as any remaining notions of affection from him, that was a long time ago, no matter what Will Caison believed.

"Right on time." She smiled and pivoted back toward her car. "How'd it go?"

"I got it."

She shot him a look.

"Don't look so surprised. I might not be a burly, gun-toting FBI agent, but I'm starting to make one hell of a cunning spy."

The brief laughter they shared dissipated with the understanding that this was no game they were playing. And while neither would tell the other just how dangerous their lives had become, they knew.

"Speaking of gun-toting FBI agents, Will's coming by later. There've been some developments. We'll need to share what we've got."

"Axell knows I was able to get the information. I think he was as surprised as you."

They reached her car and stepped inside. Lacy smoothed her wind-blown hair and started the engine before turning to Aaron. "There's no turning back now, is there?"

"No. There isn't."

It was a quiet drive back to Annandale and Lacy wondered what was going through Aaron's mind. In the moment he removed the vital information, he could've been taken right then and there. For that matter, so could she. It was a risk, however, that it seemed both were willing to take. Of course, finding themselves behind bars would do little to shed light on the truth and would do nothing to help Lacy get her children back. So they ignored the probable scenario and drove back in silence.

She pulled into the garage and killed the engine. "Welcome to the Big Brother house."

Inside, Lacy turned off the security alarm and set her purse down on the table in the foyer.

"Seems strange for Celeste and the kids to not be here." Aaron followed behind. "I guess it didn't really hit me last night, but now, at the end of the day..."

"I know. I keep telling myself that it's only temporary."

"It is, Lacy."

"Let's get set up before Will arrives. He'll want to get down to business."

"Sure. Let me just get changed. I can't stand wearing this tie." He'd already begun pulling it away from his neck.

Lacy retrieved her laptop and placed it on the kitchen table. "I'll ask Will to pick up some food. I don't have anything here." She raised her voice for Aaron to hear as he continued through the family room and to the guest room.

"Sounds good."

Her phone was still in her purse and she dug it out from the bottom where it inevitably lay. Using her work phone was out of the question, so she used the burner and requested pizza. His reply was gracious as always. "He'll be here in thirty minutes," she shouted across the room.

Aaron returned in sweatpants and a T-shirt. Lacy had already poured two glasses of wine.

"I don't know about you, but I could use this." She handed him his glass. "Okay," her first sip went down smoothly, "let's see what we've got. I'll load this up." She placed the mini card into the adapter and then into her laptop.

"Are you online?"

"No."

"Okay. And you're scanning using the programs I installed?"

"Yes, I am. I've done everything you've asked to make sure this computer isn't compromised."

"Okay. Sorry. I'm just paranoid."

"Well, it's not like you don't have reason to be." Headlights caught her attention. "That must be Will." Already in socked feet,

Lacy padded to the front door and pulled it open. "Pizza. Excellent." She stepped aside to let him in.

"Hope you don't mind. You're probably getting tired of junk food."

"Right now, my diet isn't a top priority. Come into the kitchen. We've got everything set up." Lacy shut the door and secured the deadbolt.

"Hey, Aaron. How's it going?"

"Good. Thanks, man. How are you?"

"Not bad, all things considered." He set down the pizza. "Lacy says you two had some good luck today. Should we take a look?"

As the three settled in, Lacy opened the files she'd copied. "Thanks to Aaron, I was able to get in and pull the personnel files on Kendrick and Deputy Turner." She clicked on the first one. "I didn't risk going through these at the office, so we're all seeing this for the first time."

It took them a few files before reaching something that could prove useful. "What's this?" Lacy leaned in for a better look. "Kendrick took a leave of absence three months prior to the attack."

"Does it say why?" Aaron asked.

"Family leave. Doesn't give anything more specific."

"Okay. I'll look into where he was and what he was doing during that timeframe," Will replied.

"Does it matter?" Aaron asked. "He's dead. What good will that do us?"

"It'll tell us to look for who he might have been in contact with during that time, apart from Lei Jian. If anyone else might have been involved or simply to know what he was up to. If any of it ties to Turner or anyone else at the State Department."

"Or any other agency," Lacy added.

"Yes. That too." Will stopped for a moment. "Hang on. Before we go further, take a look at Turner's file. See where he was during that time."

"Okay." Lacy pulled up the other files and the time frame in question and shook her head. "Nothing. Don't see anything unusual here."

"No? It was just a hunch," Will said. "Go on back to..." His brow creased hard as he peered at the screen. "Hang on." He pointed to a file. "Go here."

Lacy opened the file in question. "Oh my God. Turner was appointed to Deputy Secretary six months ahead of the attack."

"That's right. And look at his title prior to that," Will said.

"Undersecretary of the Office of Political Affairs." Aaron turned to them. "Kendrick's position."

CHAPTER
NINE

AN IMMEDIATE HUSH fell upon the room. A revelation of this magnitude forced them to consider the implications. Who appointed Turner to the higher post and why? The timing was perilously close to the attack. However, this exploratory mission wasn't yet complete as Aaron weighed in on its meaning.

"What I came across is beginning to make sense." Aaron handed the USB drive to Lacy. "Take a look at this."

She inserted the device and opened the files. "I don't know what I'm looking at."

"They're encrypted. Here, let me do it." He pulled the laptop toward him and began to decode the information.

"How did you manage to get this out?" Will asked.

"Suffice it to say that if I told you, I doubt you'd want to finish your food." Aaron continued to work to reveal the contents of what he'd retrieved from Langley. "Here we are." He turned the laptop for them to see. "So this is a program called Sparrow. It essentially collects information on visa applications submitted to the US embassies worldwide. Most of the security checks are performed by NSA, Homeland Security, FBI, and CIA. Others, however, go up the chain farther and are reviewed by members of the State Department."

"Now you've got my interest," Will replied.

"Good. Take, for example, this one here." Aaron pointed to the screen. "This one was submitted to the US embassy in Baghdad. As a side note, that embassy happens to be the largest and most expensive US embassy in the world."

"Right. It's been compared to Vatican City and cost the American taxpayers nearly a billion dollars," Will added.

"So this application was submitted by an Iraqi man who was employed by one of the embassy's Kuwaiti contractors back in 2014. It was forwarded for final approval by the State Department because get this. The contractor was known to have been involved in human trafficking and had several ethics violations that our government didn't want exposed. So it was expedited for approval by State and any further investigations into the man's background, or his family's, by the intelligence community, was halted."

"How does this help us now?" Will asked.

Aaron began typing again and was silent until he retrieved the relevant information. "The purpose of my example was to show you how State can get involved, which was exactly what they did here." He turned the monitor again. "For Ahsan Sajwani."

"His visa application was approved around the time Turner was promoted to Deputy Secretary," Lacy began. "Is it possible the application was put on hold until Turner's promotion? Is it reasonable to assume they were waiting it out? That maybe we're still only looking at Kendrick? He could've known this was coming. This operation could've been in the works for a year or more."

Will regarded both with apprehension. "A more pressing concern now is knowing whether Turner is Jian's next target. We don't know without a doubt that these two are connected. But if they are, I wouldn't put it past Jian to be setting his sights on the deputy secretary."

Lacy cast her gaze upward. "Who's watching us right now?"

"One of Colburn's people," Will replied.

She closed the lid on the laptop. "It's getting late. We should get some rest." Lacy began to walk toward the front door.

Will seemed to pick up on her sudden urgency to put an end to their expedition. He approached her while Aaron remained in the kitchen retrieving the storage device from Lacy's laptop. He held her gaze, knowing she was keeping something from him. "Good night, Lacy."

"Good night. Thanks for coming by."

"I'll be heading to the apartment for my shift."

"Okay." Lacy held open the door.

Upon Will's departure, she locked the door and returned to the kitchen. Her phone buzzed in her sweater pocket. It was a text from Will on the burner.

"What's wrong?"

She pursed her lips and began to type her reply. "Do we know for sure we can trust this person who's supposed to be watching out for us?"

"I trust Colburn. Don't you?" he replied.

"Right now, I don't know if we can trust anyone. What we have in our possession is dangerous."

"We don't have anything to worry about with Axell or Colburn. I trust them both with my life. And you should too."

"I'm sure you're right. Good night." And that was the end of it. She'd grown even more paranoid now because this didn't stop at a mid-level government staffer. And the problem was, she didn't know where it stopped. None of them did.

———

Within minutes, Will had arrived at the apartment where the surveillance had been set up. "Evening. How's it going?"

"Good. No concerns yet." CIA Agent Jason Hicks rose from the chair and pulled on his jacket. "Looks like the three of you had a good meeting. Will you be briefing Agent Colburn?"

"Yes."

"Okay then. Good night." Hicks took his leave.

Will tossed his coat over the chair at the workstation and began to take inventory of the cameras, confirming they were functioning and nothing suspicious caught his eye. The final check was inside Lacy's house. He understood why she was uncomfortable with this—he would have been too—but it had been her decision and this was the end result.

He spotted the two of them in the living room watching television. They weren't speaking, which seemed odd. It appeared intentional and this brought him concern. He had, quite suddenly, felt on the outside of this tight circle. It seemed Lacy was growing distrustful of those who were trying to help, possibly including himself. And that would make this much more complicated.

After several minutes, he rose from the chair to use the restroom. On his return, he noticed they were no longer in the living room. Will searched the other cameras and as he peered at the monitors, eventually landing on the upstairs, he spotted Aaron following Lacy into her bedroom. "What the...?"

Her door closed and that was it. He'd been shut out, unable to see what was happening behind that closed door. Certainly they weren't sleeping together. It didn't seem possible. Not when he knew how much she still mourned her husband.

A wave of shame passed through him as he began to feel like an intruder into her personal life. What business was it of his what she did and who she did it with? After all, those two had history and could offer one another comfort Will could not. Still, it felt off-putting and he sat down on the couch to take a moment and prioritize his thoughts. "None of my business."

———

Lacy sat on the edge of the bed next to Aaron. "What do you think?"

"I think this is getting extremely dangerous. Even more so than what we've already been through and that's saying something."

"I mean about Colburn's guy. We don't know anything about him."

"After what those guys have done for us? It'd be a disservice to them if we questioned their intentions. They both risked everything to help us. If Colburn trusts this person, then I think we should too."

"You're probably right. I feel like I'm spiraling into this deep mistrust. And I made Will feel bad about it. I shut down and I know he felt it." Lacy placed her hand on Aaron's knee and revealed a rare smile. "At least I can talk to you in here without anyone watching. I know this was my decision, one which I'm beginning to regret."

"Your feelings are justified, Lacy. I don't know what choice I would've made in your shoes. You don't want them to control you and yet, that is exactly what it seems is happening."

"I just want them back. My kids—I miss them so much. I don't know if I made the right choice—about any of this." She held his gaze. "What if we got lucky the first time and our luck's run out?"

"The people who are helping us believe we're doing the right thing and so should we. Look, why don't you try to get some sleep? Just keep these files someplace safe until we know what to do with them."

She surveyed her room. "I'll find a place to hide the USBs in here. Jay kept a box in the attic access in my closet. That'll do for now. Just don't tell anyone."

"Okay." Aaron kissed her cheek. "Good night, Lacy. I'll see you in the morning." He stood up to leave.

"Aaron?"

He stopped and turned back to her. "Yes?"

"Thank you. You've done more for me than I could ever repay."

"I love you, Lace. You know that."

————

It took Will a moment to spot that the light in the downstairs hall burned. He stood from the futon sofa and approached the monitors once again. Aaron had returned to his room and Will couldn't help but wonder what had happened. Why he cared perhaps bothered him more than what had actually happened inside Lacy's bedroom.

A knock on the door stirred him from his thoughts. He moved toward the entrance and revealed the visitor. "I wasn't expecting you so soon."

"I got your message regarding the personnel files." Axell walked past him and directly toward the monitors. "How's everything else going?"

"So far, nothing out of the ordinary."

"I wish I could've been there with you, but I can't risk a personal association with Hunter or Merrick. I still can't be sure who's watching us. What do we know right now? Anything that will help figure out what Jian's next move will be?"

"I don't know about that. But Hunter discovered that Ahsan Sajwani received a visa that was approved directly by the State Department, months prior to the attack. And Lacy was able to retrieve the Office of Personnel information on Drew Kendrick and Deputy Secretary Turner. It seems there is reason to believe he, despite his best efforts, might have been involved at arm's length with the cover-up, although we haven't figured out just how yet."

"I'd hoped that wasn't the case, but it was certainly in the back of my mind. Kendrick was an ambitious man, but his powers weren't so great that he could've bent Jian's will on his own." Axell headed into the kitchen and reached for a glass. "This does present us with a fresh set of problems."

"Are we prepared to deal with them?" Will asked.

"We'll have to be." He sipped on the bourbon that now swirled in his glass. "This doesn't change our plan, though. We still need to keep track of Sajwani's movements. When and where he will travel next. I'll continue to guide Hunter on where to look."

"What else are you hoping to find? Don't we need to push this along a little quicker? We can't wait for Sajwani to arrive. We need to launch a preemptive strike."

"This isn't Afghanistan, Caison. This is a political maneuver that we must navigate carefully and covertly."

"I'll be honest. I don't know how much longer Lacy will be able to hang on. She misses her kids and wants nothing more than for this to end as swiftly as possible."

"She's refusing to leave her home and that leaves my hands tied to certain ideas. We're diverting resources to ensure her safety rather than directing them toward solving the problem." He tossed back the rest of his drink. "I'm sure she must feel very much intruded upon, but it was her decision. The only way we expedite this is to focus our efforts on pursuing Jian, Sajwani, and now, it seems, to pursue the deputy secretary in the wake of Kendrick's death."

Will cast his gaze to the monitors, the darkened rooms inside, the murky streetscape in the subtle glow of a shrouded moon. He knew the risks of her staying in her home were growing by the day. None of them were truly safe so long as Ahsan Sajwani was still under Jian's employ. And now that they had this new information, how long would it be before their government came after them? "I'll talk to her in the morning. Get her to see reason. That things have changed and we need to adapt or risk the safety of everyone involved."

"I think you might be the only person who can convince her. Because as I see it, she and Hunter are playing off one another. Feeding off each other's fears and while they are doing what needs to be done, I believe there'll come a time when neither will be able to see the real dangers of what's happening. Lacy thinks we can keep her safe with all of this."

"You don't think so."

"It's a Band-Aid and it could be ripped off at any moment."

CHAPTER
TEN

THE VISIT to Director Mobley's office was predicated upon the evidence obtained on Turner and whether it would nudge Mobley to offer guidance on a new direction for their mutual agenda. Will needed help from the director, knowing it could only come in the form of administrative support—for now.

Mobley stood from behind his desk and offered a hand to Will. "It's good to see you again, Agent Caison. Please, sit down."

The director had been forced to swallow the bitter pill shoved down his throat by the deputy secretary under the guise of national security. And so to begin this conversation, certain nuances would need to be considered. "Thank you for meeting with me, sir. It has been a long time."

"I understand you're here in D.C. now, working for us at Headquarters."

"Yes, sir. I transferred a short time ago."

"Good. And how are you enjoying the city?"

"It's a beautiful and humbling place."

"That it is." Mobley turned serious. "I understand the reason you've come to visit based on your call, and before we go any further, I need you to understand something. Regardless of our previous meetings, a new day has dawned here in Washington. The Administration has resumed control, which, as you know, means the number one priority is the safety of our fragile economy as well as to protect the American people."

Was he hearing this right? It was beginning to sound as though Mobley drank the Kool-Aid and the idea that he was no longer an ally would present a whole host of new problems. Help was what they needed now, but as he listened, Will began to realize that help might not come. "Of course, sir, I am here to serve the people of this country and protect them."

"That being said, there are things on which we must follow through and I am entrusting you and your team to make that happen. My support in your efforts to do your job will not waver, as it would not for any other member of the Bureau." His eyes began to say more than his words could. "SSA Kelly is a team player and you will find he offers a wealth of knowledge. You would do well to take advantage of this."

With renewed faith, Will understood what had just happened. "Thank you, sir. I appreciate your support. I'll see to it that SSA Kelly is kept up to speed."

"Well, then, good luck, Agent Caison, and my door is always open." Mobley stood and again tendered a greeting.

"Goodbye, sir." The solid handshake confirmed to Will that the underlying inference of this brief meeting was fully acknowledged. Mobley was still determined to see those responsible pay for their crimes, yet needed to remain stealth in his convictions until such time as the team could prove, with utmost certainty, how far up the Hill this duplicity climbed.

As he departed, Will understood that the charges he wished to bring forth regarding the State Department needed to be impenetrable. Mobley needed absolute certainty. And right now, all they really had was that Turner was promoted and Sajwani was given a visa, but the correlation had not been clear. The central fact in this matter was that Mobley was still in support of their efforts and had essentially handed the baton to Will and SSA Kelly to get what they needed.

———

Will glanced through the window of the restaurant while Lacy finished a phone call.

"Sorry about that. You were saying?"

"My meeting with Mobley this morning. He made it clear that I was to communicate with Kelly rather than bring anything directly to him. I think he's concerned about exposure."

"What about our exposure?"

"I understand how you feel, but if Turner gets wind of his involvement, how long do you think it would take for him to garner support for Mobley's dismissal? We can't afford that. No matter what we're doing, he will be the one to pull the trigger with the secretary."

"Assuming he's not involved," she interrupted.

"Or the president. But that brings to mind the other reason why I asked you here. Lacy, I think we're harming our cause by having you stay at your house. I spoke with Axell last night. I was able to get a crew in to wire your house, but Axell thinks we're diverting resources and using up too many favors to make it possible for you to stay put. With what we've all done to keep 24-hour surveillance, well, he thinks our resources could be put to better use."

"You all think I should leave?"

"I'm just not sure how effective we're being."

"I feel like Jian will find us no matter where we hole up. At least we're prepared at my house." She raised a spoon to her lips and gently tipped the soup into her mouth.

With an abrupt, strident boom, the window came crashing down, sending shards of glass inside the restaurant. Tires screeched and smoke billowed from a motorcycle outside before it sped away. Pedestrians scattered, screaming and running, and those inside scrambled for cover.

"Get down!" Will jumped from his chair and lunged toward Lacy, pulling her from her seat and onto the ground. He threw his body over hers, shielding her from the chaos of flying glass and fleeing people. Fragments dropped on his back, the glass slicing through his shirt.

Sirens blared in the distance but grew closer. The restaurant was nearly empty with just a few of the kitchen staff still inside. Patrons fled out of the rear entrance and were now gathered in the front to witness the destruction and offer help to those who were injured.

As the commotion started to subside, Will cast a cautious eye upward and began to climb off of her. "Are you okay? Are you hurt?"

"I'm not hurt." Lacy began to rise. "But you are." She pulled his shoulder forward until he twisted enough for her to see. "You're bleeding. We have to get you some help."

A man rushed inside. "Are you two okay? What the hell just happened? Was it a drive-by or something?"

"I don't know. Did you see anything? Anything at all?" Will cringed as he pushed to return to his feet.

"No. There was the usual traffic. I was walking across the street. Then I heard a loud bang and the window just exploded. Sounded like a damn bomb."

"The man on the bike? Did you see his face?" Will pressed on.

"I'm sorry. I just didn't see." The man turned around.

"Someone had to have seen something, but sir, you need to go to the hospital."

"I'm fine. We're fine." Will helped Lacy to her feet. "Can you stand up?"

"Yes. I told you, I'm not hurt." Her face told another story. "It's Jian. He's here."

————

Day had turned into night before the team convened at the apartment that had become the epicenter of their surveillance efforts. Statements had to be given, evidence collected, and by the time it was all said and done, several hours had passed.

Lacy was shaken, yet her conviction was unaltered. "Why didn't we know he was here? Aaron was keeping tabs on Sajwani's travel. How did he slip past us?"

"We don't know Sajwani was responsible," Axell replied.

"He's been taking out all of those who knew the truth, who were involved in the cover-up. It has to be him," Aaron said. "He had to have traveled under a different passport and that's why I missed it. I should've known. Staying in Dubai after the murder of the bank president. It didn't make sense and I fucking blew it."

"The first thing we need to do is to get you both out of that house." The irony was that this was the very conversation Will had just had with Lacy. It did, however, present him with a more legitimate case and one she could not ignore. "It's time for you to leave your home, Lacy, as much as you don't want to." He began to look for assurances from Axell and Colburn. "I think we can all agree that staying there is no longer an option. Someone found us at the restaurant. Someone knew we were going to be there."

"That just proves that he can find me, no matter where I go. So why not be prepared? As we are now, in my own home."

"You're a tenacious woman, Merrick," Colburn said. "You're right about being prepared. What needs to change, however, is this." He gestured to the monitors. "This isn't really going to do us much good. We need boots on the ground. We need to find them before they find us."

"We have very little time in which to act," Axell said.

"And what are we supposed to do with what we found out regarding the State Department? Ignore it?" Aaron began to pace the room. "I put my ass on the line for that intel and so did Lacy. What if Jian wasn't behind today's attempt? What if it was our very own government? Someone who already knew what we'd found? Will, didn't you meet with Director Mobley this morning?"

"You want me to believe he had something to do with what happened today?" Will scoffed. "No way. But it does make the possibility seem more likely that someone on the inside knew where we'd be today. Jian couldn't have known. I just don't see how. He's still in Beijing, for Christ's sake."

"Then that's all the more reason to move forward quickly." Lacy was growing tired of listening to the back and forth. Decisions needed to be made and it would be up to her to make them. She was the one who opted to pursue this and she would be the one to make the call. "Axell's right. None of this has played out as we intended, so we need to change our plan. The time has come to stop being reactive. We need to be proactive."

"What are you proposing?" Axell asked.

"I believe the deputy secretary is a smart man, smarter than Kendrick. We don't know his part in all of this yet, or if he has one."

"You don't think he was involved? Then or now?" Will asked.

She raised her index finger to make clear her point. "When this reached Mobley and he attempted to arrest Kendrick, the only thing Turner was interested in was covering up what his staff had known. The obvious reason was to ensure relations with China remained intact and more importantly, to cover his ass and the secretary of state, even going so far as to suggest the president was on board with that plan. What if he had no such agreement with the president? Our entire point in moving forward was that it appeared as though someone else had to have known something. That Kendrick couldn't have acted alone. And that's why we're all standing here right now."

"Mobley would've seen through that. And besides, you saw the press conference afterward. What the president said," Will added.

"Our purpose was to find out who in our own government let Kendrick off the hook. Maybe we've been looking at this the wrong way. What if Kendrick was never really let off?"

"You think someone, maybe Turner, was working behind the scenes to get Jian freed after the elections? Let him get rid of those who were intimate with the situation," Axell said.

"I'm suggesting part of the plan, whoever's plan it was, was to do exactly that."

"Where does that leave us, Lacy?" Will asked. "What do you want to do now?"

With her arms folded across her chest and her eyes fixed upon his, Lacy knew what needed to be done. "We're going to get Turner to work with us."

Axell unleashed a hearty laugh. "You're serious? We have no idea if he's involved in this and you just want to what—ask him? You do remember what happened when I confronted Kendrick, right?"

"Yes. But we knew of his direct involvement. We don't know where Turner stands."

"And how do you propose we approach him on this particular subject?"

"We'll need Aaron to send him a message. One that only he will understand." She looked at her friend. "It's the only way we'll know where his loyalties lie."

———

Lei Jian dawdled impatiently for the minister who, it seemed, had intentionally kept him waiting.

"The minister will see you now." A man donning the MSS uniform, which displayed the ministry's logo prominently on his chest and shoulder, stood at attention before Jian.

It wasn't so long ago when it was Jian himself giving orders to guards and commanding respect. But all that changed under the new regime. He'd wondered why the premier appointed such a man to this position of power. Jian entered the minister's office.

"Take a seat, please. Why have you come to see me? Haven't I done enough for you by giving you back your freedom?"

"Of course, sir, and I am very thankful and remain loyal to your service. However, I've come here today to discuss a continuation of our previous efforts."

"You mean the efforts that led to your detention and to threatened sanctions by the US Government because you were careless? And that also led to my appointment? Perhaps it is the former minister from whom you should seek advice. I released you at the insistence of the State Council."

"And I am grateful, but if you could see just how successfully executed the idea was. And how it is still within our power to do again. This time, perhaps on a smaller scale and ensuring fewer interlopers." Jian could see that the minister was considering the idea.

"What do you hope to accomplish, Lei Jian? What can you do to further advance our infiltration into the United States?"

A hint of a smile masked Jian's face but quickly vanished. "They are still on heightened alert after the attack. I think to attempt such a thing again would be a mistake. However, there are other means of destroying their economic systems. And we've done it before, though not on such a scale." He paused. "As you know, we have operatives, many of whom fill positions within the CIA and the FBI."

"Yes. Although it wasn't long ago when thirty of them were returned home, deemed spies for the Communist Party. A mistake that I again have to assume helped to propel my position, along with your debacle."

Jian rose to anger but regained composure. This was far too important to let his ego get in the way. "That still leaves us with ample resources within the organizations and those who still conduct business inside the US. We have a great many resources to explore."

"Before you go any further, I'll need to confer with the premier. The US has focused its efforts on ISIS, Syria, and the growing instability within its own borders. There are several options to consider, yet I am intrigued to continue our efforts on the economic front. Weaken them from that aspect, and we stand to gain much more in the long term. Their dependence upon us will grow."

"Thank you, sir. I am grateful you will consider my suggestions and take them to the premier." Jian prepared to leave. "There is one other thing I would like to ask of you, Minister."

"Yes?"

"I must be able to travel freely in order to continue the work."

"After speaking with the premier, I will ask that he reconsider that penalty."

"Thank you, sir. I am most grateful." A slight bow and Jian departed.

The minister retrieved his cell phone. "I think the time has come to allow Lei Jian freedom of movement." He paused while the man on the other end spoke. "Yes, and if he is captured, which is an almost certainty, then we let the Americans do what they do best. We want him to be a reminder that we do not take orders from the US, especially from this administration. And if they again threaten sanctions, then perhaps we will remind them what it was they chose to hide from their people."

————

As he returned to his car, Jian's phone rang. "Yes, what is it?"

"They've been alerted to my arrival."

"How is that possible? You are traveling under an alias. Not even the hacker would've known that."

"The home—it's deserted. I just left there."

"Where are they? What am I paying you for, Ahsan?"

"I will find them. I don't know why they're no longer at the Merrick residence."

"I've just had a very productive conversation with the Minister. He is considering the proposal I placed before him. It is up to you to ensure the elimination of our loose ends, as you promised."

"I understand. There's one more thing, sir." He paused. "I've just been informed that an attack was carried out where the civilian FBI worker and the agent were having lunch."

"An attack? By whom?"

"I do not know. But that may have led them to flee the home."

"Find out who is after them and if it is a friend or enemy."

CHAPTER
ELEVEN

THE LAST THING Lacy wanted was to leave her home. It was the equivalent of admitting defeat. Once again, her hand was being forced and her desire for retribution was growing stronger with each passing day.

She began her trek to the other side of Headquarters, where she would meet with Will, who'd already gained the support of his new SSA, a concern, which, until Mobley's assurances, couldn't be quantified, but was now laid to rest. "Hey." She stepped into the doorway of Will's office. "You ready?"

They made their way into the Headquarters' lobby and, finally, outside to Will's car.

"Shouldn't take us long to get there. Kelly made the arrangements. I don't know exactly what information Mobley has entrusted him with, but he got the place and I didn't ask questions." Will stepped inside.

"What about Aaron?"

"He's helping take down the surveillance equipment at the apartment, where he'll stay in the interim. No one knows he's there. No one knows of that place at all, so he'll be safe. Per Axell's instructions, Aaron will go about his business as usual, except continue to track down Jian and Sajwani and gain further insight into Turner. His involvement is still key, though I don't know how much Hunter will find on him."

"There's still more to discover in those personnel files. I know there is. Aaron should focus on finding financial ties between Turner and China. That will solidify our assumptions. But I just want confirmation that he'll be safe."

"I can't offer any guarantees, Lacy. I wish I could. But I know Axell and Colburn will do their level best to protect him."

There was nothing left for her to say. They were on their way to do something she had never envisioned doing. She had joined the FBI to help find terrorists, but in a capacity that never put her own life at risk. Now she'd put her life on the line count-less times, it seemed. They were on the hunt and she would not quit until they captured their prey. Just as Lei Jian wouldn't stop until he did the same. She couldn't help but wonder who would win.

With miles of silence having passed by, Will's approach to the suburban row house was somewhat anti-climactic. Lacy had expected a sort of triumphant arrival as though the game was afoot. Instead, the somber mood was amplified, as if no one would win and, in the end, their efforts would be thwarted swiftly and without prejudice.

Will leaned toward her and peered through her passenger window. "This is the place. We should get set up." He stepped out of the car and grabbed his belongings.

They approached the steps of the front door and Will retrieved the keys from his coat pocket. Upon unlocking it, he pushed it open and stepped in first. "Let me just take a look around. Wait here." He walked inside, gun at the ready, and searched each room of the modest two-bedroom home. What made this place special was its proximity to the deputy secretary's home, whose address Lacy had furtively obtained.

"Everything appears in order." He holstered his gun. "Come on in. We need to get set up quickly. Colburn will be here soon." He glanced through the curtains of the front room window. "His place is just over there, across the street, two houses down."

"And we'll be able to pick up on his conversations?"

"Video and audio surveillance is already in place."

"Axell doesn't mess around," Lacy added.

"No. They've got the resources to operate more covertly than we do. The CIA has access to more cash than the GDP of a small country." Will opened his carrier bag and retrieved his laptop, placing it on top of a folding table. The accommodations were sparse. The home, while too rich for his blood, was listed for sale and the owners had already vacated, a spot of good luck of which Kelly had taken full advantage.

"Now we just need to wait to see who Turner is talking to," Lacy replied.

"More importantly, if he knew what Kendrick was doing before the attack." Will finished the thought that had once seemed unthinkable.

———

A young man, short in stature, but exuding the utmost confidence, approached Turner's office. "Hey, Mary, I'm here to see Mr. Turner. He's expecting me."

"Hey, Bryce, have a seat. I'll let him know you're here." She picked up the headset. "Mr. Turner, Mr. Dunn is here to see you. Thank you, sir." She returned her attention to him. "He'll be right with you."

Turner appeared only a moment later. "Bryce, thanks for

coming. Please come on in." He nodded while the man walked inside and, with a glance into the hall, closed the door to his office. "I understand you were tasked with scrubbing the correspondence from the former undersecretary, Mr. Kendrick?"

"Yes, sir. As you know, I've been working on that for the FBI since they made the request."

"I'm sure it's a very unpleasant task at that. And did you find something of value?"

"I—I'm not sure, sir. I thought it best to bring this to you directly. Frankly, I'm not sure how to handle this." He handed over the flash drive.

Turner flipped the drive between his fingers. "Does anyone else know you have this or is aware of what its contents are?"

"No, sir."

"Then why don't you enlighten me? You must be greatly concerned by whatever is contained on here." He moved to his desk and inserted the drive into his computer.

"There are several documents on there, sir. Would you like for me to pull up the one that brought me here to you today?"

Turner pushed back in his chair and away from his desk. "Go right ahead."

The young man, not older than thirty, approached the desk and leaned in to retrieve the document in question. "This is it, sir." He stepped away again.

Turner leaned in close for a better view and began to read the letter. His previous expression, which revealed only mild concern, now appeared deadpan. "You say you found this on Kendrick's computer?"

"Yes, sir. And because his position is still vacant, none of what he had has been scoured in some time. The file had, of course, been deleted, but in accordance with FBI requests for information, I had to restore all the files. They still have the authority, depending on what we find, to confiscate the computers. Which, I imagine, after they see this, they will do so."

Turner had intentionally left the position vacant, dependent upon the outcome of the election. It was a decision he now regretted because this information would likely have been discovered much earlier had someone been appointed to the office. Now there was a young staffer, eager to prove his loyalty so that he might one day have his favors repaid, who had brought it to him. "I appreciate you bringing this to my attention. This should and will be forwarded to the agent in charge. In the meantime, I trust you'll come to me with any further findings of this nature?"

"Yes, sir. That is my intention. Undersecretary Kendrick was a good man, in my humble opinion, and I'm sure this wasn't intended to undermine your position." The man began to leave.

"Thank you, Bryce. Your cooperation is very much appreciated." Turner waited for him to close the door and quickly returned his attention to the screen.

Dear Mr. Secretary,

I tender this resignation with a heavy heart. My entire adult life has been in the service of this country and now my time has come to an end. It was never my intention to do harm to any American citizen, but to protect them first with my military service and; secondly, with my service as the Undersecretary to the Office of Political Affairs, protecting each and every citizen with the choices I made in this office. However, I succumbed to the temptations that often plague those who choose public office. Power. Plain and simple. My desire for power outweighed my need to do good. I, and I alone, am responsible for the attack on the mall in Fairfax, Virginia. While I did not perform the act myself, I did nothing to prevent it. There were others aware of my actions who chose to stay silent and that, sir, is what I wish to confess to you now.

Turner could read no more. This was not the letter he'd seen upon Kendrick's resignation and the one forwarded to the president. It was a clear attempt to preserve his life, made after his resignation. This would do irreparable harm to the department, himself, and the entire administration.

This indeed had been Kendrick's insurance policy, meant to be found in the event of his death, which he must've surmised would come about sooner rather than later. However, what Kendrick hadn't banked on was the letter's discovery by an ambitious young staffer. This was where Turner found luck.

"Damn it!" He was left with no choice but to finish the job Kendrick had half-heartedly attempted and that was to permanently destroy this letter and pray he could keep the young man on his side and under his control. Kendrick was cunning in his efforts and, had it worked, Turner could no longer hide behind his carefully crafted lie.

He retrieved the flash drive and placed it in his pocket as he prepared to leave for the day. It had been a long and arduous day filled with questions about Kendrick's death and post-election appointments when his biggest concern was the return of Lei Jian. Turner grabbed the rest of his things and walked out into the main part of the office. "I'm heading home. Have a good night."

"Good night, Mr. Turner."

He was already stepping inside the elevators and scarcely heard the reply. His mind was preoccupied with far more pressing matters. It wasn't until he reached his car and began driving home that he realized he hadn't shut down his computer. Was there a way someone might be able to see what he'd seen? No, not possible. It was on a USB and he had that drive with him now. Perhaps it was paranoia.

———

Will noticed Turner's car pulling onto his driveway. "He's home."

"And still no sign of Sajwani?" Lacy asked.

"No. Nothing yet. It's still early."

"I just hope we're right and that it was Sajwani who came after us at the restaurant."

"I suppose we'll know our assumption was correct if we see him there tonight, at Turner's home. If it isn't, we'll have another problem on our hands," Will continued.

"There's no question it would be a huge risk for Sajwani to go after the deputy secretary."

"But that doesn't mean he won't. Jian is after revenge and Sajwani will do whatever it takes to keep his boss happy."

The two began to study the monitor, which panned from different cameras hidden inside Turner's home. It was a quick and dirty job for which Colburn's team had been responsible and had been extremely effective. The unsanctioned surveillance of a high-ranking member of the State Department would see both him and Axell jailed on the grounds of treason if those cameras were discovered before any practical evidence against him was found. Lacy didn't think even Mobley could help them if that happened.

Will peered through the window and spotted a car approaching. "Colburn's here. Good timing." He opened the door. "Turner just arrived home. We've been monitoring him for the past several minutes."

"How's Aaron?" Lacy asked.

"Safe. I confirmed with Axell only a few minutes ago. He dug around and retrieved Turner's records prior to his appointment as Deputy Secretary. Axell thinks there could be a link between him and the Chinese and that's what Hunter's working on." He continued inside, placing takeout bags on the table and shedding his coat. "Thought you guys might be hungry."

"I could eat." Lacy offered a warm smile. "Thank you."

Colburn turned in the direction of the window. "Did you see that? It was a light; a flash of something caught my eye. Caison, you seeing anything on the monitor?"

"No." He moved toward the window to join him and peered down. "I don't see—wait. I do now." He looked to Colburn. "You think that's him? You think that's Sajwani?"

CHAPTER
TWELVE

WHEN THE KNOCK sounded at the door, Turner's wife glowered at him. "We're having dinner. You aren't expecting someone, are you?"

"No. I'll see who it is." Turner pushed away from the table and walked toward the door, rendering a glance over his shoulder before opening it. "What are you doing here? My family is home. You need to leave right now."

"We need to talk and it can't wait."

"Who is it?" his wife shouted.

"Just work. I'll only be a minute." Turner stepped outside and closed his door. "What is it? What's so important you needed to come to my home while I'm eating dinner with my family?"

"I think you know. Are we going to have a problem with that young man?"

"No. Of course not. It's taken care of."

"Have you destroyed the file?"

"Yes. I told you before, you need to let me do my job. I've taken care of the letter. No one will know of its existence."

"Just remember that you have as much, if not more, to lose

than we do. Our arrangement is simple. But only so long as you keep to your end of the bargain."

"I've given you no reason to doubt me, have I? I didn't know he'd emailed himself the letter. How could I? It's been removed from the files. The FBI will have no cause to confiscate the computer. Kendrick is no longer a problem for us."

"Unfortunately, Kendrick brought it on himself. You know as well as I do how anxious he'd become. How long do you think it would have been before he demanded money to keep quiet?"

"Yes. And look at where it got him."

"Then we are in agreement. I'll leave you to your dinner. It smells delicious, by the way. I will assure our colleagues, then, that the young staffer will not reveal what he knows. And if he does, you will be held accountable."

Turner closed the door and walked back inside, fixing an artificial smile on his face.

"Everything all right?" his wife asked.

"Yes. Everything's fine."

———

With the lights turned low so as not to be noticed, Will continued to peer through the window. "I don't know who he is, but he's leaving now. What the hell letter was he talking about? And it seems clear he believed Kendrick posed a threat." Will turned back. "Is he connected to his murder?"

"There's the sixty-four-thousand-dollar question. We have the visitor on surveillance footage," Colburn began. "We'll run him through facial recognition to see what it picks up."

"I don't think it was Ahsan Sajwani." Lacy returned to the monitors. "This guy was shorter, fuller. And if it was, I think Turner would be dead."

"The overcoat could've made him appear stouter than Sajwani. But in any case, I wouldn't be so sure Turner would have been killed on his front porch." Colburn said. "Taking out a sitting Deputy Secretary would create chaos for Jian, the MSS, and the entire intelligence community after Kendrick had just been killed. Regardless of who it was, we know Turner's hiding something. Whatever this letter he referred to was, we need to get our hands on it as soon as possible. For now, Will, run his image through FACE and NGI and I'll get Hunter to run him through our systems. Something will turn up."

"What's on the agenda for tomorrow, then?" Lacy asked.

"Will, you're going to need to get access into Kendrick's home," Colburn said.

"What about the agent in charge of the investigation? He's not going to let me waltz right in and start nosing around."

"Sure he will. And you're going to make sure he does." Colburn smiled. "While you're busy with that, Lacy and I will wait until Turner's place is empty and have a look around there for this mysterious letter." He turned to her. "Assuming you're up for that?"

"Why wouldn't I be?"

"Good. Then we should get some rest."

———

Will considered how to approach the agent as he drove to the Kendrick home, which his widow had already vacated. While it was no longer considered an active crime scene, as the feds had already come through in a whirlwind gathering of evidence, it was still considered to be off-limits to anyone other than those involved in the investigation. Even the family had to garner permission to enter. This was a former diplomat and, as such, was a top priority for the FBI team. So it was no surprise when Will needed the agent's permission to enter and also insisted he stand side-by-side while Will searched the home.

He pulled alongside the edge of the road where the front lawn abutted a curbless, rural street. The home was set back a fair distance and was shrouded by tall live oaks, though he could see through them now that the branches were bare.

With no other vehicles in sight, he stepped out in search of his contact, the agent heading up the investigation, SSA Adam Fraser. It wasn't until he reached for his cell to make the call in an attempt to locate the man did he appear from the side of the home.

"Agent Caison?"

Will began walking to meet him. "Yes. You must be Agent Fraser. I didn't see another car and thought I was alone." He offered his hand on approach. "Thank you for meeting me. I'm sure you're very busy with this investigation."

"Yes, we are. But it seems you have friends in high places, and so here I am."

This wasn't going well at the onset. It was clear the man was irritated to be meeting someone of lesser authority on a site that was in his jurisdiction at the Washington Field Office, not Counterterrorism at Headquarters.

"I apologize if I'm wasting your time, Agent Fraser. This won't take long."

Fraser started back toward the entrance of the home. "What is it that you're hoping to find, Agent Caison? My team has done a thorough job here."

"I'm sure they have, sir. My instructions were to photograph the location of where the body was found and to retrieve copies of any surveillance footage you were able to obtain."

"I could've sent you that without your having to drive all the way out here." Fraser stopped at the door. "Tell me why someone from CTD is really here."

———

Lacy hovered over the monitors and finally turned to Colburn. "Everyone's out."

"It's about time. Let's get started." He retrieved the key.

"How did you get that?"

"Wasn't hard. I entered the deputy's office while he and his staff were in a meeting and scanned his house key. He'd left his keys in his coat pocket—an easy pick. From there, I used a 3D printer, and *voila*." He held the key in his hand. "A fully functional key."

"I'm glad you're working with us." She slid on her coat. "I suppose you know the alarm code too?"

"Why yes, yes I do. We needed that before we could install any of the cameras."

"Right." She followed him out the door.

As they left the home, Colburn walked across the street, surveying their surroundings in an effort to spot anyone who might be watching them. "You remember what we discussed?"

"Yes. We're looking for anything that ties him to Jian or China. And of course, this mysterious letter."

"Right. He told whoever visited him last night that he'd destroyed it. But my guess is that he didn't and is probably keeping this letter on his own personal server for safekeeping. And if we don't find it, I'll bet a dollar to a dime we'll find something to prove he's working in his own best interests."

They made it to the other side of the street and Colburn began, "Most people keep their important docs in a filing cabinet in an office, but I suspect, because of the deputy's position, he keeps his documents either in a safe in his house or a safety deposit box at a bank."

"Let's hope we find something in there. Otherwise, we're just committing another felony. But hey, who's counting?" Lacy joined him at the steps of Turner's home.

———

As the words left Agent Fraser's mouth, Will knew the question would come first and foremost. Fortunately, he'd already produced an answer he hoped would pass muster. "I understand your concern. You're in charge of this investigation. If I were you, I'd question me as well. The best I can say is that there are concerns about appearances from the State Department. Those which the FBI director wants to clear up."

"Appearances?"

"Because of Kendrick's uncharacteristic and sudden resignation and the whirlwind of rumors surrounding it, so shortly after the mall attack, the director wants to be sure of complete transparency coming from the Bureau and, of course, to eliminate any question that this might have been terrorist-related as a result. I'm not here to double your or your team's efforts. I'm simply here to offer a second set of eyes—from the Counterterrorism Division. And so we're to act jointly, in part, on this investigation. But as far as I'm concerned, I'm only here to take a look at the crime scene, take a few shots, and have a look around his den, where he was last seen by his wife. And finally, discuss with you any theories on a suspect."

"And that's it?" His eyes conveyed doubt in Will's answer.

"That's it. Feel free to call my boss, SSA Kelly. Hell, you can call Director Mobley, if you like."

That seemed to do the trick. Throwing around Mobley's name was enough to make just about anyone back down.

"No. That's fine. If that's the way Headquarters wants it." Fraser opened the front door. "Come in. Take a look around."

"Thanks."

Will had a keen eye for details, a skill that had served him well during the mall attack investigation. In fact, he was the one to discover Jay Merrick's carrier bag, which contained the man's final gift to his wife. It also contained the flash drive, which he'd turned over to IT. And in the end, it was Lacy who realized what was on that drive and was the very reason he was here right now.

"Have you received the phone records yet?" He began to study the room, dissecting each corner, every book, every knickknack, and what he'd hoped to find was anything that might point to communications prior to his death with Jian or his people.

"Yes, I'm happy to send that information over to you," Fraser replied.

"What about his wife? Have you spoken to her regarding any recent visitors to the home?"

"Yes. She said no one ever came over. Their children are in college and it was just the two of them. She said everyone in D.C. seemed to treat them like outcasts since his resignation."

"Had he seemed agitated that day? Did she say?"

"No. Of course, he'd been holed up in here, she said, for the majority of the day. Said he often came in here to be alone. That he wasn't the same since leaving his position."

Will continued to look around. "And you guys scoured his laptop?"

"You're more than welcome to get a copy of the report from Computer Forensics. They didn't find anything that might explain why he was murdered."

Will immediately thought of the letter. It seemed like

Kendrick hadn't kept a copy here, or they would likely have already discovered it. He approached a bookcase and furrowed his brow at one of the titles. He cocked his head slightly to read the words on the spine. It was a book on the Chinese economy. And as he continued to peruse the shelf, he noted others of similar topics.

"You see something?" Fraser asked.

"No. Just interesting reading he has here." Will turned from the bookcase. "You want to take me outside where his body was found?"

———

With the turn of a 3D printed key, and entering four little numbers on a keypad, they were inside Turner's impressive home. Colburn walked inside ahead of Lacy and moved straight for the home office. "Let's start in here. We're looking for the server. Probably only used as a backup, but most of these guys have something where they can transfer data from their work laptops."

"Isn't that illegal?"

"Depends on the usage and what's stored. I back up files onto my own server; nothing classified, of course." He winked. "But I wouldn't use a cloud-based system if my life depended on it. Too many people out there like our friend Hunter."

Lacy smiled. "I suppose so. But even if we find one, how are we supposed to get into it?"

"We don't need to. And I already know there is one because we found it yesterday when we set up surveillance." Colburn walked toward a small closet inside the office. "See. Here it is." He knelt and pulled the server out with gloved hands. He reached around the back and retrieved a dongle; essentially, a small USB the size one would find when using a wireless mouse. "I've got it."

"What is that?"

"A keylogger. We popped this baby in yesterday too, figuring we'd want to know what Turner was keeping."

"A hardware keylogger. Wow. Old school. Nice, but definitely old school."

"Sometimes the old ways are best." Colburn pushed up to his feet. "We can take a look and see what's on it when we get back. No need to reinstall it because Hunter will be able to pull the passwords and get remote access from that point."

"Well then, we should focus on finding any sort of financial information. Get an idea if and from whom he might be taking money." Lacy opened the small lateral filing cabinet near the closet. She rifled through the files and then immediately knew she'd found what they were looking for. Lacy retrieved the file marked "Jan," undoubtedly, his wife's name, and began perusing the file. "I think I got something here." She pulled out her cell phone and took pictures of the documents. "Looks like bank statements to me, and they're in his wife's name."

"Perfect." Colburn turned his attention outside at the sight of movement. "Oh hell, we're not alone. Put that back. We need to get the hell out of here."

Fraser led the way to the shore of the lake. "This was where his wife found him."

Will began to examine the area. Mud covered much of the grounds, a few footprints presumably from him and his wife when she found him were visible. He looked to the left. "Would anyone have seen someone approach from this direction?"

"I believe so. As you can see, the road fronting the home is just ahead of where you're looking right now. But we're thinking the killer approached from this side." He turned toward the right.

"What makes you think that?"

"Because he was strangled first. Means the killer would've had to stay out of Kendrick's periphery until he was close enough."

"He was shot too. How many times?"

"Just the one." He pointed to the area on his side as an indicator of where the bullet would've struck Kendrick. "Right here. We did find the shell casing over here a few feet to the right."

"What was the caliber?"

".40. Probably a Glock, but I'm still waiting on forensics. Silencer fitted too."

Will recalled the shots fired at the restaurant. Before the police arrived, he'd found one of the shell casings nearby, and being uncertain of his level of trust for just about anyone at this point, he slipped it into his pocket. He'd discovered it was also a .40 caliber and knowing that these two weapons, at least, the ammunition, were a match, made it seem all the more likely that they were dealing with the same assassin.

CHAPTER
THIRTEEN

THE UNEXPECTED GUESTS were moving in on Lacy and Agent Colburn's territory, which was to say that it seemed they were all looking for the same thing. Lacy ducked below the line of sight and followed Colburn out of the room and toward the back of the home where a set of French doors would be their only way out.

"Who is it?" Her words were imbued with panic. "Is one of them Sajwani?"

"No. Just go—quickly." He opened the back door and they fled into the yard and toward the fence. Colburn leaned over and laced his fingers. "Jump."

She placed her left foot into his cradled hands and gripped the top of the fence while he pushed her up. His strength was greater than she'd expected when her body was catapulted over and she stumbled to the ground. "Hurry!" Lacy stared at the fence, waiting for Colburn to hop over.

In a split second, his head appeared and she was never so grateful to see his salty hair. He tumbled over the top and landed with an awkward thud, slamming his knee on a jutting stone. Lacy helped him to his feet. "Are you okay? Can you walk?"

He winced in pain now that the full weight of his body rested on his knees. Blood dripped from a gash. With a nod of assurance, he pointed ahead, mouthing the word "go."

Lacy started toward a side gate at the neighboring house. The sound of their steps on the brick pavers that lay over much of the grounds was unavoidable and whoever had come must've heard them, but they were left with no choice except to flee as quickly as possible.

"Hold up!" Colburn approached the gate first, still appearing to be in pain. He peered over the gate. "Let's try this again." He helped her over and struggled to pull himself up but soon joined her. "We need to make it across without them spotting us. They're in Turner's backyard already, so I think we have time before they realize where we are. We'll go to the end of the street, then cross over and back to the house."

Lacy began to jog but realized how far Colburn had trailed. When she stopped and turned back, he motioned for her to continue. In defiance, she shook her head, but he persisted and finally Lacy knew she had to keep going.

At the end of the road, she took another look back and saw that Colburn was still lagging. The time had come to cross to the other side of the street. The house was in sight and they would be safe soon. She surveyed the area and spotted no one approaching. Her heart told her to stop and wait for him, believing that perhaps they had made it and were now in the clear, so she did.

When Colburn caught up to her, his face masked in disappointment. "I told you to keep going."

"I can't leave you behind." She grabbed his arm and led the way across the two-lane road. "Who the hell is coming after us?"

"I don't know, but I'll find out. Let's just get back to the house."

Now on the other side of the street, both cast their gaze toward Turner's home. A car was parked in front, but still no one appeared.

"They're looking for the letter. They have to be," Lacy said.

"We're almost there. Just keep going." Colburn returned his attention to the building ahead. "Stop!"

Lacy whipped back toward him. "What is it?" Upon turning her eye in the same direction, her heart sank.

He quickly handed her the dongle. "Lacy—run." Colburn stood tall and moved in front of her.

"I'm sorry." She ran in between the adjacent building for shelter and continued through the alleyway. A gunshot sounded, startling her, and she turned back. "No!" Her eyes darted back and forth as she reached the end of the alley. To her left was the house, but the risk of going back there now was too great. On her right was the unknown. She was in an unfamiliar place and had no idea what lay ahead, but the unknown was her only option.

———

A final inspection along the banks of the murky lake and Will felt he'd gotten all he was going to get and needed to get back to Lacy and Colburn. "Thank you, Agent Fraser. I think I've gotten what I needed."

"I can still have my team send you whatever you need for a full assessment on the status of our investigation."

"Thank you. I'd appreciate that. In the meantime, I'd better head back and let you do the same." Will started toward the house again.

"I'm sorry if I was defensive." Fraser walked alongside him "I do understand the severity of this case. A retired diplomat, who frankly retired under somewhat inauspicious circumstances. I've heard the rumors, as I'm sure you have as well."

"No need to apologize. We're all working toward the same goal here. And whatever the truth is, it will come out." They reached the front of the home. "Thank you for your cooperation." He began to walk toward his car and, with a final glance at the stately home, Will drove off, heading back to the house.

A message sounded on his cell phone—a missed call in a part of town with a weak cell phone signal. "Shit." He glanced at the caller ID and listened to the voicemail Lacy had left him.

"Someone showed up at Turner's house when we were still there. We got out, but something happened to Colburn. Got split up. I need help. They're after me now."

The call was cut short. "Damn it!" He pressed her contact info and waited for her to answer. "Come on. Pick up!" The call went to voicemail and he slammed on the steering wheel. There was only one person he knew who could ping her phone, but Aaron was at Langley and cell phones weren't allowed in the building where he worked. He would have to find another way to get to her and fast.

———

Sirens approached in the distance, probably due to the gunshot that rang out, which would have been unusual in this part of town. Lacy kept moving. Her legs were wearing out as she pushed to get farther away. She needed to find a safe place to hole up.

The sun was above her head as the morning quickly turned to afternoon. Lacy believed she'd outrun them, though remained in the shadows as a precaution. A firehouse was just ahead and it would offer her a location to convey if she tried Will once again.

This time, he answered. "Lacy! I've been out of range. I'm so sorry. Thank God you called. Are you okay? Where are you?"

"I've tried to stay off the grid, but I'm heading toward a fire station up the road. I ran for miles, maybe five or six from where we were. Will, I think they killed Agent Colburn."

"Is it safe for you to stay there? I'm heading your way now."

"I think I'll be safe. My God, Will, he saved my life. Keith Colburn saved my life and now he's gone."

"Just hang in there, Lacy. I'm on my way."

Within minutes, she spotted Will's car approaching. Walking out from behind a large tree and toward the sidewalk, she reached the car and opened the passenger door. "What took you so long?" Her face was masked in relief.

"I'm so sorry I wasn't here."

She stepped inside, tired and drenched in sweat from having run so far and so fast. "We have to find Agent Colburn."

"We'll head back toward the house and see if anyone is still there looking for you." Will began to pull away. "Did you see him get shot?"

"No. He told me to run—and I did. I should've stayed with him, Will. I abandoned him."

"You did the right thing. If you would've been hurt too..." He stopped. "Did you two find anything in Turner's house?"

"Yes. He had a keylogger installed yesterday on Turner's server when they put in the cameras. And I have a picture of a bank statement in his wife's name. That was as far as we got because someone showed up."

"Do you know who it was who shot him?"

"No. Colburn heard two people approach the house, and that was when he told me to run out to the back. We jumped into the neighboring yard and escaped out onto the street. But when we tried to make it back to the house, someone was waiting for us."

"That's when he told you to run?"

She nodded. "He handed me the keylogger device and I ran. After I was, I don't know, maybe half a block away, was when I heard the gunshot."

"Then you don't know who was hit. Could've been the other guy."

"If it wasn't Agent Colburn, don't you think he would've reached out to one of us by now?"

With notable distress, he replied, "Probably."

"I don't think it's safe to go back to the house, Will. They had to know we were staying there. How else would we have been stopped only steps away from it?"

He shook his head. "No one knew where the hell we were."

"Someone did."

———

Axell stood behind his desk. His hands were balled into fists with knuckles pressing hard on its surface. The call had come from Caison, and while neither knew for sure the fate that had befallen his friend and colleague, Axell felt betrayed. Who in their small circle of trusted associates had given away their location? The problem still lay in the fact that he didn't know who exactly was after them.

His first instinct was to call Colburn's cell phone but feared that could jeopardize whatever situation he might be in. If Colburn had been free to call, he would've already. Instead, Axell left his office and made his way to see Hunter. He'd tried to maintain distance to avoid the appearance of a personal relationship, but all that had now been tossed out the window. All he cared about was finding Agent Colburn.

He spotted Hunter at his desk inside the small, compartmentalized unit in which he worked. "Hunter?" Axell leaned over his desk. "I need you to find Colburn. Now."

Aaron seemed to understand the urgency and began to locate Colburn's cell phone. After several minutes, he was able to spot his last location. "I pinged his phone and this was his location as of an hour ago."

"Where is he now?"

"There's no signal. Either his phone is off, or..."

"Right." Axell didn't wait because he already knew the ending of that sentence. "You're coming with me."

The two left in haste as Aaron tried to ignore the eyes of his colleagues who followed them. "Where are we going?" He struggled to keep up.

"I told Caison to check out the area around the house and Turner's home. We'll meet up with them nearby and assess the situation."

"Oh God, what happened?"

"I don't know. But I'm sure as hell going to find out."

They jumped into Axell's car. He sped out of the parking lot and drove toward the house.

"Have you been in contact with anyone outside of our team?" Axell asked.

"No. Of course not. No one knew what I was doing. I made sure of it. Did I screw something up? I swear I was careful."

"I just need to be sure you weren't being watched." Axell turned to him. "What about the supervisor who trained you? You said she might've seen what you were working on the other day."

"Maybe. But I don't think so. I mean, no. I'm sure she didn't."

"Then who?"

The rhetorical question hung in the air until they reached the rendezvous point. As soon as Axell rolled to a stop, the two jumped out.

Will and Lacy met them halfway.

"Any word from Agent Colburn?" Lacy asked.

Axell cast his gaze down and shook his head. After a moment when all seemed to reflect on the probable answer as to why no one had heard from him, Axell continued, "Is anyone waiting for us?"

"Not that I could tell," Will replied. "I drove the perimeter but not the actual street in case we were recognized, but we saw no one."

"You and I need to hoof it and get to the house. If they knew about it, it would've been ransacked already."

"What can we do?" Lacy asked.

"Wait in Caison's car for now. I'll contact you when I know it's safe for you to join us."

"And if it's not? If you end up in the same situation as Agent Colburn?'

"We don't know what's happened to him yet, Lacy," Will said.

"If..." Axell raised his hands to preempt the growing tensions. "If we don't make contact inside of thirty minutes, I want you two to see SSA Kelly." He turned to Will. "You said he had Mobley's assurances?"

"Yes."

"Good. Because right now, I have no idea who the hell we can trust."

———

They made it to the front of the row house and walked up the steps. Both had guns brandished, ready to fend off anyone who might be lying in wait. Making it this far had been the easy part. It seemed if someone was after them, they'd opted to keep themselves concealed for the time being. Still, there was no sign of

Agent Colburn and both grew despondent at the most likely outcome.

Axell raised his index finger to his lips as he reached for the handle. It was unlocked and they were under no illusions that this was a good sign. With a measured hand, he pushed it open.

Will stood shoulder to shoulder with him, aiming his weapon through the opening of the door. Both stepped over the threshold and grasped the devastating scene.

"Oh God." Axell lowered his weapon and rushed to his friend's side.

Agent Keith Colburn was bound to a chair, his head hung low, beaten and bloodied. Axell placed his fingers on Colburn's neck. A moment later, he turned to Will. "He's gone."

"Son of a bitch. Whoever did this has to be the same person, or was with the same people as the man at Turner's last night. It had to be someone in Jian's ranks, but how the fuck did they find us?" He pushed his fingers through his hair and turned away.

"There's no way it was Jian's people, or Sajwani, or anyone like that. No way he could've known about this place. We're the only ones who knew, except for Kelly. He set this place up for us."

"And Colburn's guy. Agent Hicks. Do you know him? He knew we were coming here, didn't he? Colburn trusted him."

Axell ignored the questions being hurled at him because he knew it was Caison's anger overriding any cohesive thoughts. Instead, he began to search the ransacked home. What little furniture they had had been overturned. The monitors lying on the ground smashed. "I don't know if it was Hicks or not. But if it was him and he's not dead already, he's about to be."

CHAPTER
FOURTEEN

COLBURN'S BODY had been placed on the floor and covered in a sheet. Lacy sat next to him, legs crossed and staring in disbelief that he was gone. And only hours after he'd helped her flee those responsible for killing him. He'd saved her life as he had done only months ago, but this time, it cost him his.

"I can't stay here anymore. I can't look at him." Lacy wiped away her tears and finally stood up. Her legs filled with pins and needles, but she paid no attention to the discomfort. "Do we still have nothing from facial recognition on the images of the man from last night? I mean, come on. He has to have been one of the men who came after us today. Why don't we know who he is yet? Why the hell are we sitting here, still knowing nothing?"

"While I was at Kendrick's home, Agent Fraser told me the shell casing they found was a from .40 caliber bullet. It's the same as the casing I took from the shooting at the restaurant. We may not know who this is, but it's looking like we could be dealing with the same assailant. But right now, it's starting to feel like the Wild goddam West. Like there's a bounty on all our heads."

Axell continued to pace the small living room, glancing

through the window as the sun was beginning to set. "I have to take care of Colburn. I have to get him out of here."

"You think you can find out the type of bullet used to..." Will couldn't finish the sentence.

"Yes. It'll take some time, a day, at least." Axell regarded his friend. "Damnit. I'll have to get word to his family—and to his boss."

"Look, there might be a way to find out who went after these two and who took Colburn from us." Will peered at the body, still stunned. "Agent Fraser, I think we can use him."

Axell cast a wary eye at him. "How?"

"He made some comments regarding rumors and such about Kendrick, and I think he might have been fishing for information. Maybe he's grown suspicious of Turner himself."

Lacy had almost forgotten about the keylogger and the photos. "Wait." She pulled the device from her pocket. "What about this? This is what Keith handed to me before I took off without him. Maybe we should see if this letter is on here or if anything else turns up that will give us some idea of who did this to him. Whatever is on that letter seems awfully damn important."

"Right. Shit." Aaron took it from her and looked around. "The laptops are destroyed. Unless anyone's got another computer handy, this won't do us any good right now."

"Give me some time. Let me take care of my friend. I'll get more equipment. Caison, you said you thought Fraser could be of use. What do you want to do?"

"Well, there will be a report of a break-in at Turner's home once his family returns and realizes the alarm is off and the door unlocked. I don't know what they did inside if they took anything or what; regardless, a report will go out. And because Turner is who he is, FBI will be called. Meaning I could reach out to Fraser and tell him I heard about the break-in and ask him if there's a chance someone could be after Turner too. That'll whet his appetite given what I think I know about him already. Then, if we can find this letter and figure out if it's important—which at this point, we have to assume it is—I'll show him."

"No way. You don't know him, Will. You don't know what he might do," Lacy said.

"I understand what you're saying. But you said yourself we need to get Turner to work with us. Now's our chance."

"You wanted me to send him a message," Aaron began. "Well, depending on what we find, I'll send him a message that someone's after him too. A text from an unknown number. There are a lot of ways I can get to him, or at least get it to Fraser."

Axell looked to Lacy. "I think this is our answer. We need someone on the inside. Someone who can help Turner navigate through this mess while passing along information to us that we can use to identify Colburn's killers and, hopefully, the one who came after you two. Could be one and the same. But before you reach out to Fraser and Caison, let me run background. Make sure he's one of the good guys. Then we can discuss how much to divulge and get him to make nice with Turner."

Aaron held the device between his thumb and index finger. "Then I'd better figure out what we have on this keylogger as quickly as possible. We'll need it to sway this Agent Fraser."

"My friend is dead. They're after us and, right now, this is the only shot we have at getting to the bottom of Turner's involvement."

"Okay. I can see when I'm outnumbered. Then we'd better get to it." She looked again at Colburn and her eyes reddened. "The longer we sit here, the more likely they'll come back for the rest of us."

———

Yet another in a string of temporary surroundings, this time they landed exactly where they should've been days ago, but Lacy insisted on staying at her home. While the vacant house across from Turner's home was burned, the only place left was to go to Will's new apartment. And as the evening wore on, they waited for Axell's return. He did what he needed to do to take care of Keith Colburn and now they were at a standstill until he returned with an air-gapped computer. All the information they needed could be on that keylogger.

"He's here." Will jumped from his couch. "He just texted me."

"Thank God." Lacy stood up and turned toward the door. "I was afraid something...never mind. He's here now."

"Yes. He is." Will opened the door. "Good to see you, man. Everything go okay?"

"I made his station chief aware of what happened, indirectly. She and I go way back and she said she would take care of things. I left it at that." Axell raised the box in his hands. "Also, I stole this from inventory at our office. No one will ever know it's gone." His congenial smile soon faded.

"Did you find Hicks?" Lacy asked.

"No. I asked Ward about him. She's the station chief. She says he's loyal and if she thinks so, then I do too. Colburn had no reason to doubt him either. So he's not our leak."

"Okay. Aaron, you want to get that set up and we can see what's on the logger?"

"On it."

Within minutes, Aaron had the laptop running. "I've got it set up to re-route us all over creation if we need to access the internet. But for the purposes of accessing the keylogger, we shouldn't need to, assuming there's also a screenshot program on here, which I'm sure there is. Lacy, can I have the dongle?"

"Here."

Aaron loaded the device and pulled up whatever Turner had keyed when it was plugged into his server. "Looks like he didn't do much in the hours this was on his system, but this does contain a screenshot program, so let me see what I can find in there." He continued to type while the others hovered over his shoulder. "I really don't like it when you guys watch over me like this. I feel like I'm at Langley."

Almost in unison, the three pulled back and replied, "Sorry."

"Well, I think I found it." Aaron pushed away from the laptop. "This is a letter from Drew Kendrick addressed to the secretary of state. It's dated two weeks prior to his murder."

Lacy and the others pushed in to read it, but she was the first to speak. "This was why he was killed."

"I'd have to agree with you." Axell continued to read it. "He admits he knew about the attack and looked the other way."

"This throws Turner under the bus too." Will stepped back. "Says he knew about it."

"I'd say that would be enough to get you killed in this town." Axell looked at Will. "This is what you need to show Fraser. Get him on board. We need him now. He's clean as far as I can tell."

"Wait, shouldn't we take this to Mobley? How much more evidence do we need?"

"Lacy, we always knew Turner wanted to keep this quiet. That's why he forced Mobley to let Kendrick go and did whatever deal he could with the Chinese and the president and whoever else. The problem for us is knowing if it stops with Turner."

"Will's right," Aaron began. "Maybe Turner ordered Kendrick's murder. We still don't know, although this letter is compelling evidence. But that doesn't explain why someone broke into his house to get this. It means someone else knows about it too. It just feels like we've got more than one enemy here. Turner, Lei Jian, and who else?"

"Okay. Let's just tackle one problem at a time. I'll set up a meeting with Fraser. He gets Turner to talk and we might actually get somewhere."

———

Will sipped on the coffee while he waited for Fraser to respond to the proposal.

"I don't know what to say, frankly. This all seems very conspiratorial if you ask me. And I'm not one to put much stock in those theories."

"I understand where you're coming from, Adam, believe me. If I hadn't been through what I've been through since the mall attack, I'd be saying the exact same thing." Will leaned over the table. "Look, you and I both know that there was a lot of shady dealings where Kendrick was concerned and I'm sure you've already seen some of that in your investigation."

"To be honest, most of the things I've come across have been redacted. And that alone gives me pause."

"Exactly. Now I don't know how Turner fits into this, except it seems clear he knew, or that's what Kendrick wanted us to believe. But someone broke into his house, looking for a letter." Will pushed a mini SD card toward him. "We got that letter and I think you need to see it and decide for yourself. Go ahead; check it out."

Fraser eyed him before picking up the card and inserting it into his cell phone. After a few moments, he opened the file and began to read the letter.

Will watched as the color drained from Fraser's face. He knew then that he had him.

"Are you shitting me with this?" Fraser asked.

Will shook his head.

"Holy shit." He rubbed his forehead. "And no one knows you have this?"

Will shook his head again. "No one. Turner thinks he's the only one who's seen it and whoever visited him the night before last. At least, as far as I know."

Fraser was quiet again, staring at his phone. "Okay. What do you need me to do?"

"Whoever broke into his house is after me and my friends. We lost someone yesterday as a result. That's why I need your help. Turner's in this and I just need your help to get him to talk to us."

Fraser nodded. "Okay. I can get a meeting with him. He knows I'm running the show on Kendrick. I'll figure out a way to get him to open up. Maybe feed him some line about finding something in Kendrick's home. I don't know. Is there anything else I should know before I get myself wrapped up in this?"

"Just get Turner to talk, for now. There's more to this than I can get into here."

"But if I do this, you need to let me in on that."

"You might not want in. Trust me on that, brother."

———

Wendell Turner crisscrossed his office at the State Department, hands clasped behind his back and eyes down at the floor. "I sent my family away. People are going to ask questions as to why I slept in my office last night. If word gets out about the break-in, they'll launch an investigation. No one can know about this."

"I understand where you're coming from, Mr. Turner, and that's why I'm here. As I said before, I can help you get through this. What I found at Kendrick's home is troubling, but I know people who can help. No one wants you to take the fall for whatever it was Drew Kendrick was involved in."

"How do I know I can trust them? You think I don't already know who you're talking to? I know all about Agent Caison and his people. There isn't a chance in hell they'll help me. They blame me for protecting the president after Kendrick was taken into custody. How do I know they weren't the ones who broke in?"

"I think you know that's not the case, Mr. Turner. And I won't lie: Caison doesn't trust you. But this is your chance to clear the air. Someone came to your house looking for something. And I'll bet there's a high probability that you'll be dead, just like Kendrick, if we don't get help."

Turner sat down in his chair and rested his head in his hands. "I should've ended this when I had the chance."

"You chose to protect the president. No one will fault you for that."

Turner huffed. "You sure about that? I put politics over the safety of this country, over the truth. Could you forgive that?"

"It doesn't matter what I could forgive. Kendrick is dead. Your house was ransacked. They'll find you and they'll kill you too. No one knew where Kendrick was either, and yet he was found."

"A few people knew."

Fraser leaned over Turner's desk. "Let me reach out to my friends. Let me get the help we need to put an end to this once and for all. Who else do you have to turn to?"

———

The meeting was due to take place at a secure safe house Fraser had arranged about an hour south of Will's apartment in downtown D.C. where they'd waited almost twenty-four hours since he set up the deal.

"We need to go now. They'll be there soon."

"Another safe house?" Aaron asked

"You have a better idea?" Will asked. "The place near Turner's home is compromised and we can't stay here in my apartment forever. How long do you think it'll take to find us? We have to know who came after us or we're not safe. And you still have no idea where Sajwani is. Maybe do your job so we stand a fighting chance and don't have to cut and run at every turn."

"Hey, I got eyes on me all day, every day. You won't be the one going to prison for doing the shit you're asking me to do. I will."

"Do we really need this right now?" Lacy began. "Aaron, I know you're doing your best. We all are. And with Colburn gone, we're all on edge. Will and I were targeted at that restaurant and we've got people coming at us from every angle. Turning against one another won't solve our problem. Let's just go to the safe house. I agree that we can't stay here. Unfortunately, we have to stay on the move and, as much as I thought we could avoid that, I was wrong."

"I'll call Axell and have him meet us here and then we'll leave." Will brushed past Aaron as they eyed one another.

Tensions were high and Lacy could feel the team beginning to crack under the pressure. The death of their friend was bringing back the reality of the dangers they still faced.

———

In the darkening skies, Will spotted the meeting place. "This is it. Up ahead."

A cottage-style home, demure and rather nondescript, was set far back from the road. The brick-paved driveway was blocked by a low entry gate secured by a simple padlock.

Aaron pulled himself forward from the rear seat. "Doesn't exactly look like Fort Knox. Do you need to call and tell him we're here?"

At that moment, Agent Fraser appeared and opened the gates. He waved them inside and again secured the lock.

Axell stopped behind another vehicle parked in front of the single-car garage. A row of trees lined the property where it faced the street in the sparse community. Lights were on in the home's two front windows and as he pulled out his keys, Fraser returned to the porch. He began to step out. "Caison, you and I need to go first." He looked into the rear seat. "You two stay here until we give the 'all clear.'"

There were times when Lacy would object to being told to stay put, but this was not one of those times. She'd learned to trust Agent Axell and when he said it was best to stay put, then it was probably best.

Lacy tried to peer around them as they met with Fraser and all stood at the entrance, discussing something. But it seemed they were intentionally blocking her view, or blocking the view of Aaron and her.

She continued to peer, shifting her head for a clear view. Finally, Will turned and motioned for them to get out of the car. "There's our signal."

They stepped out onto the driveway and the nip in the night air sent a chill through Lacy's body. A final confirmation from Will suggested they continue forward until they all stood beneath the porch that was illuminated by a single hanging light.

"This is Lacy Merrick," Will began. "Lacy, this is Agent Adam Fraser."

She eyed the man and finally offered her hand. "Agent Fraser."

"Ms. Merrick."

"It's Mrs."

"Apologies, Mrs. Merrick." He turned to Aaron. "And you must be the hacker, Aaron Hunter. Pleasure to meet you."

"Same here."

"I'm sure you all would like to get out of the cold." Fraser stepped aside. "Come in. We have a lot to discuss."

It wasn't until they'd all entered the modest home that the deputy secretary made an appearance. Lacy regarded him with a mixture of revulsion and distrust.

"I can tell by the look on your faces that I'm the last person you wanted to see." Turner continued into the room. "I can only imagine what you must think of me. And before you say anything, I'd just like to convey my deepest apologies." He turned to Lacy. "To you, Mrs. Merrick, for the loss of your husband. And to you, Agent Axell, for your very recent loss of Agent Colburn. If I had known..."

"Doesn't matter now, Mr. Turner," Axell began. "All that matters now is that we understand one another, that we're all here for the same reason."

"I believe we are, Agent Axell."

"Why?" Lacy stepped closer, unable to slow her rising anger. "Why didn't you tell the people what happened at the mall? How could you have lied to them? To the families?"

"Lacy." Aaron reached for her arm, but she pulled it away.

"No. He should know what he's done. And in case you haven't realized it yet, Mr. Deputy Secretary, we're all here right now because of that lie. Because of you, I lost my husband and now we've lost a friend. What the hell are you going to do about it?"

"Your anger is understandable, Mrs. Merrick. Despite what you might believe, I'm angry too. Yes, I hid the truth and that will endure on my conscience for the rest of my days." He looked to the others. "I did what I did for the good of the country. I was under the false impression that if I kept the truth hidden, jobs would be saved from the throes of yet another economic downturn, only the likes we hadn't seen since the Great Depression. I wanted to avoid what could well have been a war between two superpowers. Mrs. Merrick, I wanted to avoid the downfall of our country."

Lacy laughed in outrage. "You're kidding me, right?" She turned to her friends. "He wanted to save his career and his political party. End of story." She refocused her attention. "One of your subordinates in the State Department took money and God knows what else to look the other way while Chinese operatives working under the direction of the MSS blew up one of our malls. And then he had the audacity to make it look like another Islamic terrorist attack. You didn't hide the truth for the protection of our country. You hid it *despite* that. And now, what, you want our help because Lei Jian was freed? Because someone ransacked your house? I bet it never occurred to you that he'd want to settle old scores and get back at the man who made sure his own government locked him up."

She turned her back on him. "I hope he finds you and whoever else is after you. And I hope he kills you."

"All right." Axell stood between them. "This isn't helping anyone right now." He gently reached for Lacy. "Maybe you're right. Maybe the only reason Turner came forward was that they found him." He looked to the man himself. "Who were you talking to that night? The night before your house was broken into? He came to you looking for information about the letter. The one on your server."

"I don't know who you're talking about."

"You clearly don't understand who you're dealing with right now, Mr. Turner," Lacy replied. "We know someone came to your door and you spoke to him outside. That's how we knew you were hiding something."

"It was you people. You were the ones who broke in." Turner looked at Fraser. "Why the hell am I here? I thought you were trying to help?"

"I am. And all of you are in someone's line of sight. That's why you're here. But you need to tell them the truth."

Turner looked upon the glowering eyes of Lacy and her colleagues. "He was my assistant. He knew about the letter because he brought it to me. I can't believe you were watching me. How the hell am I supposed to trust any of you?"

"We could say the same thing about you," Aaron replied.

"How about we stop pointing fingers and get down to business?" Will began. "We know Ahsan Sajwani killed the bank president in Panama. We assumed he killed Kendrick and that was what set this whole plan in motion. But after the break-in, what if our assumptions were wrong?"

"What do you mean, wrong? Who else would've killed the bank president?" Aaron said. "Who else would've killed Drew Kendrick?"

"What is it you're getting at, Caison?" Axell appeared to be catching on to his stream of thought.

"I believe Lei Jian and Ahsan Sajwani are doing their best to get rid of everyone associated with the attack and that includes us, but maybe not you, Turner. It would serve no advantage to rid himself of a powerful political figure, which would undoubtedly end in further sanctions against his country. I think we have another enemy. The enemy who got into your house and searched for that letter and anything else they could find. Someone who wants to be sure Turner never comes forward with the letter Kendrick left. Someone who could easily spin his death on another cause." He finally looked at his FBI colleague, Agent Fraser.

"You think it's someone on the inside?"

"Inside?" She glanced between the men. "The FBI? You think it's someone in the Bureau?"

"We can't rule it out. Unless you have any other ideas, Mr. Turner?"

"The reason I'm here is to find out. I don't know any more than you do who got into my home. No one else knows about the letter, apart from my assistant, which I already told you visited me the other night. Fraser came to me and said we needed to work together and it seems you all are in the dark as much as I am. You really think someone inside the FBI is working against all of us?"

"Anything's possible," Lacy replied. "Just look at what's happened so far."

"Mr. Turner, I'll need you to provide the names of those you've been in contact with at the Bureau regarding the Kendrick investigation. Apart from Fraser, of course. We can start there. Also, you'll need to provide us the name of your assistant."

"He's not involved in this."

"He is now. He knows and we need to know what his agenda is too," Axell continued.

"Fine. What am I supposed to do now? Stay in my office?"

"Frankly, I don't give a shit where you go," Lacy said.

Will eyed her. "We're in the same boat, Mr. Turner. We've been forced to stay on the move and I think the best thing you can do now is check into a hotel. Somewhere outside the city, until we can get more information."

"I think we've had enough for tonight. It's late," Fraser began. "This is a start, but what we have to remember here is that we're all working toward the same goal. And that is finding out who's after all of you." Fraser headed toward the door. "I'll get him settled in a hotel. Caison, as we discussed, it's best if you all stay here. You'll be safe." He opened the door. "Mr. Turner?"

After they left, Will closed the door.

Lacy eyed the car through the window as it pulled away. "He's lying. We all know that whoever came to his door was no assistant."

"Yeah. I got that impression too," Axell replied. "None of this has gone the way any of us had expected. So we need to take this steaming pile of horseshit and turn it into fertilizer. Turner will have to give us his contacts at the Bureau. See if we can find anything out on that front, assuming, Will, your theory is right. We'll continue to try and locate Sajwani and stop screwing around with him."

"Got it," Will replied. "Let me talk to Fraser. I'll get him to keep dibs on Turner. He knows more than he let on. I think we can all agree on that. But my theory hasn't changed. It's all we've got right now."

CHAPTER
FIFTEEN

THE SMALL HOUSE that was meant to hold no more than four or five people was near capacity with their crew. And it was Agent Fraser who secured the new accommodations. Laptops strewn about, papers, photos. While it would, to anyone on the outside, seem a chaotic environment, to the team inside, their plans were set and their tasks assigned.

Aaron's eyes flickered open when a light in the kitchen burned. It was dim enough, perhaps a range hood light, that it didn't seem to wake Caison, but Aaron knew right away it was Lacy. He pulled the blanket from his legs and stood up from the chair as quietly as he could, padding into the kitchen. "Hey." He placed a hand on her shoulder while she stood facing the refrigerator. "You okay?"

Her eyes conveyed the hurt, anger, and betrayal she felt at this moment. It seemed they were being hunted from every angle and were running out of places to turn. "Couldn't sleep. You?"

Aaron pointed to the light on the range hood. "Saw the light."

"Sorry. Didn't mean to wake you. I couldn't see a thing in this place."

"That's okay. Come here." He reached around and pulled her close. "I hope to God this is over soon. I just want to go home."

She pulled back and their eyes locked. "I want my kids. I want to get back to my normal life. I just don't know if it'll be there when this is over."

"Your kids will be and that's all that matters. You can start over, Lacy. We will put this in the rearview, I promise."

She leaned into him again, resting her head on his chest. A few sobs that it seemed she'd tried hard to keep inside managed to escape. But only for a moment, and Lacy pulled herself together again, as she had so many times this past year. "I still can't believe Keith is gone."

"Shhh." He brushed her dark hair, which had grown to her shoulders now. "None of us can. You should try to get some sleep. God knows when we'll get the chance again. I have a feeling, after tomorrow, everything will be different."

Lacy peered up at him. "I think you might be right—again." Her smile was tender but all too brief, and she made her way back to one of the two bedrooms. Axell had claimed the second, leaving Aaron and Will to fend for themselves in the living room, where Will still slept on the sofa.

Aaron watched her walk down the hall and disappear into the room before turning back and heading to the uncomfortable side chair that he doubted would allow for any decent sleep.

"Hey. She all right?" Will whispered.

"Not really. But I don't think any of us are. Are we?" Aaron tossed the blanket over his legs and shuffled into the chair in hopes of finding comfort. "Hopefully, she'll get some sleep. You should too. Night, Will."

"Night."

———

Lacy had reason to be suspicious of everyone around her. The idea that there could be someone in the Bureau after them hardly seemed fathomable. But she could not afford to overlook anyone. Even if that person might not be a direct culprit, someone in her department could be handing over information about her. "Stop." She closed her eyes and grasped the edge of her desk with her hands. The paranoia that continued to feast on all rational thought was compounded by a lack of sleep, and the fact that she'd lost a friend who'd saved her life. Assuming Will was correct, and it made all the sense in the world, it was a bitter pill to swallow.

A meeting had been called that Lacy was required to attend and the time had come to do the job she was being paid to do and try to leave the rest behind for the time being. She grabbed her tablet and headed toward the conference room. Inside, she spotted Michelle and a few members of her team, whom she'd felt she'd abandoned as of late.

"Okay, I think everyone's here and we can get started." Michelle made her way to the door, closed it behind her, and returned to the head of the conference table. "Thank you all for clearing your schedules. I apologize for the short notice." Sitting down, she continued, "As you all know, Lacy was at the restaurant that was hit a few days ago by an as-of-yet-unknown suspect. And another of our colleagues, a field agent, was with her. Fortunately, both were unharmed." She nodded to Lacy. "However, what that means is heightened security measures for the city, which has already been on high alert since the Fairfax mall attack. We have been tasked with additional duties, which include monitoring the usual sites and locales, but will also now include an additional level of observation. It's for our friends in the field, special agents who call upon us to dig deeper, to find the threats—even before they become threats—and alert them as soon as possible."

Lacy waited for this unusual request she was about to impart upon her and her colleagues, who, in the end, were still civilians.

"We are being tasked to blanket our city. Decipher and decode data transmitted within the twenty-four-hour period prior to and after the shooting."

"You're talking thousands upon thousands of pieces of information, most of which are likely unrelated to the event itself. How are we supposed to manage that amount of data and actually find something viable? It's needle-in-a-haystack type of stuff." Brian Eckhart was Lacy's equal up until her recent promotion, which he'd desperately wanted.

"You're right. It is. But what they don't want is another attack, which is what they're calling the shooting. It was no drive-by, gang member-style shooting. This was a calculated and targeted maneuver, possibly aimed at two of our own." She eyed Lacy. "And it'll be your job to find that out." Michelle rose from her chair. "Thank you all. I'll let you get to it."

Lacy waited for the room to clear. "Michelle, can I have a quick word?"

"Come back to my office. Better to talk there."

They arrived in her office and Michelle closed the door behind them before returning to her desk. "Have a seat. I can only imagine how you must be feeling right now after the restaurant and, of course, the mall attack. I wouldn't blame you for asking that you work on another assignment."

"Is that what you want?"

"Not at all. I want you to do what you think you should. Word has come down directly from CTD. We don't know if you were the target and it's a priority that we find out as soon as possible."

"I have to say something that, well, I'm not quite sure how you'll take it."

"Go on."

"I believe I was the target, and I think you do too. Things are happening right now. Things I haven't told you about—that have put me at risk. And not just me, but others."

Michelle folded her arms and leaned back. "I won't do you the disservice of construing that your presence at the restaurant was a coincidence, but who? And why?"

"First of all, can you tell me who's in charge of this investigation?"

"SSA Kelly, and he's working with SSA Delgado."

"Kelly?" Lacy began to wonder why Will hadn't said anything about this. Kelly was his boss. Why was he keeping him out of the loop?

"You seem surprised."

"A little. Listen, I know we've talked before and you said I could come to you with anything. Trust you with anything."

"And I meant it."

She was fearful to say anything further. Especially without consulting with the others, but she knew she could trust Michelle. "What if I needed to know a little bit more about SSA Kelly, and Delgado, for that matter? He took over after Mendez was unceremoniously dumped from the mall investigation."

Michelle regarded Lacy with apprehension. "I guess it depends on what type of information you need to know."

"Requests have to go through you for approval. This, however, is not a request that can appear on any paper trail or electronic trail. If I needed it, could you get me access to what they've asked for since arriving here?"

"You want to know what they've been doing? What they've been working on?"

"Yes."

Michelle cast her gaze down. "I'm assuming you're asking this because you have good reason to."

"You and I both know this hasn't ended; just been put on hold."

"I'll see what I can do, but, yeah, I think I can help you."

———

Lei Jian peered through the window of his office. His hands clasped behind his back as though he were handcuffed. While he'd spent the past several months in just such a predicament, today he was no longer a prisoner, but he was beginning to feel like one again. "I am useless here. Someone is working against us and we have to know who."

He turned toward the speakerphone. "Do you know who was responsible for the intrusion into the deputy secretary's home yet?"

"No. Not yet. I seem to be obstructed at every turn. I have been made aware, however, that one of the CIA agents has been killed."

"And who gave you this information?"

"Our friend who has helped us before. Word reached him earlier today."

"I have to go there."

"Sir, I implore you, do not travel. Your passport has been revoked. You will not be allowed to travel in any event."

"Ahh, you see that is where you are wrong." He began to meander inside his office. "The minister and I have begun to see eye to eye once again. He has come around to the fact that there are things that must be taken care of in order for us to move forward."

"It would be all too easy for the other CIA agent to track you down. There's too much risk."

"Your warning is duly noted, my friend. However, these roadblocks that have kept us from completing our mission have become cumbersome and I believe it must come down to me to make them disappear."

There was silence on the other end of the line.

"Ahsan? Are you still there?"

"Yes, sir. I will wait for your arrival then, sir."

"Don't worry, Ahsan. This will be over soon and you will be able to return home and I will again return to the position of which I was unfairly robbed."

CHAPTER
SIXTEEN

THE FACT that the safe house would be Lacy's home for an indefinite period of time made her all the more anxious to resolve her current predicament. Like the others, she wanted to go home, and getting her children back was her biggest priority. She hadn't attempted to reach out to Jay's sister in the past week and began to wonder if Olivia and Jackson believed she was never coming back. To a child, time moved slowly and that must have rung true for them. Day after day in a new home, in a new school. It must've felt like they'd been gone for an eternity. And it was beginning to feel that way for her too.

The route back to the safe house was to be continually altered in an effort to evade followers. Today, it would add an extra twenty minutes to the journey and she was ready for it to end. Alone with her thoughts, she drove along the secluded roads. It would've been so very easy to just keep going; get her kids and drive all night. Perhaps that was what a good mother would do—not try to save the world, but save her own family.

She unlocked the gate and continued through, noticing Aaron's car already in the driveway. Pulling around to the side of the home, Lacy stepped out and made her way to the front door. While she did feel fairly safe here—the barrier the trees provided, the remote area—a constant threat loomed and it had begun to take its toll. Pressing on would be one of the most difficult decisions she would have to make, but press on she would because Keith Colburn deserved it. Her husband deserved it.

Inside, the warmth enveloped her, soothing her shivering nerves, but offering little more than physical comfort. Aaron was the first to offer a welcoming smile. "Did you just get here?"

"A little while ago. How'd it go today?"

As soon as she closed the door, Will and Trevor appeared from the kitchen. "Looks like I'm the last one to the party."

"We're all taking different routes and leaving at different times," Axell said. "It's the only way to be sure we have no tails."

"I have some interesting news we need to discuss." She hadn't spoken to Will about the meeting, assuming it was best to keep him at a distance at work in the event she was being watched there too, which she'd begun to feel was highly likely now. "We've been asked to analyze information and data that was transmitted twenty-four hours prior to and after the restaurant shooting."

"I'm not surprised by that," Will said. "I heard it was being investigated as an attack, although my team hasn't been asked to take part."

"Which is unusual, don't you think?" Axell replied.

"Not really. We have multiple teams, and the fact that I was there means they probably don't want me involved in the investigation."

Axell grunted his displeasure.

"So who's running the show?" Will asked her.

"SSA Kelly is coordinating with Delgado."

Will's expression hardened. "Delgado? The same man who replaced Mendez?"

"That's right. Now do you think it's unusual?" Lacy replied.

They returned to the living room and Lacy sat down. "I asked Vogel for a favor, one she granted late this afternoon."

"You talked to her about this?" Aaron said.

"You know how she helped us before. I have no reason not to trust her now."

"Lacy, we can't keep bringing people in on this. Jesus!" He turned away from her. "You're putting everyone in danger."

"Like we haven't been in danger every minute of every day since Jian's release?" Her defenses shot up.

"Okay, let's just calm down and take a step back." Will turned to Lacy. "What was the favor and how is it going to help us?"

"She's given me clearance to view the requests Kelly and Delgado have made in the past six months."

"Requests?" Axell asked.

"Yes. Each department of the Bureau submits to the Cyber Division requests for information, analysis—things like that. We process them and present reports back but not before reviewing them with Michelle so that she's aware of everything coming and going through the department. Prior to the attack, I analyzed web traffic coming into the East Coast region from IP addresses in red-flag countries, among other requests made by other divisions. Now I review the information from my team and submit it to Michelle for final analysis."

"And she gave you authorization to view these requisitions?" Axell continued.

"Yes. However, I won't be able to access it until tomorrow. It was too late in the day and I had to be sure and leave at the right time, per our agreement."

"Right." Aaron finally turned and rejoined the conversation, appearing to have calmed down. "I can get you into the FBI's server. You don't need to wait until tomorrow. I know you can't risk accessing information from here, but it won't be under your login or originating from this location."

"Can anyone trace anything back to here?" Axell asked.

"Not the way I do it."

"You've done that before, Hunter, and it ended in an ambush," Will added.

"That wasn't his fault. That was mine for not ensuring a fully vetted connection to the CIA secure net. That's not on Hunter; that's on me," Axell replied.

"I can do this, Will. I've got decent skills, and I thought I was pretty good, but since going to work as a technical analyst, I've seen things I never considered before. Ways around, ways inside. It's made me better than I was. If I was a layperson, seeing that stuff for the first time, I'd be scared to death of my own government."

"I already am," Lacy replied. "Aaron, if you think we can do it safely, then let's do it. The sooner the better. These are the only two variables in our equation and I'm hoping one of them will shed some light on who's after us besides Lei Jian. We don't have anything yet from Turner, is that right?"

"Nothing yet," Axell began. "He's stalling and I think it's time we get Fraser to push him along. Yesterday, I only thought he was hiding something. Now I know he is."

While Aaron began to set up his laptop, Will approached Lacy. "Can I talk to you for a minute?" He began to walk toward her bedroom.

Lacy followed with curiosity and once they reached her room, she began, "Why do I get the feeling something happened that you're not telling me? Or that you don't want the others to know."

Will closing the door made her feel all the more uncomfortable and her nerves shot up on end. The two sat down on the edge of the bed.

"I want you to know that I had someone check on your kids."

"What?" Her eyes immediately welled. "Are they okay?"

"Yes. Yes, they're fine. They're more than fine. He said they seemed happy."

She placed her hand over her mouth and took a moment to let the news sink in. With a calming breath, she continued, "How did you? I didn't tell anyone. My God, if you found out..."

"I'm sorry. I—I shouldn't have kept this from you, but when we were at your house, I checked the burner you kept in the foyer, knowing that we were being listened to. I didn't want to just ask where you'd sent them and I figured you had to have made a call or two to set it up. I thought if you knew how they were, it would settle your mind. So I called in a favor with a friend in New York, where the calls were made. You don't have a large family and I remember seeing Jay's sister at the funeral. Anyway, he drove by the house in Long Island."

"They're okay? They looked okay? Like they were eating?"

He smiled and chuckled a little. "Yes. He said they appeared healthy and happy."

She held his gaze. "I should be pissed at you. You know that, right?"

He nodded.

"If I can't have confidence in you to be straight with me, Will, then what do we have?"

"I know. I'm sorry. I didn't want you to worry about them. That's all."

Her prolonged silence finally ended when she wrapped her arms around him. "Thank you. You have no idea what it means to me knowing they're okay."

He pushed her back gently as her emotions began to spill over. "Hey, hey. It's okay." With a gentle touch, he wiped away a fallen tear from her cheek. "This is more than any of us should have to bear especially you."

"It has impacted everyone, including Trevor. He's trying to be stoic, but I know the loss of Keith hurt him. It hurt all of us."

"Of course, it did. But you're a mother, Lacy, and your children are young and they need you. And right now, you're off fighting the evils of this world and, someday, they will know what you've done for this country. And don't worry. I covered my tracks."

Lacy averted her eyes from the intensity of his stare. "We should get back out there and see if Aaron's ready."

"Sure. Yeah. Let's go."

"There you guys are."

Aaron noted their return and Lacy spotted an unusually wary look mask his face. She dismissed the uncomfortable exchange and continued, "You ready?"

"Yeah. Okay, so what I need from you is the server address."

That was the easy part. As Lacy relayed the information, she wondered how he planned to gain access. She'd always simply logged on with her own credentials but knew that each and every time she did, the information was kept on file. If someone on the inside was operating against them, surely this person would be monitoring her activity, delving into every piece of data she'd reviewed, written a report on, or forwarded to any other member of the Bureau. The frightening part was that if all of this were true, she'd probably been monitored since coming back to work after the attack.

Aaron began to work his magic and Lacy, while fairly well versed in such things, knew her skills paled in comparison.

"What's it like there?"

Aaron stopped. "At the CIA?" He glanced at Axell for a moment as if to make sure it was okay to speak on the subject.

"Incredible. Brilliant minds with extraordinary abilities. And it seems they're all there for one thing—to protect the country."

"Do you think they wield too much power? I feel like that at the Bureau sometimes. Like we're invading our own citizens."

"Because of what they know and what they have access to?" Aaron replied. "There's a sense of a humble fear—well, respect really—for what they're doing. For me, being an outsider and, of course, knowing what I know now, I think they have tremendous power and if someone came along who had an agenda, it would be dangerous."

"You mean like you do?" Will asked.

"Exactly."

"Okay, Lacy, what's the password you use to log on to the server?"

"Won't they be able to tell it's me if I enter my password?"

"Yes. Your initial log-on will be authenticated. They'll know you're in the mainframe. However, once I'm inside, I'll overwrite the authentication protocol by using SAML. It allows me to navigate to different portals, like, say, the database we need access to inside the FBI's server without secondary authentication."

"Okay, okay, I get it." She did to a certain extent, but more importantly, Aaron was prone to delving deep into that world if left unchecked. And there was no time for that right now. "I'll type it in."

"You afraid I'll hack into the FBI's server on a regular basis?"

"Maybe." She smiled. "I'm in."

"Great." Aaron began typing again. "Let me see where it is we need to go." A few minutes later, he'd finished. "And we're in."

"You mind if I take the captain's chair?" Lacy asked.

"Be my guest." Aaron stood and gestured for her to take a seat.

Lacy knew the system well and wasted no time getting to the information she needed. "Okay, here are the requests that have come from Kelly." She began to scroll through. "We should save this. You have a flash drive?"

Aaron placed it in the machine.

"I'm going back to the point where I returned to work. I figure if someone's looking, that's when it started."

"Agreed." Axell hunched over her shoulder. "What kind of requests would you be looking for?"

"Anything relating to me, which will have my employee number only. No name. Anything relating to Will. And finally, anything relating to the mall attack and, most recently, the shooting at the restaurant."

Will stood at attention and folded his arms across his chest. "I don't think it's Kelly. He and Mendez have known each other a long time. They're friends. He helped to expedite my transfer."

"Then that's all the more reason to be concerned, Caison." Axell cocked his head. "The ones who you trust the most are the ones who end up stabbing you in the back."

"Maybe in your line of work. Not mine."

"Don't be so naïve. This isn't Afghanistan. These people are not your brothers in arms." Axell pulled upright again. "You've been at this what, two, two and a half years? I've been at it for twenty-five. I hate to burst your bubble, but in this line of work, our line of work? Trusting someone can get you killed."

Trevor Axell was a grizzled and hardened man, and Lacy had occasionally heard this line of rhetoric come from him before, but nothing so harsh, and to direct it to Will, who yes, was still new to the game, but had already been through more than his share. This wasn't Axell. This was anger at the loss of Agent Colburn talking now and this was how he dealt with it, good or bad.

"I haven't seen anything unusual. In fact, I'm not seeing much from SSA Kelly at all, not for my department." She turned to Will.

"It could be that Delgado asked him for help and not the other way around."

"Which would make sense if he wanted to keep tabs on me too," Will added.

"I agree. I'll move on to Martin Delgado." She pulled up a new screen and typed in the commands. "He came here, what, about two or three weeks after the attack?"

"Sounds about right. That was when Mendez was shipped back home."

"Right. And you know, Aaron and I met him that day, the day we got the audio files from Porter. You remember that, Aaron?"

"How could I forget? I nearly pissed my pants when Vogel showed up with him." Appearing slightly embarrassed, Aaron turned to the others. "I didn't. Just so you know."

Lacy smiled and continued, "Anyway, I didn't trust him then."

"What makes you say that?" Will asked.

"I knew he was doing his job. They were never going to tell me anything about the investigation once I got booted out. But just his demeanor. The way he talked. Condescending as hell and just kind of an asshole."

"We need more than the fact that he's an asshole," Will replied. "But I understand your meaning."

Lacy continued to view the information. "This is my employee number, here." She pointed to the screen. "This request was made in June. After the attack, and after I returned to work."

"What's it asking?"

"It's a request to look into the online activity from my workstation." She turned to Will. "Looks like he wanted to keep an eye on what I was doing."

"And he could just ask that and no one would question it?" Aaron said.

"Oh yeah. We're routinely screened for security checks. We're civilian employees, remember? And there's still quite a bit of animosity between us and the law enforcement side of the Bureau. Been that way for a long time."

"Okay. So that's not unusual."

"No." She continued to scroll. "But this does appear more frequently than I would have expected. Another request thirty days later, then again in October."

"That was when I put in for my transfer," Will said.

"Holy hell." Lacy shook her head. "Take a look at this."

"What is it we're looking at here, Lace?" Aaron asked.

"My number is in here more than fifteen times since October. And look at this, Will. Since you got here, he's put in four requests. That's your number, right?"

"Yep. Hell, I've only been here a few weeks."

"I know."

"So we think this is our guy?"

"Hang on. Let's reel this in for a moment," Axell began. "What do you see on there that makes you believe he's after you?"

"You see this column here?" She pointed to the right side of the screen. "These are codes. These numbers designate the type of request. For example, security checks are coded with the numbers starting with 7. Here, you see these? These all start with 3."

"And that means what?"

"Security risk assessment. This gives them authorization to monitor, essentially keylog, my workstation. Record calls coming into my office line and maybe even my work cell phone. Goddamn it." She peered at the screen again. "He's been watching me for weeks."

"So what do we do? How the hell are we going to go after him?" Aaron asked.

"Before we jump the gun, I'll need to get some intel on Delgado," Axell began. "If he's got ties to anyone at the MSS, or, and let's not forget this, anyone inside the State Department. Even if this is the man who's coming for us, he's not coming alone. Someone's given him orders and that's who I'll need to find."

"What should I do?" Lacy asked.

"Be careful who you communicate with and how. But, Lacy, you still have a job to do. If you change any behavior, he'll know we're onto him. Don't use your work cell to call any of us, not even Caison. Your laptop at the office? Don't use it to email any of us or look at anything that might raise a red flag." Axell began to pace the room. "I'll find out who he's working for. Hunter, you'll look for a way to keep tabs on him. I don't care how you do it, just get it done."

Axell turned to Will. "And as for you, Caison, because he's now working with your boss, I suggest you stick close to him and find out what information Kelly's passing along."

"We still have Deputy Secretary Turner to consider in all this. I'll get with Agent Fraser and find out who in Turner's inner circle knows this guy. I still think this leads to him or his department in some fashion. And since he's not very forthcoming at the moment..."

"We still have Lei Jian and Ahsan Sajwani to deal with," Axell started. "Hunter, look, I know you're busting your ass in there, but we have to know where they are. What they're doing. I realize I'm asking a lot here and that the more you do, the more eyes will be on you. But we'll have to cross that bridge when we get to it. The more we discover, the worse this gets, and I don't know how much time we have before it blows up in our faces."

CHAPTER
SEVENTEEN

THE SHOTS FIRED into the restaurant were meant either as a warning for Will and Lacy or the shooter simply didn't have time to fire off another round with better aim. Regardless, the bullet casing Will recovered in secret needed to be identified and the best place for that was the forensics lab at Headquarters. A vast facility with cutting-edge technology, the technicians there were the best of the best.

The unit in charge of handling that type of evidence was the FTU, the Firearms-Toolmarks Unit. The idea was to determine if the casing came from the same gun as the one found at Kendrick's home and then find out to whom the gun belonged.

"Excuse me?" Will approached a technician who came highly recommended by his friend in the Operations Center, Agent Porter. A man who, for his help with audio surveillance, had been instrumental in proving Kendrick's involvement in the attack.

"Yes?"

"I've been told you're the one to see with regard to ballistics."

The man pulled away from his monitor. "Oh yeah? Who you been talking to?"

"A buddy of mine in the Ops Center." Will retrieved the plastic bag that contained the casing. "I need to trace the weapon this came from, more specifically, the owner of that weapon."

The technician took hold of the bag and began to examine it. "It's a Smith and Wesson .40 caliber cartridge likely from a Glock 22. Where'd you find it? What case is this for?"

"I'm working on the restaurant shooting in Downtown D.C. I was the agent there at the time."

"Right. I heard about that. And you've been assigned to investigate a shooting that you happened to have been involved in?"

"Can you help me or not?" Will needed to avoid any further inquiries because he had no such authorization.

"The question isn't if; it's when. How soon do you need this?"

"It's a priority. They want to rule out a lone-wolf terrorist attack."

"It has very few indications of that. Single shooter, no dead, few injured. Sounds more like a drive-by gang-related shooting rather than terrorism."

"Except for one thing. I was the target and I work in CTD."

The man appeared sheepish and again examined the casing. "Of course. I can have something for you by tomorrow. I'll have to analyze the striations, upload the images, and enter the information into NIBIN."

Will recalled that from his Quantico days. The National Integrated Ballistics Information Network was a massive database utilized by not only the Bureau but also the ATF and DEA. Details on weapons, bullets, and casings; all of it compared and analyzed and then uploaded to find matches to other crimes. That was what Will needed to know. Did the cartridge match the gun used to kill Drew Kendrick and, pending information from Axell, was it also used to kill Agent Colburn?

"Thank you. I appreciate your help." He began to walk away.

"Oh, and if there is a match to a weapon used in another crime, I ask that you give me a heads-up on that first."

"No problem."

———

The death of Agent Colburn still haunted Aaron. He'd felt responsible because his job was simple—get a location on Ahsan Sajwani. While no one knew for sure if he was the culprit, it didn't matter. Agent Axell had entrusted him to find the man. But he was paralyzed with fear of being caught and hadn't done enough. It would only be a matter of time before they all realized he wasn't cut out for this job, no matter how highly he touted his own skills. Apparently, it wasn't as simple as he'd led them to believe.

"Hey, man." A colleague brushed past him. "Didn't mean to startle you. You all right?"

"Yeah, yeah, I'm fine. Just concentrating and wasn't expecting you. Sorry." He logged off his computer and stood. "I gotta take a piss." Noting his colleague's look of growing concern, Aaron quickly departed, making his way to the bathrooms. It was the only place he could be sure he was truly alone. His stomach turned and his head was light. Little sleep, little appetite, and shattered nerves were a dangerous combination.

He walked into a stall and pressed against the door, locking it quickly. Thoughts of what had already happened: Colburn's death, the attempt on Lacy and Will's life. The feelings mixed with his churning gut and he thought he was going to lose it. Why couldn't they just get this out into the open? Why did every move they made have to be like something from a James Bond movie?

Cracks in his casual veneer were growing and he wondered how long before everyone else noticed too. What would Lacy think of him? She'd been so strong, losing her husband, sending her children away. And here he was, ready to toss his lunch because he was tinkering around inside highly secure databases. His past was riddled with suspect, borderline illegal dealings, but this was the CI fucking A, and they didn't screw around. Treason, life in prison. Yeah, he was afraid of Jian and Sajwani, but not nearly as afraid as he was of the people upstairs who glared down at all of them, watching and waiting. "Stop. Just get your shit together and do your job!" He pulled away from the stall door and inhaled a breath to gather himself. Finally, he re-emerged and approached the washbasins, where he splashed water on his face.

A man appeared from an adjacent stall and regarded Aaron. "Are you okay, sir?"

"Fine. I'm fine, thank you." Aaron pressed a paper towel against his face and tossed it into the trash. After a final acknowledgment to the concerned man, he left the restroom. Embarrassed and ashamed of the breakdown, Aaron soon returned and got back to work. His "come to Jesus" moment had arrived. All their lives were at stake and if he cared about Lacy the way he believed he did, then it was time to man up and do what he had come here to do, even if it meant going to prison for it.

Aaron input Sajwani's passport number with the knowledge that they believed he was still in Dubai, although at this point, that seemed highly unlikely. The problem lay in the fact that Sajwani could be traveling under a different passport. Running the facial recognition program to determine any aliases he might be traveling under would be the only way to know for sure. That would take time, which meant his work log would reflect the task and offer more ammunition to those who might be watching.

Aaron scanned the photo from the passport into the database in search of a match to any other passports in the system. Those in the CIA's periphery were generally US passport holders who had traveled to Watch List countries. However, those who had arrived in the US from suspect countries were also included, making the search cumbersome, to say the least.

Several images appeared on the screen with percentages next to them. These percentages were calculated based on the possibility of an exact match. And as Aaron peered intently at the information, he was certain he had found his target. Sajwani wasn't traveling under his own passport issued by the UAE, but one issued by the Chinese government. He'd arrived in the US two days ago, according to the stamp from the Reagan International Airport. Which confirmed a more pressing concern—that he was in D.C.

———

A knock on his door and the CEO of the Dalian Company, Shen Yang, peered over his glasses. "Yes?"

A young man wearing a black tie and neatly pressed white oxford opened the door. "Pardon the interruption, sir, but I have Mr. Delgado here to see you. He insists that it's urgent."

With a wave of his hand, Yang signaled his consent and waited for Delgado to be escorted inside. "What is so urgent, Agent Delgado, that you insisted on interrupting my day?"

Delgado entered the office and waited for the assistant to close the door. "Apologies, sir, but this couldn't wait."

"Have a seat."

"I've just been informed that Lei Jian is making plans to travel here in the coming days. I've been tracking the whereabouts of his right-hand man, Ahsan Sajwani, who is in Washington as we speak. If both are here, I can assure you that this will bring bigger troubles than those we face from the likes of Lacy Merrick and Agent Will Caison."

Yang leaned back in his chair and removed his glasses. "You're missing one crucial element in this equation. The minister has allowed this to happen for a reason. You and I both know Jian has become more trouble than he's worth. While he performed his tasks, his ego has gotten in the way. He misses the power he used to have and is looking to regain that. The minister knows this."

"What are you saying? He wants Jian to come here and cause problems?"

"What I'm saying, Agent Delgado, is that you've been hired to do a job for us. That job now entails handling this situation as you see fit. Or rather, as you know it must be handled. Unfortunately for us, what had started as a relatively straightforward plan has veered off into a vain effort on the part of Jian to seek retribution for his imprisonment. Now it is up to us, or rather, you to fix the problem."

"Of course." Delgado stood. "Thank you for your time, sir."

"Before you leave, what is your progress regarding the letter found on Kendrick's laptop?"

"Deputy Secretary Turner's home has been searched and his server destroyed. If he had a copy of the file, he no longer does."

"Thank you, Agent Delgado, and if there's nothing else..."

"No, sir. Goodbye, sir." Delgado left the office and walked through the corridors of the Dalian Company until he finally exited through to the parking garage. He retrieved his cell phone. "I need to see you. Thank you. I'll be there shortly."

————

A black SUV appeared from the parking structure and Lacy recognized it as Delgado's. With the help of Michelle Vogel, she received his schedule, and when she noted an entry that simply indicated "out of office," following him was a priority.

No one knew she'd followed him to the Dalian Company

offices in Alexandria, but somehow, she wasn't surprised by his arrival here. Their attempts to dominate the space currently occupied by Nova Investments were obvious after the attack. It was, after all, the intent of Lei Jian's entire agenda to unseat the Arab-held leader and replace it with their own leader in the Asia-Pacific market in retail development.

What was surprising, however, was that it appeared the Dalian company was pulling Delgado's strings and that it was likely he was monitoring her as a result of that relationship. She'd believed it was someone in government, perhaps above Turner, who was responsible for Delgado's surveillance of her every move. And now the battle between the two fronts appeared to be a battle between two factions of the Chinese government. One side with the FBI in its pocket, and the other who'd put Lei Jian in charge. Still, none of this could be possible without help from someone in the current administration. There wasn't a chance in hell someone in State, or higher, didn't know about this.

Delgado's SUV passed by her as she instinctively crouched below her driver's window and, upon looking up again, noted he was heading north. Perhaps he would now be on his way to whoever else had purchased his sedition.

She pressed the ignition button and her Lexus purred to life. Lacy headed north and continued to follow him from a safe distance. Will would have been proud of her. No field training and yet she was acting like a field agent. Then again, he just might think her foolish. Delgado was a dangerous man with powerful friends, but she'd faced down these very same people before and she was about to do it again.

The drive continued for some time and she wondered where he was going. The hour was approaching 3 pm and if she wasn't back at the safe house by six, they'd all come looking for her.

As Lacy exited the highway with Delgado still three cars

ahead, she noted the sign. "Langley?" She'd just exited into the community of McLean in Fairfax County, Virginia. While commonly known as CIA headquarters, Langley was also part of the community of McLean, from which many D.C. workers commuted. "What the hell are you doing here?"

Delgado finally turned off the main road and onto a smaller residential street. Lacy had to drop farther back to avoid detection. The stately colonial homes with grand circular drives were spaced widely apart, making it all the more difficult for her to remain concealed.

The SUV pulled onto a cobblestone driveway and around to the front of the home. Lacy stayed back, almost too far back to see, but she'd been prepared. In the center console was a compact pair of binoculars that she purchased only today in anticipation that she might need them. It was a good call.

The house was shrouded in greenery and tall trees, most of which had shed their leaves, a small measure of luck that provided better visuals. She watched him leave his car and another gentleman stepped out onto the driveway to meet him. The men shook hands. She didn't recognize the other man and began to take pictures with her cell phone. At that moment, she'd realized the binoculars were a good start, but what she really needed right now was a zoom lens.

She took a few more shots of the two men and the house. It was the best she could do. There was no way to hear what they were saying and she wasn't a lip reader and the moment they walked inside, it was over. The door promptly closed.

Lacy waited a few moments to confirm she was all clear to pull away. The sun was lowering quickly and she was miles away from the safe house. With traffic, it would be close. She decided to leave a message with Aaron, taking every precaution, of course, and utilizing one of many burners she had in her possession. He wasn't allowed to carry his cell inside the building, so she would leave him a message. "Hey, it's me. Listen, I might be running a little late. Don't worry; everything's fine. I'll see you later. Bye."

Her concern for Aaron had grown considerably since he started at CIA headquarters. And it wasn't lost on her that she was only minutes from him right now, but in the end, it was far too risky to try to see him. For all she knew, there were eyes on him there, just as there were eyes on her at the Bureau.

CHAPTER
EIGHTEEN

LACY OPENED the door of the house to all eyes in her direction. "I'm late, I know. But I have a good reason."

"Before you tell us, Hunter found him. Sajwani, and he's here in Washington. Arrived two days ago, before we were hit at the restaurant," Will said.

She looked to Aaron, who seemed reassured and appeared to have regained some of his former confidence. "Good. At least we know he's here. Not that it puts me at ease. It does lend credence to the fact that we think he was the shooter from the restaurant. Timing's right, anyway. That means, however, what I've got will only muddy the already dirty waters." She handed her phone to Aaron. "You mind pulling up some of these pictures? They're from a distance and I can't say how clear they are, but maybe you can do something with them."

Axell paced the room while Aaron manipulated the photos Lacy had taken in an effort to identify the other man. "You took these pictures?"

"Yes, I was in McLean," Lacy answered.

"Do you have any idea how dangerous that was? What could've happened to you?"

"If this guy thinks he can watch my every move, then turn-about's fair play. Look, I get that you think I took on an unnecessary risk, but what choice was there? We're that much closer to understanding his role in this now, thanks to me." She looked to Will and it appeared he was in agreement with Axell. "You think I made a mistake too?"

"I don't think you should've gone alone, that's all."

"This is the best I can do." Aaron turned to Lacy. "The resolution of the camera on your phone isn't great."

Axell peered over his shoulder. "You say you were in McLean?"

"Yes. He was at the Dalian offices first, which makes me think he's working for them, something we hadn't considered before, and probably a point of concern. After he left the Dalian offices, this was where he went."

Axell continued to stare at it, and in a flash of sudden recognition, he bolted upright. "Holy shit."

"What? What is it? You know that guy?" Will asked.

Axell began shaking his head.

"Who is it? Trevor, you have to tell us. Who is Delgado working with?" Lacy pressed him for an answer, but he seemed to be in shock.

Axell began to rub his stubbly chin and continued to stare at the photo. "I don't believe it. There has to be an explanation."

"Trevor, please."

He turned to her. "You're telling me you saw Delgado at the Dalian Company, then he goes here? This man is my boss—indirectly. And I think we just stepped into some seriously deep horse-shit now."

"What?" She peered again at the grainy image of the men shaking hands.

"Much of what I do requires me to act as a liaison between the FBI and the Directorate of Operations branch of the CIA. After 9/11, there was a lot of blame placed on the fact that several agencies had information, and yet none seemed to connect the dots. So that was addressed by creating departments within the intelligence agencies whose job it was to coordinate with one another. That was how I came to meet Agent Caison."

"So, he's part of the CIA talking with someone we believe is a traitor working for the FBI? You weren't kidding. This is deep shit."

"He isn't just anyone," Axell continued. "He's Camden Meeks, a department head, who calls the shots. My boss's boss." He turned away. "I need a minute to think."

"Do you think it's possible Delgado's playing both sides?" Will asked him.

Axell turned back. "Martin Delgado isn't clever enough to do that. I looked into him, Caison. After what Lacy discovered last night, I did some digging. This guy's in it for the money. He came out of Quantico seven years ago, barely passing. Was sent to New York. Didn't make any friends. Then he was sent to the D.C. office. Again, no love lost when he left. Finally, it turns out he gets promoted to Supervisory Special Agent."

"How the hell did that happen?" Will asked.

"Good question. Got a letter of recommendation from the US Attorney General's office on how great a job he'd done assisting them on some investigation and, *voila*, he's now an SSA."

"How did he end up at FBI headquarters?" Lacy asked. "He shows up out of the blue and takes over for Mendez? Sounds like he wasn't even working in counterterrorism."

"He wasn't," Axell continued.

"Somebody got to him and it probably didn't take much. Be careful around him, Lacy. Whatever you do, don't follow him again."

"If I hadn't followed him, Will, we wouldn't know what or who we're really dealing with here."

"She's right. I don't agree with your methods, but I can't dispute the fact that this puts us ahead in the game. Now we just got to figure out how the hell we move forward. And how Dalian fits into this freak show."

"We have Sajwani and now this," Lacy began. "I think the storm's coming."

———

Axell tossed the cigarette out of his driver's side window and pulled away from the safe house. There were things he needed to take care of now that he knew he was being played. It was Meeks who suggested he be put in charge of coordination with the State Department and the FBI Counterterrorism Unit after the mall attack.

It wasn't until Agent Caison came to him that day when it all changed. He'd realized then that the case had begun to reek of a cover-up. When he learned that former ambassador Lei Jian had been doling out money, he'd begun to piece together the fact that State was pushing for closure, and then, of course, the shit hit the fan.

He'd been around long enough to know that the covert wars and regime manipulations were part and parcel of the agency. But this was different. Someone was working with the MSS to destroy the country from the inside. Not through war, but through economic dependency—a far more effective tool.

The odds were mounting ever higher against them and he

knew their chances of success were dwindling. He was nothing if not pragmatic. He'd nearly been taken out by Kendrick's men, which, as it turned out, were really Jian's men. His friend and colleague was dead and now the time had come to dispense with the clandestine operations in which he'd enlisted the help of the hacker, Aaron Hunter. The time had come to take matters into his own hands. The time had come for him to recall his earlier days in Syria, Egypt, and the rest, where trusting anyone would get you killed. If Meeks was involved in this, then who knew how far up the ladder this went? Kendrick must've made a deal with him. The question now was, who did Meeks make a deal with?

———

Ahsan Sajwani waited in his car alongside the curb. Lei Jian was due any moment, his flight having arrived. A lanky man from a country where the temperatures often hovered in the hundreds during the summer, he placed his hands in front of the vent to warm them on this cold November night. This was a mistake, Jian flying here. He was putting himself and the mission at great risk. The chances of his arrival going unnoticed were slim and none. The former ambassador, who was already being watched by his own country, was undoubtedly being watched by this one. But once Jian had made up his mind, Ahsan knew it could not be changed. And so he waited, like the good little servant he was.

What had Jian hoped to accomplish by coming here? That was what he could not understand. His mission was clear and it was only a matter of time before he located the woman and the FBI agent. What Ahsan had not counted on was that someone else was after those whom he hunted. Perhaps Jian could now shed light on that. He had many ties within the MSS as well as US ties. It seemed they were all working toward the same goal but via different avenues. And now the time had come to pool the resources, assuming the end goal was, in fact, the same.

Ahsan spotted Jian exit through the terminal doors and flashed his headlights to catch his attention. It was the first time he'd seen Jian travel alone and not be surrounded by an entourage willing to kill anyone who had the appearance of posing a threat. But not here. Jian would have to keep a low profile and this was a good sign.

Ahsan stepped out, walking around to the curb to meet him. "Hello, sir. Let me get your bag for you." He placed Jian's luggage in the trunk of the car and opened the passenger door for him. "It's good to see you, sir. Please." He closed the door and returned to the driver's side.

"Thank you, Ahsan. It is late and I am tired from the long flight, but it's the first time in more than six months that I've been allowed to travel freely. I can't tell you how good that feels."

"I'm sure it does, sir. Where would you like to go?"

"I'll be staying in the same hotel as you if that won't be a problem."

"Of course not." Ahsan keyed the ignition and pulled away. As they began the drive through downtown D.C., he couldn't help but question the plans of his superior. "Sir, what are your intentions and how will you be able to stay out of the periphery of the CIA and FBI? I'm sure if they do not know you are here, they will very soon."

"I understand your concern. And the reasons I am here are to ensure, first of all, that our loose ends are tied and, secondly, to rebuild my relationship with Shen Yang. He must be made to understand that we are still on track and that completing the mission is our priority. We've made it past only the first phase and there is still much work to be done."

"You are not concerned with the US government learning of your arrival or plans?"

"Why would I be? Isn't that why you're here?" He looked to Ahsan. "You finish your job and I will work to complete mine."

———

Will returned to the forensics lab, anticipating the results of the ballistics testing on the bullet casing he retrieved at the restaurant. Today would bring changes to the way they'd been operating up until this point. Axell was on the warpath, determined to understand the relationship Delgado had with one of his own. Hunter was still keeping tabs on Sajwani while attempting to locate Jian and Lacy; well, Lacy was a whole other reason for concern. He'd begun to believe that it was too dangerous for her to show her face anywhere and yet she'd insisted on continuing to work. Changing her mind was out of the question, that much he knew. But he'd hoped his point had gotten across last night and that she would take greater precautions at her office. Delgado couldn't be trusted and was already watching her every move. If he found out what she'd done yesterday, Will was confident Lacy would already be dead.

He approached the technician. "You said you got the results?"

He reached for the report. "It was a match to the ballistics report filed on the Kendrick case. Looks like you're dealing with the same weapon."

"Thank you. I appreciate this more than you could know." Will began to walk away but stopped short. "Listen, this still needs to stay confidential."

"Of course."

Will left the lab and headed back toward his office, making the call he'd been waiting to make. "Hey, it's Caison. Can I meet with you today?" He paused. "The sooner the better. You're going to want to see this." With a nod, he ended the call.

"Caison." A colleague approached him in the hall. "Kelly wants to see you—now."

The urgent summons wasn't a good sign and Will picked up the pace. "Sir, you wanted to see me?" He stepped inside Kelly's office.

"Close the door and have a seat."

Will took a seat and grew concerned over Kelly's somber guise. "Is everything all right?"

"You know I've been tasked with working with SSA Delgado on the restaurant shooting. Updating him, etc."

"Yes."

"Apparently, a report reached his desk first thing this morning."

At that moment, Will knew exactly what that report contained. "Let me guess, it was a report authorized by me?"

"Will, you should've come to me with this. I could've run it without question. But you?" He shook his head. "This was supposed to be done without your involvement, and for good reason."

"I didn't think." Will turned away. "Guess Axell was right. You can't trust anyone."

"Sorry?"

"Nothing. What's he planning on doing with the report?"

"It's not what he plans on doing with the report; it's what he plans on doing with you. And that is to recommend disciplinary action."

"Are you serious? With what that guy has done?"

"What do you mean?"

"I mean..." Will stopped. "Nothing. What are my choices, sir? Can I continue doing what I've been doing?"

"Leave this with me. I'll take care of Delgado. I'll let him know you were working on it because of the simple fact that you were there. You were the one who was almost killed. He would be doing the same thing." He paused for a moment. "But I'm telling you, Caison, this needs to be wrapped up sooner rather than later. You catch my drift?"

"I understand. It will be, sir. Thank you." Will stood. "I'm supposed to meet with Agent Fraser from WFO. Am I still authorized to do so?"

Kelly nodded. "I suggest you keep it brief."

———

The line Lacy had crossed yesterday couldn't be uncrossed and the real concern was that Delgado would find out if he hadn't already. She could've used Aaron's expertise right about now, but he had his hands full. So the time had come for her to put her own skills to use. She was no novice in the computer hacking arena and had reminded Aaron of that fact in the recent past.

Lacy needed to know how Delgado fit in with the Dalian Company. Was he getting money from them? Were they blackmailing him? The only way to know was to get into his computer and find out. If she got what she needed, this could end now and she could take the information to Director Mobley. The deputy secretary would be more than happy to lay blame at someone else's feet. Of course, the whole idea of this was to put people like Turner in prison for treason, just like she'd tried to do with Drew Kendrick. Kendrick might have been the one responsible for keeping silent on the truth, but Turner knew now and had evidence in his possession.

So maybe the time had come to do what she should have done months ago, to get what she needed on Turner and now Delgado. Once she did that, she knew exactly what to do with it.

CHAPTER
NINETEEN

WITH THE CONSTANT shadow of surveillance looming, Lacy made her way to Michelle's office, rather than risk a phone call or email. She was an ally and was about to call in yet another favor. "Michelle?"

"Lacy, come on in."

"I need to head out for the day."

"Sure. I'll just make a note that you're in meetings all day. Don't worry about things around here. Go do what you need to do."

"I appreciate that, thank you." She began to turn.

"Lacy? There is one thing. You remember me mentioning the dedication ceremony at the site?"

"I do." It lingered in the back of her mind, but she hadn't given it much thought, all things considered.

"It's been scheduled for a week from Friday. I know that with everything else, this probably doesn't feel like the time, but I have to ask. They still want you to speak. You're part of the FBI and you lost someone. They think it would be a good idea."

Her mind flashed back to the moment she stood at what had

since been called "ground zero," and while most people thought of the Towers when they heard that phrase, Lacy thought of the blast at the mall, and the boy Jay tried to save—well, did save, as it turned out.

It had taken at least a month, but the boy's father had tracked Lacy down through various resources that had been set up to help the victims. The boy's mother died in the blast, but he told his father that a man saved him and described Jay.

Those were the things that came to mind whenever she heard the phrase all Americans had known to be a day of sadness and strength. That was what she tried to remember. The strength. But to speak of it in front of so many. It would not be easy. Not to mention that so much was going on that Michelle simply had no idea about. And that was by design. Lacy couldn't place that kind of burden on her. It was far too dangerous and Michelle had a family too. Lacy would not put them at risk as she had her own.

"A week from Friday?"

Michelle nodded.

"I'll have to prepare something." Lacy could feel her chest tightening at the thought. Not simply of having to speak, but rather would she still be alive to do so? "Okay. Yes, I'll speak. It's the least I can do for the other families." She made her way back into the corridor and was ready to do what needed to be done to get to the bottom of Agent Delgado's connections.

Lacy didn't make any calls. Didn't tell anyone that she was heading back to the safe house. They all had their plates full, and she didn't want the distraction or to be convinced this was not the way forward. It was the only way forward, and it was about time Lacy took matters into her own hands. Her appreciation for Will, Aaron, and Trevor was boundless, but this she needed to do because it could not stand. Delgado could not—would not get away with this.

———

Will entered the Washington Field Office and made his way to the information desk. "I'm here to see Agent Fraser. Field Ops, CID."

"I'll let him know you're here." The security officer made the call.

Will moved about the lobby while awaiting authorization and peered into the corridor that led to the elevators. A woman stepped out and headed in his direction. At first, it hadn't occurred to him who this person was, but a moment of recognition surged and he did a double take.

As she drew near, he knew. "Kate? Kate Reid? Oh my God."

"Will Caison?" Kate shook her head in disbelief. "What on earth? What are you doing here?"

"I'm working with an agent in CID. Man, look at you. How long has it been?"

"Since Quantico. And I think last we spoke was what, at least a year ago." She embraced him before pulling back to take in the sight she hadn't seen in some time. "I can't believe you're here. I thought you were working in Louisville."

"I was, up until a few weeks ago. Put in for a transfer to Headquarters. Still working in CTD, though. I worked on the mall attack investigation."

"Of course. That was an awful thing. Much too close to home."

"You have no idea, Kate. I just can't believe you're standing in front of me. You been here since graduation?"

"I have, but I'm not sure how much longer I'll be here. Probation's up, so, you know."

"Right. Yeah." From the corner of his eye, Will spotted Agent Fraser's approach. "Boy, I really hate to cut this short, but I've got a meeting. Listen, maybe I can give you a call sometime? Now that we're both in D.C."

"I'd like that very much." Kate smiled. "It was so good to see you. You take care of yourself." She began to walk away. "I'll be waiting for that call. You still owe me for those beers I bought you at the graduation party."

"You got it."

Fraser approached. "Agent Caison. Thanks for coming down." He offered a greeting. "You know Agent Reid?"

"Yeah. We were at Quantico together."

"Wow. Small world. Come on; I'll show you back to my office."

Will glanced over his shoulder as Kate left the building. "Sure is." Returning his attention, he noticed Fraser several steps ahead and jogged to catch up. "By the way, we have a problem."

"I figured that was why you were here." Fraser pushed the button for the elevator and stepped on as the doors parted.

"The lab tech gave Delgado the ballistics results." Will joined him and watched the numbers climb.

"How do you know?"

"Kelly called me into his office this morning. Said Delgado asked him why I was looking into it. Fortunately, he told him it was because I was there and wanted answers."

"You think he bought it?"

"I wasn't with him, so it's hard to say, but I hope so."

They stepped off the elevator and Fraser led the way to his office.

"I assume, then, that the casings were a match." Fraser entered his office and waited for Will before closing the door behind him. "Which means."

"This means the person who killed Kendrick is most likely the same one who came after us in the restaurant. The problem is, we still don't know who that is."

"No registry on the weapon?"

"No, and it's not standard issue FBI either, as you probably already know."

"Right." He cast his gaze away. "Which puts us back at Square One. And I'm still working on Turner, but I just don't think I've gained his full trust."

"We may not be entirely back at Square One. Delgado is connected to the Dalian Company somehow. Lacy followed him yesterday. It's becoming clearer that they're tied to the MSS."

"What? Caison, you got to tell me everything. Maybe if I know, Turner will confide in me. You're asking me to put my ass on the line without knowing all the details."

"Okay, okay. But before we go down that road, she also discovered something else."

"And that is?"

"Like I said, she followed him to the Dalian offices. He was there for a while, meeting with someone, we don't know who, but then he drove out to McLean and met with a CIA Counterterrorism official. A Camden Meeks."

"Well, what the hell is Axell going to do about that?"

"I'm leaving that up to him. It hit him hard, though. First, he loses Colburn and then finds out his own people are involved. This thing is going to come to a head and fast."

"Right, well, you're not leaving until you give me everything. Give me something I can use to get Turner to trust me."

———

Alone in the house that had begun to feel more like a prison, Lacy sat at the workstation where Aaron had set up a secure laptop. The time had come to find out if Delgado was being extorted by or was on the receiving end of money from the Chinese-based Dalian company, a company that had signed with Argus Solutions and had been Jay's largest account.

The deeper she delved into this conspiracy, the darker her feelings became about the motivations of governments, whether elected by their people or appointed by a leader. All seemed corrupt. Nothing like what she used to believe after joining the FBI. But the time had come to expose this corruption and no threats would stop her this time.

Her heart raced as she doubted her own expertise in an area in which she hadn't worked for quite some time. But she'd been watching Aaron, learning from him as he'd taught her when they were younger. And so she began. Delgado was smart enough not to have any social media accounts, which Lacy quickly learned. Moving on, she instead opted to search for financial records, which meant getting inside the credit bureaus to find out which banks he used. Sounded simple enough, except it would require Lacy to find out Delgado's social security number. Aaron had already attempted to find his information in the Office of Personnel Management files, but Delgado's were marked SIC and neither had that clearance, nor could they get it. And no matter how good a hacker he was, SIC was well outside of his ability to hack. So, now it was up to Lacy to dig around and put her tradecraft to use. The first part was easy. She knew Delgado, based on what she'd already learned, had been born in Massachusetts, meaning his social security number would begin with numbers ranging from 010-034. Social security numbers were assigned in much the same way as zip codes, by area. Those numbers encompassed those born prior to 2011 in Massachusetts. But things would get a little more difficult from there.

Delgado was born after 1962 when the second set of numbers were revised to reflect *when* a child was born in a state and not assigned based upon his or her nationality, a practice that had contributed to the earliest forms of identity theft. This meant that Lacy could dwindle, based on the year of his birth, the second set of numbers. The Social Security Death Master File was public information, and with that, she was able to eliminate the numbers already assigned, because once a person had died, their number would never again be used. And now, through the process of elimination and Delgado's birth date, Lacy now had the first three and the second two numbers. She was getting close now.

Finally, the last four numbers. These would prove the most challenging because they were randomly generated. However, by utilizing the year of Delgado's birth and reconciling it with the Death Master File, the process of elimination became easier. The final part of this scenario involved utilizing a random number generator. She already had the first five digits and had excluded the numbers issued that year in the Death Master File. While the combination was extensive, Lacy further eliminated numbers based on a simple equation. Using a validator issued by the Social Security office for the purposes of employment background checks, Lacy could now enter the most likely numbers based on the pattern she had developed.

There was, however, a limit to the number of times she was allowed to enter a sequence. But there was a simple workaround for this too. Proxy servers. Aaron had set up a service that would disguise their IP address and give the appearance that another IP was being used in another part of the country. This allowed her to use multiple IP addresses to access the validator. She recalled a conversation she'd had with Aaron and Jay back in school. At the time, identity thefts were on the rise and they discussed the reason for this was the fact that Social Security numbers were never used twice. And with the increasing speed at which programs could run combinations of numbers, they realized that the most vulnerable to identity theft were those born after 2000. They knew then there would come a time when the entire system of issuing numbers would have to be revamped.

Lacy checked the time. Will and Aaron would be there inside the hour. But she was getting closer. One of these combinations would be it. It had to be or else today was for nothing. Accessing the social security number of someone with top clearance was no easy task. If this failed, she had nothing else in her arsenal.

Her attention was returned when she finally got a hit. "This is it. Holy hell—I did it." She wrote down the number and now the easy part could begin—running a credit check. This would tell her what banks he used via identified loans. From there, she would need Aaron to get into them. He'd done it before like it was second nature to him. But she had the number, and now she could find out if Delgado was on the take as others had been in this game.

She heard the door open, immediately shut down the computer, and shot up from her chair.

Aaron made his way inside. "Good. You're already here." He approached her. "What's wrong? You're looking at me funny. Did something happen today?"

"Aaron, I got hold of Delgado's social security number. I need your help to find out if he's taking money from the Dalian Company."

"How did you get that? You didn't ask anyone, did you?"

"Of course not. I do have skills, you know. I figured it out."

"Wow. Okay. I never doubted you." He patted her on the shoulder. "Come on, then. Let's get to it." He rubbed his hands together and blew on his fingers.

"What are you doing?"

"This is my ritual. It's what I do." He smiled and sat down. "So, what's the number?"

———

Agent Axell sat in the guest chair, studying the woman across from him. "We've been friends for a long time, Elizabeth."

"We have."

"And when I told you about Colburn, you did what needed to be done to make sure his family was taken care of."

"I did. Why don't you ask what it is you came here to ask, Trevor?"

"I need your help and I don't know who else to turn to. I have reason to believe Camden Meeks is involved in dealings with a foreign entity and getting the help of someone in the FBI."

"What?" Her smile wasn't because she was pleased, but because it seemed hardly believable. "What kind of dealings?"

"You're the station chief, and you're the only one who can authorize a team to look into this. I want to lead that team."

"You're not a field agent anymore, Trevor. And this is not something I can just shoot from the hip and hope it all turns out okay. You know what you're asking?"

"Yes. I know exactly what I'm asking. I'm asking you to do this for Keith. I've found myself involved in something that I thought I could take on alone. And I have, but I've discovered that Meeks could be compromised —likely is compromised. But I need to know for sure and I need resources. Resources I can't get on my own—not anymore."

She took in a long breath. "I don't want to know anything, you understand? Not unless you get something concrete. This one will have to be off the books and I'll have to figure out a way to keep it as such until you do."

"Thank you, Elizabeth." Axell stood and began to leave.

"If Meeks is involved in whatever it is you're working on, chances are, you'll end up like Keith Colburn."

"Not if I can help it."

CHAPTER
TWENTY

LACY peered through the front window and into the darkness. "Why isn't he back yet? He should've been here a half hour ago." She dropped the curtains and turned to Aaron. "I don't like this. We have to call him, make sure he's okay."

"Maybe you're right." Aaron reached for the burner phone. "He needs to know what we found. Here, you call him."

Lacy dialed his number and the line rang. She turned her attention to Aaron and shook her head. "He's not answering. Son of a bitch. He's not answering."

"It's okay, Lace, just take a breath. Let's think for a minute. Did you talk to him at all today?"

"No."

"So you have no idea what his schedule was like?"

"No, I don't. I'm sorry. I left early to come here and find out what the hell Delgado has himself wrapped up in."

"I'm not trying to upset you, Lacy. I'm just looking for a reason as to why Will isn't here yet."

"I know. I'm sorry. I guess I'm more worried than I thought. What about Axell? You think he might know?" She didn't wait for a reply and tried him. "Trevor? It's Lacy. Have you heard from Will today? He's not here and, well, he should've been almost forty-five minutes ago." She listened, nodding her head a few times. "Okay, I will. Thank you." She ended the call. "He hasn't heard from him either. Says he's working on something right now but will call back later."

Aaron began to pace the living room. "Okay. I'm sure there's a good reason why he didn't stick to the plan. You said yourself that you broke protocol and came here earlier, right? And you had a good reason. So let's not jump the gun here. If we haven't heard from him in the next hour, we'll—I don't know—we'll figure something out."

Lacy's eyes began to redden. "If something happened to him. I just couldn't..."

"He's fine, Lacy. I'm sure he's fine." He examined her for a moment. "Do you have feelings for him? I mean, it's none of my business, but I was just..."

"Of course I do. He's my friend."

"You know that's not what I meant. Look, I'm not judging. After everything we've been through, I wouldn't do that. You shouldn't be alone for the rest of your life. It would be easy to understand if you did feel something for him."

"He's my friend. You're my friend and so is Trevor. So can we just drop it? Please?"

"Yeah, sorry." Aaron walked into the kitchen and poured a glass of water.

"Headlights!" She peered through the window. "Aaron, I see headlights. That has to be him." She waited as the car approached. "It's him. Gotta be." Her worst fear had abated. If someone else she cared for died because of this, there was no telling what it would do to her and she was grateful not to have to find out.

The door opened and Will walked inside.

"Where the hell have you been? You have any idea how terrified I was that something happened to you? Why didn't you call one of us? For God's sake!"

Aaron returned from the kitchen. "Yeah. You had us pretty freaked out there for a while."

"I'm sorry. I should've called. I just didn't have the opportunity. There's some things we need to discuss."

"Same here." Lacy turned to Aaron. "We were able to get something of interest on Delgado. He's receiving money from the Dalian Company. They're paying him for something, but we just don't know what that is yet."

Will furrowed his brow. "How did you find this out?" He raised a hand. "Never mind. I'm asking a hacker how he got information."

"It wasn't just me," Aaron replied. "Lacy did most of the work."

Will continued inside. "Guess that helps solidify my findings. I was with Fraser."

"What is it? The weapon?" Lacy asked.

"We did have a match with the restaurant shooting and Kendrick, but no way to trace who the gun belongs to. But, because Fraser is working on the Kendrick investigation, it allotted him some flexibility for following up on potential leads, even if the potential was nominal at best."

"Are you saying you and Fraser did some digging around on your own with regard to Delgado?"

"Under the guise that it pertained to the investigation—yes. At the very least, to rule out Delgado and refocus our efforts on Sajwani."

"And?" Lacy pressed on.

"And, according to a background check on weapons he owns, we discovered he, at one time, owned a Glock 22. Those generally fire .40 caliber bullets, same as the one from the restaurant and Kendrick's home."

"That's a pretty common handgun."

"That's true. However, he was on record as having sold his last year. We obtained the serial number of that weapon and found out that he'd sold it to a gun shop owner."

"Okay. Sorry, you're obviously getting at some sort of a connection here, but I'm not seeing it," Lacy continued.

"Fraser and I visited that gun shop this afternoon, which was why you couldn't reach me. We began looking at the inventory and everything seemed legitimate until I spotted one that clearly had the original serial number scraped off and replaced. I've seen it before, so I knew what to look for. This made me start to question the shop owner's legitimacy. And after a bit of questioning, and our assurances that we would not pursue any case against him, we questioned him about Delgado's Glock. He remembered it. And remembered that Delgado had asked him to remove the serial number and he'd buy it back, only with cash and off the record, and for a lot more than he'd sold it for, leaving the record of sale to the gun shop owner, but not its resale back to Delgado."

"And that's what he did? Sold it back to him?"

Will nodded. "I think he used that weapon to kill Kendrick. I also think Kendrick knew him because there were no signs, according to Fraser, of Kendrick attempting to flee. I mean, who the hell wouldn't run when you see someone coming at you with a gun, right? Which, to me, means he knew him. He knew his killer."

"You're also then saying that it was Delgado who shot up the restaurant."

"It was a professional hit. He was wearing a motorcycle helmet, no plates on the bike. He knew what he was doing, which also leads me to believe it was a warning shot."

"And, because he was monitoring me, he knew we would be there." Astonishment bore down on her. "Son of a bitch. That gives us all the more reason to believe he's working for Jian and so is the Dalian Company. You can't tell me those two aren't in bed together. Makes perfect sense. Jian wanted Dalian to replace Nova Investments. I guess it wasn't Ahsan Sajwani after all, but still one of Jian's men, so there's that."

"I did talk to Axell just before you arrived," Lacy said. "He said he was working on something but didn't say what, and I could only guess it had to do with this Camden Meeks. He should know what we found. It might help him."

"Should I tally this up for us, then? The MSS, CIA, and FBI are after us." Aaron looked to Lacy. "What the hell chance do we have of making it through this?"

"We've hit one hell of a nerve. There's no denying that. And it brings to mind something I want to do that might help put the nail in the coffin. The dedication ceremony for the mall memorial," Lacy replied.

"Dedication ceremony?"

"I've been asked to speak at it." She turned to Will. "Can you believe that? They want me to speak because I work for the Bureau and I lost Jay."

"Why am I just now hearing about this?" Aaron asked.

"Because I'd forgotten about it when Michelle asked me a few weeks ago. And just today, she asked again. Said the ground-breaking was due to be next Friday."

"What is it you'd like to do, Lacy?" Will asked.

"Exactly what I should've done six months ago."

———

Axell pulled his keys from his pants pocket. "You ready to go?"

"You've got a lot of balls putting this together." Agent Hicks grabbed his coat.

"Hey, if you don't want to be a part of this, then I'll find someone who does. Colburn was your friend too and I thought Elizabeth said you could be trusted."

"No offense, man. I can be. Don't you worry about that. Keith was a hell of a friend and if this shit is real, then I got your back 110 percent."

"Good. We don't have much time. He and his wife are at a charity event. We have to make our move now, or we won't get another chance." Axell pushed through the doors of the Washington station lobby and toward his car. "We get in and get out. From there, the rest will be up to me. You won't need to get your hands dirty."

"Axell, I'm sorry, man. I want to do this. If what you say is true, and the chief believes it could be true as well, then we've got a major fucking problem here."

"Thank you, Hicks. That's what we're about to find out." Axell wanted to check in with Lacy, just to be sure they heard from Caison, but he didn't know just how much he could trust Hicks, even if Colburn had. All Hicks knew was that Colburn was killed and that Meeks might have had a part in it. He wouldn't reveal anything more to a kid he knew very little about. Except that, the kid seemed like kind of a prick.

By the time they reached McLean, Axell's thoughts turned to Meeks and if his involvement had anything to do with the loss of Agent Colburn. He regretted ever pulling Colburn in, but what was done was done and his friend was gone. All he could do now was try to get him justice. And if it meant getting justice for Jay Merrick too, then all the better.

"This is it." Axell killed the lights and rolled to a stop just before the house. "Looks pretty quiet around here. Good news for us." He pulled the keys from the ignition. "Get your shit. Let's get this done."

————

The knock on the door alarmed Will as he pushed up from the sofa and peeked out of the window. "Who the hell is that?"

Aaron mumbled something in his sleep.

The door opened and Will yanked his weapon from the table, aiming it at Axell's head. "Axell? I almost blew your damn head off, man."

"Sorry. I have a key, but I thought it'd be worse if I just came in without knocking."

Lacy emerged from the hall in a t-shirt and shorts she'd been wearing for days now. "Trevor. What are you doing here? Is everything okay?"

He continued inside and headed straight for the workstation. "I've got Meeks under surveillance." He began clicking on the keyboard and eventually images of the man's house appeared.

"Oh my God. When did you do this?"

"Tonight."

"How?"

"Don't ask." Axell continued to type. "We're listening to him as well. I'll know who he's talking to and who comes to see him." He turned to Lacy. "That's why I couldn't talk earlier. But I see that Caison turned up."

"Yeah. Late, but he had a reason. We're getting close now, Trevor. Will has turned up some things and so have we."

"Good. I've got all night. Let's talk."

————

Lacy anticipated a response from Axell, one that was late in coming. It was as though he was considering all that they now knew and what they could do about it. "We have the proof on Delgado. He started getting money from Dalian shortly after the attack, after his transfer to Headquarters. I don't know if they're related, but if they needed someone on the inside, they found him. I think it's time we inform Director Mobley."

"I agree we have enough to take Delgado down, and we will, but I need him. I need to know what part he's playing with Meeks. We'll find out soon and, when we do, we can move in on him."

"I am so sick of waiting!" Lacy threw her arms up. "How many more people have to die before we do something, Trevor? Will? Aaron's risking his life every day to keep tabs on Sajwani and searching for Jian. My every move is being monitored by a man we now know is working with Dalian and by all accounts, the CIA. I mean, do you even hear what you're saying right now?"

"Lacy, if we move now, without knowing the full extent of the CIA's involvement, I won't be able to protect you—any of you. Not even myself. This changes things whether you want to believe it or not. For months, we've been working on untangling this web of deceit to find all those who were involved in the mall attack. Doing it for the victims, including your husband. But this is big, Lacy. We won't win if we go up against my people. I have to understand Meeks' part. Otherwise, we will lose this fight."

"So what do we do now?" Will asked. "What is our next move? Lacy's right. This has to end. Too many people know. Too many people had a hand in what happened. We can't stay here forever. Lacy can't be away from her children forever. Axell, we need a plan. One that we can act on swiftly and decisively because as I see it, we're running out of time."

"I've been in situations like this before and the outcome is never what you think it will be."

"Trevor," Lacy began, "I know how much Agent Colburn meant to you. It was my life he saved and I want to bring justice for him the same as I want to for my husband and all the others who were killed in the attack. But Delgado is after me. Sajwani is after all of us and God knows when they'll find us this time. What do you need, Trevor? What do you need in order for us to bring this to an end?"

"You want to act now?" Axell looked for consensus among those whom he'd been trying to protect. "Then we go after Delgado. Not tomorrow, not the next day—now. We get him now."

———

Getting a location on Delgado had been easy. Lacy had acquired his social security number, address, discovered he had a penchant for dropping bills at strip clubs, and could probably glean a fairly accurate bathroom schedule, given more time. The team moved quickly and was now waiting outside of his home.

"We get in, we get the information, and we get out. Understood?" Axell said. "Hunter, I want you to stay here and listen in." He handed him the headset. "If things start going tits up, I want you to call on Kelly. We know he's got our backs. But if we can keep his hands clean for the time being, then it will serve us better for the long game."

"Lacy, you sure you want to go with them?" Aaron asked.

"You're damn right I do. He's been watching me and I intend to find out why."

"Let's just get this over with." Will stepped out of the SUV. The residential street was quiet in the pre-dawn hour.

Lacy and Axell moved quickly to join him. She turned back to Aaron and nodded. It was no secret he didn't like what was about to happen, but there was no stopping her this time. She'd been chased for so long by too many people wanting to see harm come to her. It was time to turn the tables. No more running.

Axell signaled them to follow as they quietly approached the front of the home. "There will probably be a security system, but I can bypass it quickly, and when I do, you two need to move in and clear the house."

"Clear it?" Lacy asked.

"Make sure no one else is in there."

"He doesn't have a wife or kids," she replied.

"Still, we need to be sure no one else is inside. If there is, then we'll have to guarantee whoever it is doesn't get in the way."

"Understood." As much as she'd wanted this to happen—demanded that this happen, her fear was real. But she had to put it behind her because this man was the key to a lock they'd struggled to open themselves.

CHAPTER
TWENTY-ONE

BLINDED BY THE DARKNESS, Lacy moved at a snail's pace inside the two-story home of the man who had been paid to watch her every move and perhaps put an end to her, if given the chance.

Axell was the first to ascend the stairs while she and Will cleared the house. He stopped and turned back toward them and simply nodded as if to indicate all was going to plan.

Lacy had no idea if this was the way it was supposed to go or not and had to rely on the men who were trained in these activities. Will gestured for her to go left while he went right. He raised his gun, almost waving it before her until she finally understood what he was doing. He wanted her to have her gun ready. While still a novice on the subject of guns, knowing what was at stake gave her more confidence and she held it at the ready.

She continued in the darkness, her eyes adjusting until she could see more than the hand in front of her face. The first floor was clear and the quiet was disrupted by Axell's footfalls above her. She soon rejoined Will.

He returned the acknowledgment that it seemed all clear. The question now was should they go upstairs, or wait for Axell at the bottom?

A thump on the ceiling above diverted their attention. Will began to run up the stairs and she followed. Her heart pumped fast with fear of what they would find.

"This way!" Will shouted as he approached a bedroom from where the sound came.

Inside, Delgado was on the floor. Axell held the collar of his undershirt and had his gun pointed at the back of his head. Will flipped on the light and the momentary flash burned Lacy's eyes.

"Get up!" Axell yanked on the shirt. "Get the fuck up!" His gun pressed into Delgado's back. "Caison, get over here. Help me get him to the chair."

Will rushed to Delgado and grabbed him by the arm.

"You have no idea what you've gotten yourself into." Delgado peered at him. "And her? You might as well say goodbye now. She won't be around for long."

"Shut up." Will dragged him and tossed him into the chair, waiting for Axell to make the next move, but his stance was firm and unmoving. "How do you want to handle this?"

Axell continued to aim his weapon at Delgado, appearing ready to wipe the smug expression clean off his face. "We know you're taking money from the Dalian Company. We also know you're working with someone in the CIA. Now what I want to know is—why."

Delgado shot a glance at Lacy. "I knew you were smarter than they thought you were. You should know that I never underestimated you, Merrick."

"Don't you dare talk to her," Will said. "Answer the fucking question."

"Did I hit a sore spot, Caison? Oh yeah, I know all about you too. The reason you transferred to Washington, leaving a promising career at Louisville. And for what? Her?" He leered at Lacy again. "She must be a hell of a lay. Guess she didn't waste much time, did you, Mrs. Merrick?"

With the back of his hand, Will cracked his fist against Delgado's cheek, leaving a cut that began to spill blood.

"That's enough!" Axell said. "If you want to survive this, I suggest you answer the question."

"See, that's where you've got it wrong, CIA Agent Trevor Axell. You're under the mistaken impression that any of us are going to make it out of this alive. As I said, you have no idea who you're dealing with."

"Enlighten me."

Delgado pressed his middle finger against the cut on his cheek and peered at the blood. "Assistant Director Meeks came to me after Lei Jian was released. He knew I was in bed with Dalian. I was supposed to tell him what they were planning."

"You're lying," Will began. "We know you own the weapon that killed Undersecretary Kendrick. The same weapon used in attempt to kill Lacy Merrick and me."

"Kendrick was going to be killed by Lei Jian's men anyway. I went there to stop him from going public. He'd already written the letter."

"So you killed him when he refused?" Axell asked.

"No. I was there to talk to him at Meeks' insistence. We both knew Jian was trying to get rid of everyone involved in the attack, including all of you."

"Are you saying you didn't kill Kendrick? It was your weapon," Will added.

"I did have a weapon on me. However, I left my gun in the car because I had no intention of using it; not that day anyway. But when I returned, the gun was gone and my window smashed. By the time I'd gotten back to Kendrick, he was dead, and I couldn't be seen there, so I fled."

"Why have you been surveilling me, then?" Lacy moved forward, her hands trembling, but still, she aimed her gun at him.

"Because we knew you were a target too. When Jian was released, I reached out to Kendrick to warn him to keep his mouth shut and that we'd do what we could to protect him from any retaliation from Jian. It wasn't until Ahsan Sajwani went after the Panama Bank president that the assistant director realized what was going to happen. We have assets who were able to get to the bottom of Marquez's death. After Kendrick was snuffed out, we knew what Jian had planned and were trying to protect you and your colleagues."

"Why are you taking money from the Dalian Company, then? What are you to them?"

He eyed her and it seemed he'd been rendered speechless for a moment.

"Oh, you didn't think we knew about that? You passing along all this information to them?"

"Ever hear of a double agent, Mrs. Merrick? Well, that's what I am. Actually, you could say I'm a triple agent. I work for the FBI and the CIA on domestic terrorist matters like the mall attack. We knew Dalian had a hand in it, thanks in part to what you discovered, but had nothing solid on them."

"Were you the one who broke into Turner's house? Did you kill Agent Colburn?" Axell pressed his finger against the trigger.

"No. I was later informed of the incident by my contact at Dalian. They sent someone to get the file at Turner's home the night before but left because his family was there. The next day, they came back for it. He'd been talking to them; a connection I was trying to uncover, via my own in with Dalian. No one expected Merrick and Agent Colburn to be there. You see, you should've let the big boys handle this because now it's a giant clus-terfuck and it's your fault."

"The hell it is! You knew Colburn was killed by those assholes and you did nothing?" Axell raised his gun to Delgado's head.

"Whoa, just hang on, Axell," Will started. "You and Dalian knew what Jian wanted to do and were happy to let him do it until the letter of resignation was discovered. Then, for whatever reason, the game changed. You and whoever you're working with want to keep it a secret just like Turner did and the president."

"You think the president knows about this? You're wrong. He was advised by the secretary of state, who was advised by Deputy Secretary Turner. The president did what he was told."

Delgado peered at Lacy once again. "It was my job to keep you on a short leash, which got a lot harder once your boyfriend over here arrived. But you're wrong about one thing, Caison. We had no intention of letting Dalian's people or Lei Jian come after you. Colburn was an accident. If I'd known he was there..."

Lacy moved in and kicked Delgado in the gut. "You're a piece of shit traitor. My husband is dead because of people like you. Spinning lies, telling half-truths, all in the name of national security."

He coughed a few times before returning his sights to Lacy. "You keep telling yourself that. The only reason you're still alive is because I made it so."

"Okay, I've had enough of this shit," Axell began. "You're going to tell me where Sajwani is and you're going to tell me who at Dalian Company killed Colburn. And then we're going to see Meeks."

Will shot him a worried glance. "What if he's lying?"

"I've known Meeks a long time and I know he's a man who loves this country and would do anything to protect it."

"If I knew where Sajwani was, don't you think he'd be dead by now? Besides, I thought you guys were working on that. Isn't that why you've got that second-rate hacker working for you at Langley?" Delgado smiled. "You're not the only one with an ace up her sleeve, Merrick. We know about him too. You should know that, Axell. You've been at this game a long time."

"You're right. I have." He reached for Delgado and pulled him to his feet. "You're coming with us."

———

The sun had begun to rise when they returned to the safe house with Delgado in tow. The priority now was to ensure the man was telling the truth and the only way to do that was to see what intelligence had been gathered from Meeks' home.

"You bugged his house?" Delgado, in cuffs, remained seated on the couch. "You've got some marbles, I'll give you that much. Is that how you found me?"

"No. I found you," Lacy said. "I'm one of those second-rate hackers too." She looked at Aaron and revealed a smile imbued with conviction.

"You, Merrick, were the only one we couldn't get a read on. Sure, we knew about Nova Investments and what you found with regard to the money. That was excellent work, by the way. But when you returned to Headquarters, that was when we knew there could be problems. This could've all gone away if you'd just let it go. We would've taken care of Dalian and the MSS."

She glared at him. "Would that have happened before or after they attacked us again? Would you have told the American people the truth then?"

"I can see you want nothing more than to put a bullet in my head right now, and I don't blame you. But know this; we are on the same team, whether you want to believe it or not."

"Does Director Mobley know about your little deal with the CIA?" she asked.

"No. No one does. That's how this works."

Axell sat down at the workstation and began to retrieve the audio files captured while they were extracting Delgado.

"Who authorized you to bug him?" Delgado asked. "There's not a chance in hell you got the manpower and the equipment without someone's okay."

Axell turned to him and back to the monitor.

"Doesn't matter. I'll find out."

As the files played, Axell seemed to grow concerned that he would find nothing and that he would have to take this man's word for it, but he couldn't. Not yet. He'd felt as though Delgado had bested him and he didn't care for that at all.

The audio went static for a moment, as though too much sound suddenly filled the house. A gunshot rang out and a woman screamed. Axell jumped from the seat as he listened. "What the...?"

Will leaped toward him. "What the hell was that?"

Even Delgado's face expressed shock.

"Holy shit. It's Meeks' wife." Another shot was fired and the screaming stopped. Axell lunged toward Delgado. "Who was that? Who came after him?" He began to choke the man. "Who the fuck just killed Meeks?"

"Axell!" Will tried to yank him off and turned to Aaron. "Help me over here!"

The two finally managed to pull Axell off of Delgado after he nearly choked the life out of him.

Delgado coughed and used his elbow to push himself back up. "It had to be Sajwani. It had to be. Somehow, Jian found out."

"Why? Why would he go after the assistant director?" Axell shouted.

"I don't know, all right!" Delgado squirmed. "Get these cuffs off me. Goddamn it!"

"We have to call 911." Lacy reached for her cell. "For God's sake, we have to help him."

Axell knocked the phone from her hands. "No! If Jian found him, then he'll find you. I'll do it. I don't know how long ago this was. Doesn't matter. I'll do it." He stepped into the kitchen and placed a call on another burner.

"Oh my God. What the hell are we going to do?" Lacy's voice quivered.

Aaron tried to offer comfort, but she pushed him away.

"No. No. We can't have lost another one. No!"

"This isn't your fault, Lacy." Will approached her. "This is Lei Jian's fault and Delgado's and everyone else who's been trying to keep this secret." He turned to Delgado. "And for what? Huh? So China can keep sending us garbage? Cheap shit that people buy up because they can't afford anything made in America?"

"You can blame me all you want, Caison. But we got a real fucking problem here. You think the death of the Meekses will go unnoticed? A high-ranking CIA official?" He shook his head.

Axell returned. "That depends on who killed him, now, doesn't it?"

———

Wendell Turner poured a shot of vodka into a glass and tossed it back in a single gulp. He turned toward the window of his office and peered out over the lights of D.C. A knock sounded on his door, which pulled his attention from the lighted streetscape.

"It's me, sir. It's Bryce Dunn."

Turner approached the door and opened it. "Come in." He peered into the empty corridor. "Anyone follow you?"

"No, sir. I made sure of it."

"Good."

"It's done, sir."

"Then it won't be long before Agent Axell is taken into custody. It's a shame a good man had to die, but this is on them, and the careless work of Agent Martin Delgado. Yang's suspicions were correct." He poured another drink. "They'll start looking into Colburn's death too and it'll be all too easy to jump to the conclusion that Axell committed the crimes. We won't have to worry about him anymore and I doubt any of his colleagues either once we inform Jian of their whereabouts."

"No, sir. This will die the way it should have died with Undersecretary Kendrick."

"Agreed. And we can finally move on as a nation from this horrible tragedy."

CHAPTER
TWENTY-TWO

THE LIGHTS of downtown Washington were a welcome distraction for Lei Jian as he peered through the window of the hotel room while Ahsan Sajwani finished a call.

"Turner has followed through with his end of the bargain."

"We know where the agent and the woman are?" Jian turned toward him.

"We do, sir. We will need to act quickly because once they arrest the CIA agent, our targets will realize they are not safe where they're at and we can't afford to lose them again."

"Agreed. Then you will do what needs to be done and we can finally end this."

Sajwani nodded and tossed a duffle bag onto the bed. "They'll be heavily armed and the safe house well-guarded."

"I know I do not need to tell you how to do your job, Ahsan, so I will leave it in your very capable hands. I will meet with our new friend, Mr. Turner, first thing in the morning and ensure we are in agreement as to the events of the days ahead." Jian began to leave. "None of us can afford any mistakes, Ahsan. I will not go back to the minister having failed to deliver on my promise. You would do well to remember that."

Once Jian departed, Sajwani placed two weapons inside the duffle bag—an automatic rifle and a 9mm handgun. Depending upon the situation, one was a precise instrument, and the other was intended for maximum carnage. He'd underestimated these adversaries before and would not make that mistake again so he had to prepare for the worst. However, this was a job that required more than one person, but he would not get help. Jian had few people left in his charge, several turning against him at the moment of his capture. Why Ahsan had been loyal was simple. His endgame was the same and, through his loyalty, he maintained hope of rising above the title of right hand to Lei Jian, a certainty once this mission was complete. Jian would regain his power and Ahsan would be rewarded and rewarded handsomely.

———

The writing on the wall had become clear to Axell. As he sat on the couch, elbows against his knees and listening to the others in the room for whom he'd felt responsible, there was little time to act. He finally stood and inserted himself between Caison and Delgado, who appeared ready to go to blows. "It's clear we're all on the same side here, even if we arrived from different places. We have a high-ranking CIA official who is now dead. I was in his house only hours earlier. You two can't tell me you haven't figured out who they're going to come after, can you?"

Will retreated. "Who turned on you? Hicks?"

"I don't think so. No, this was a carefully crafted set-up by someone who wants to get me out of the way in order to get to you."

"I think Agent Delgado knows more than he's letting on." Lacy turned to him. "Don't you? You met with Meeks the other day. Why?"

"I already told you why."

"Right, because you're on everyone's side."

"Are you inferring I had something to do with the assistant director's murder?"

"I'm simply implying that you were one of the last people to see him. I'm not saying you did it. Obviously. You were with us. But that doesn't mean you don't know anything about it."

"You're insane. You think I had anything to do with it? I'm the one who's been keeping an eye on you. Making sure you and your little friends weren't doing anything stupid. How the hell should I know who went after Meeks or why?"

Will lunged forward, but Axell stopped him. "Enough. This isn't getting us anywhere. Whoever had him killed probably knows about us. All of us. Delgado, you were working with the assistant director, and who else? Who else at the Bureau knows what you are?"

"No one. That's kind of the point. I was working undercover for the CIA."

"And you were taking money from the Dalian Company," Lacy added. "You haven't explained that yet."

"At the risk of sounding like a fucking broken record, it was part of the deal. The assistant director knew about the money. It wasn't a secret. I'll tell you what." Delgado's face darkened with growing frustration. "You all can sit here and chastise me, or we can figure out who killed Meeks. Because I can guarantee you, and I'm sure Agent Axell will agree, that whoever it is will be coming after us."

"Get your things together," Axell began. "We have to leave." He waited for them to move. "Now!"

Lacy returned to the bedroom where she packed the few items

she'd had with her. Where they would go now remained unclear, but she agreed that it was now too dangerous to stay put. Still, something about Delgado wasn't sitting right. Like he knew more and yet was refusing to share. Why and to what end? It seemed like he was, despite all she'd believed, protecting her and Will.

"Lacy, it's time to go." Will appeared in the doorway.

"Where can we go this time?" Lacy moved toward him, bag tossed over her shoulder. "I can't go home. Can't stay here. Where is there left that's safe for us, Will?"

"Axell has a friend."

"No. No way are we involving anyone else in this. I won't be responsible for another death. Especially another friend of Trevor's. No. We'll have to find someplace else. A hotel, something else."

"They'll find us at a hotel."

"Not if we're careful."

The front door burst open and a gun began to fire. A thump sounded on the floor. Someone had been hit.

"Get down!" Will pulled Lacy to the ground and threw himself in front of her. "Stay here! Don't move!"

"No! Will!" She reached for his arm, but he'd already slipped away from her. Her heart raced. Her friends were out there, yelling and screaming and guns firing. Someone had come for them, just as Axell said. But she was still inside the bedroom and didn't know who was out there. The time to hide was over. Lacy would not let them take another away from her. She crawled on her knees into the hall. Will was already out of sight, but she spotted Aaron on the floor. It was he who'd hit the ground, and it looked like he was struck in the shoulder. He shook his head when he spotted her, demanding with his eyes that she not come any farther.

Ignoring him, Lacy inched closer, listening to the struggle, and finally peered around the corner. The room was in tatters and the three men had taken down the intruder. It only took a moment to realize who it was. Will was tying the man's hands behind his back while Delgado bound his feet. She'd only ever seen this man in pictures, images captured on closed-circuit television, but there was no question in her mind that this was Ahsan Sajwani and he'd come to kill them. But coming alone was a foolish move on the part of a man who'd been so elusive up to now.

When she was confident it was safe for her to rise, she did so and rushed into the living room, where Will stood over this man. "Where's Axell?"

"With Delgado, checking the perimeter for anyone else," Will replied.

"How did he find us?" She stared at Sajwani, a reedy man with eyes full of hate as he stared back. "How did you find us?"

Sajwani smiled but didn't speak.

Will threw an uppercut that connected hard against Sajwani's chin. "She asked you a damn question."

Lacy heard Aaron moan behind her and ran to him. "Oh, God. Are you okay?" She peered at his shoulder. "You're bleeding. Will, Aaron needs help."

"Hey, buddy." Will approached and began to examine Aaron's shoulder. "Looks like the bullet just grazed you. You'll be all right. Can you stand up?"

Aaron nodded. "Yeah. Yeah, I can get up."

"We need to get you cleaned up and see how bad this is." Lacy began to walk toward the kitchen.

Axell opened the front door and walked in with Delgado trailing. "If he came with someone else, that someone else is long gone." He continued inside and stood in front of their prisoner. "Ahsan Sajwani. Nice to finally meet you. Took you long enough to find us."

He spat blood at Axell's feet and returned a smile.

"Were you the one who killed Agent Colburn? Camden Meeks and his wife?"

"I don't know what you are talking about."

Axell bent down so the two could meet eye to eye. "Sure you do, Ahsan. Your boss, Lei Jian, sent you to Turner's house. That was you, right? And earlier tonight too? The assistant director? Boy, going after such a high-value target makes you some kind of fucking idiot, doesn't it? You want the whole of the CIA after you because that's what's going to happen."

"I didn't kill your friend or anyone in the CIA."

"I already told you, Axell," Delgado began. "It was someone from Dalian. You need to back the hell off."

Axell pulled upright again but kept his eyes fixed on Sajwani. "Then maybe you should tell us who at Dalian was responsible. You know those guys, right? I'm sure you'd like to get out of here; go back home to whatever country you came from, eh, Hadji?"

"Axell, come on," Will said.

"You think this asshole deserves to be treated with respect, Caison? He just fucking tried to kill you and all of us in here. But hey, I don't want to be insensitive."

"That's not what I mean. You're pissed and so am I, but we need him."

"We don't need him." Axell kicked Sajwani's feet out from under him. "And guess what, Hadji? Time for you to go meet your maker." Axell aimed his weapon between Sajwani's eyes.

"Stop!" Lacy leaped toward him. "Trevor. We can use him to our advantage. He didn't kill Agent Colburn. I know I didn't get a good look at the person, but like I told you before, it wasn't him."

"I don't give a shit anymore. This guy." Axell shook his head. "He's perpetuating the stereotype, isn't he? Lets his boss blame some terrorist group to get everyone all up in arms about radical

Islamic terrorism when it was the Chinese all along? You got on board with Jian back in Dubai, right? Thought, hey, why not screw over the Americans? And then Jian was released. That's why you came back. Started taking out everyone who knew the truth."

"Does it really matter? You will all be dead by morning."

"Is that right, Ahsan?" Axell raised his weapon again. "Are there more of you coming? Because it seems to me Lei Jian doesn't have as many friends as he used to. You see, I have friends in Beijing. They've told me things."

Sajwani turned away.

"They've told me that Jian was only released because the new minister wanted the Americans to bring him down so he could keep his hands clean. Make it look like he kept his end of the deal. I do give the minister credit. He didn't like what Jian did. Put hundreds of hours of negotiation at risk and for what? To gain a better position for your Dalian Company? Hardly seems worth it. So I don't believe you when you say we'll all be dead by morning. Because as I look at you now, it's not looking like you're capable of doing it. So, again I ask you, did you kill the assistant director?"

"No."

"Then who did?"

"That would be the same people who killed your friend, Agent Colburn."

Axell pulled the trigger and a blast of gunfire rang out. Sajwani slumped in his chair and Lacy recoiled as blood splattered across her face.

Will turned to Axell in utter shock. "What the hell did you just do?"

"We couldn't let him go. He wasn't going to tell us anything anyway."

CHAPTER
TWENTY-THREE

BALTIMORE, the place where it all began, was where Lacy now found herself. They were forced to flee yet another location, leaving behind the mess Axell created for someone else to clean up. Someone who had done it for him before. Turned out, there was a lot she didn't know about Trevor Axell. Regardless of what he'd done, she still had faith in him. Her own theories about what the intelligence community and the government were capable of doing had made a seismic shift since this began. While the ultimate goal was to ensure safety for American citizens, it often seemed that achieving those goals required hands to be dirtied. Perhaps that was just the way of it. Because certainly, those from whom they protected the citizens hadn't kept their hands clean.

"You should eat something."

Lacy returned from her drifting thoughts as she perched on the bed in the motel room. A dingy, rundown motel, they settled in two adjoining rooms—like fugitives. "How's your shoulder?" She examined Aaron's arm that Axell had bandaged up.

"It's fine. I'm fine. Really." He presented her with a wrapped sandwich. "You need to eat, Lacy."

Delgado peered at her. "He's right. Tomorrow won't be any easier and you'll need your strength."

"With Sajwani gone," Axell began, "Jian will come after all of us with greater numbers. And we have to assume he's getting help. Probably from Dalian. They may have started at opposite ends of the spectrum, but what they want now is the same thing. And that is for us to be out of the way—for good. And it won't be long before the murder of the assistant director is pinned on me. I won't be able to stay here. It'll put all of you in more danger than you already face."

"You can't go, Trevor; we need you here—with us," Lacy replied. "Who else is left for us to turn to? As I see it now, we're dead in the water. Am I wrong?"

"You're not entirely wrong." Delgado sat up in his chair. "Look, I know what you think of me and there's nothing I can do to change that except to say that I can help. Despite what you believe, I am with you on this."

"What can you do for us?" Will asked.

"I agree with Axell, that Jian will come back at us harder than before. But the three of us need to return to Headquarters in the morning," Delgado said.

"Are you serious?" Aaron asked.

"It's important we go back. Look, I don't think it'll be safe for you to return to Langley. Everyone knows that Axell got you in. Don't think they won't make the connection. You'll be stripped of your credentials and, at best, detained. This battle is far from over, but I can help. Dalian sent someone after Turner to get the Kendrick letter. And whoever that was likely killed Agent Colburn."

Axell regarded him, appearing uncertain of any real level of trust. "And what can you do about that?"

"If the Dalian CEO, Shen Yang, ordered the murder of Meeks, which is possible, then I'm burned. I won't be able to go back there. If it was someone in Jian's employ, then I stand a chance of discovering if they are working in concert for the same end. Get the Kendrick letter and finish off anyone who knows the truth. And that could include Turner." Delgado reached for his phone. "Let me make a few calls. It's late, but the people I know don't sleep." He headed toward the door.

"I'm coming with you." Axell followed. "Don't think that you've earned my trust because you sure as shit haven't." He palmed his gun while Delgado dialed a number on his phone.

Delgado eyed the weapon. "You think if I wanted any of you dead you'd all still be breathing?"

"Don't flatter yourself."

"Look, Axell, Meeks was a good man. What we were trying to do was the right thing, and that was to get something we could use on the Dalian Company to put Shen Yang away or sent home."

"So they could let him go like they did Lei Jian?"

"*Touché.* However, my point is, that as far as I know, Jian had no real connections to Yang. He was acting on behalf of the ministry, or what he believed the ministry wanted. And I'm starting to get the impression that Dalian may, in fact, want Jian dead. Put this whole thing to bed so they can continue digging in their heels here in the US." He raised his phone to his ear. "Yeah, it's me. I got to know, man, we got bodies piling up over here. CIA bodies that are going to create problems for us." He looked at Axell as he listened. "I heard Jian might be back. You think he's responsible?"

Axell never let his gaze fall away. He was trying to get a read on Delgado.

"Okay, man, thanks. Watch your back." Delgado ended the

call. "Look, I knew they were sending someone to Turner's house to get the file. That was when I realized the two were connected in some way. Turner and the Dalian Company. Yet another pile of crap I had to wade through to get to the bottom of Jian's return. I didn't know they killed Colburn until later."

"And you said nothing? Not to Meeks or anyone else? What was that call about, then?"

"It was my informant, inside Dalian. Word is, Turner's playing nice with Dalian right now because it seems like everyone but the damn president knows about Kendrick's letter. But it doesn't seem like there's anything more to it than that."

"Bullshit." Axell turned away.

"Before you decided to blow Sajwani's brains out, he said Meeks was killed by the same people who killed Colburn, meaning someone at Dalian. Which also means that I am burned. And that's probably the last time I'll talk to that guy. He's as good as dead."

"And Turner lied about who was there that night. He came to see us, looking for help after his house was broken into. Said it was just his assistant." Axell began to fit the pieces together. "Why was he looking for cover unless he's afraid of Dalian now?"

"Funny how Sajwani found you and your team after you all met with Turner. Like someone told Jian himself."

Axell marched back inside. "Son of a bitch."

"Well?" Lacy noted their return and Axell's troubled expression.

"I don't know what the hell to think anymore."

"Why? What happened?" Will replied.

"It's Turner. We need eyes on him. There's a good chance he was the one who gave us up. Why? I don't know. But we'd better find out fast."

"Next week is the groundbreaking ceremony for the memorial," Lacy began.

"That's still days away. A lot can happen in that amount of time."

"Hear me out. There's no doubt in my mind that whoever killed Meeks will pin it on you, Axell."

"We agree on that."

"What I can't be sure of is Agent Fraser's intentions. Will, you trust him?"

"I do."

"Good. We're going to need his help on this."

————

They'd come to an agreement late in the night not to raise suspicions at Headquarters with a disappearing act. And so as Lacy appeared at Michelle's door, her note of surprise was to be expected.

"Lacy, come in." Michelle glanced into the hall as she pulled Lacy in and closed the door behind her. "I heard what happened to the CIA official. Please tell me your friend is all right—Aaron?"

"He's fine. When did you find out?"

"It's all anyone can talk about."

"And the prevailing theory?"

"General consensus seems to be that he was targeted like they believe Undersecretary Kendrick was. Is that true?"

"I don't know, Michelle, but you're going to want to sit down for this. I'm working with SSA Delgado and..."

"Delgado? I thought he was the problem."

"I thought so too, but now—I hope I'm right in assuming he's been helping us indirectly. That's why I'm here."

"What can I do? Lacy, this is getting so far out of control.

Maybe it's time to come forward with what you have. I'm concerned for your safety and your friends."

"I wish I could. This is so much bigger than I ever believed. I can't begin to explain everything but just know I'm working to end this as quickly as possible. And that brings me to why I'm here. I need the agenda for the groundbreaking ceremony later this week. I need to know everyone who will be there, the timing of the speeches—everything."

"I don't like the sound of this. What are you planning?"

"It's better if you don't know. I need to be able to trust you, Michelle. If not, then you might as well sign my death warrant."

"Of course you can trust me. Haven't I shown you that already?"

"Yes. I'm sorry. I'm just feeling, well, like I'm running out of options."

"I'll get you the information. Where can I contact you?"

"I'll be in touch. It's best if I keep you at arm's length—for your own safety."

"I may not be fighting this fight with you, but I am here. I'll do what I can. I always have." She reached for Lacy's arm. "Give me the day and I'll get what you need."

"Thank you. I'll be in touch soon."

————

Lei Jian waited for confirmation, which eventually came in the form of a picture that had been texted to him, that Ahsan Sajwani was dead. The man who had reached out to him to relay this upsetting information wanted to discuss their options. However, hesitation persisted because this informer was the very same man who'd helped Jian be taken into custody by his own government. The question was, how could he trust this man to help? But he had little wiggle room at the moment. Without Sajwani, he faced an uphill battle.

Jian assessed the hotel room, peering at the belongings of his loyal friend who was now gone. The decision was made. He would wait to meet with the deputy secretary for now and instead would call upon the very people whom he'd tried to help. Shen Yang had the ear of the minister and extensive resources, both of which would be of great value to him.

Jian made the call and now stood beneath the hotel awning, waiting for the car to arrive. Upon making the journey, he was escorted into Yang's office.

His swift arrival was greeted with a temperate response. "Ambassador, very good to see you again."

"Is it?" Jian entered the office, eyeing the men who accompanied him.

"You may leave." Yang motioned for the men to depart. "Please, Ambassador, sit down. We have a great deal to discuss."

"Indeed, we do." He placed his cell phone on Yang's desk, opened to the photo that had been sent to him. "I have lost a very loyal friend and colleague, who was sympathetic to our concerns."

Yang examined the image. "I'm sorry to hear this, especially after the successful execution of our initial plans. However, your return to the US was ill-advised. It is not safe for you here. The Americans have lost very important and influential people. Your arrival will undoubtedly be detected. After all, it is no secret that you were released and that the minister reinstated your ability to travel."

"Yes. While he and I agree, it is beginning to feel as though many are working against me. Which is why I'm here. I believe I have a new ally. That *we* have a new ally." Jian eyed Yang as he tried to assess his position. "You and your investors have benefited greatly from the declining revenue of Liwa Properties here in the US."

Yang nodded. "We have."

"Meanwhile, I was made the scapegoat while you sat here and reaped the rewards."

"What is it that you want, Mr. Ambassador?"

"Support. I am to meet with Deputy Secretary Turner and discuss the terms of a new deal. I would be foolish to take on such a task alone and I understand the minister's hands are tied."

"Is that what he told you?"

"Pardon?" Jian's eyes flickered with an air of suspicion.

Yang continued, "First you must tell me, did you authorize the murder of the CIA official?"

"Of course not. I can assure you of my absolute lack of involvement in that situation. My intentions have been clear from the start. And I do not wish to have the entirety of the Central Intelligence Agency coming after me for something I did not do, nor did I authorize."

"Then who did?"

"I suspect it had something to do with the deputy secretary. Or else why would he approach me? I had no arrangement with him prior. Only his subordinate. He knew I was here. Someone had to have told him. I cannot say whose side this man is truly on, except his own."

"And you trust him?"

Jian laughed. "No. I do not. However, he wishes to maintain power in his office. And because of that, he will cooperate in any means necessary to eliminate the remaining individuals who were aware of my arrangement with the now-deceased undersecretary. This was something that should have been taken care of long ago, but there were unforeseen circumstances. And I am here to rectify them."

"So you would like me to provide you with security to ensure your safety?"

"Among other things."

"Such as? Please, Jian. We are both too tired to dance around the issue."

"I need people who will implement orders as well as ensure my safety."

"Like Ahsan Sajwani?"

"Yes."

Yang seemed to consider the request. "I have people who will do as I ask without question. Those are the people you will want by your side when the time comes. And what, then, is the benefit to me, should you accept the offer of help?"

"As I said, Dalian has benefited greatly from the decline of your competitor. Allowing even greater investment in the United States, as was our initial goal. A goal set forth by the previous minister as well as the premier."

Yang smiled. "So I have already reaped the rewards and to request anything additional would be disrespectful. I see." He paused. "The last thing I want to do is disrespect you, Ambassador, or the premier. I will make the arrangements now."

"Thank you. I am to meet with Deputy Turner in a matter of hours to discuss our options."

As Jian departed, Yang retrieved his phone. "Jian was just in my office." He paused. "Yes. His goal has not changed; however, he has lost his only ally and has called upon me for assistance and I have provided him with that." He nodded. "I agree. It won't be long before they find him and take care of the problem for us. And perhaps that will also include the deputy secretary."

————

All signs pointed to Trevor Axell as the man responsible for killing the Assistant Director of Operations, Camden Meeks. The Washington station chief's hands were tied and she could not cover for him regarding the requests he made to surveil Meeks' home. In fact, Elizabeth Ward was about to be drawn and quartered for her sanctioning of the activity, regardless of the fact that it had been off the books. She'd placed her trust in Axell that he was on the right track and it had backfired spectacularly.

He was ready to face the charges head-on as he sat in his office in defiance of the recommendations from his cohorts. His instructions were clear and Lacy knew what needed to be done and she had every intention of following through on her promise. In the end, she had become as loyal a friend as he'd had. But until they could find a resolution, he would face the music in an attempt to offer distraction to the likes of Deputy Turner. He banked on Turner moving forward knowing Axell was out of his way.

And as far as Aaron Hunter was concerned, his immediate future at the CIA was safe, for the moment. There were those behind the scenes, those who were certain of Axell's innocence who would offer cover to the hacker to finish what he started.

It wasn't long before several FBI agents approached, as well as the CIA director himself. Axell stood from his desk. "Sir." He placed his hands behind his back.

"You're under arrest for the murders of Camden and Jinny Meeks." The director peered into Axell's eyes. "I sure as hell hope you weren't the one who pulled the trigger, Agent Axell. Because if you were, I'd be the one to put you away. You understand that?"

"I do, sir."

The agents took him by the arms and led him out of his office. His colleagues and friends lined the halls as he was escorted out, their expressions shocked; some teary-eyed with disbelief. He hoped Lacy could do what she had set out to do. He was putting his life in her hands now.

————

Night had settled on a day that made Lacy feel as if all had been lost. All they had worked toward—snatched from them. And a truth that still clawed its way from deep inside a well, only to be drowned with more tragedy and betrayal. She sat in the car parked in front of the derelict hotel room where Aaron and Will waited. But no Trevor Axell. Word had already reached her via Aaron that he had been taken into custody.

"We should go inside now." Delgado pulled the keys from the ignition and stepped out.

Lacy joined him as the two approached the door, both looking over their shoulders. They walked inside to see the defeated faces of those who remained true to the cause.

Aaron quickly stood on her arrival and approached, not offering words, but a warm embrace that she needed so much. "He made sure I wouldn't be touched. Taking care of everyone else, as usual."

She smiled and pulled from the embrace. "I'm glad because we need you now more than ever."

"This will be over soon," Will said. "We'll get him back. I promise."

"I know we will. Any word from Fraser?" Her emotions were beginning to get the better of her and she refused to let them see her weakness. Her thoughts turned to her children as they had so frequently since she sent them away.

"Fraser said Turner has a meeting scheduled for 8 pm with a junior staff member, a kid by the name of Bryce Dunn. He thinks there'll be another in attendance, but he hasn't been able to find out who yet."

"Will he have ears on that meeting?"

"Yes. Turner seems to have placed his faith in Fraser. He'll be there too. I don't know what he did to gain his confidence, but whatever it was, it worked."

Delgado dropped his keys on the table and fell into the chair. "Good. We need all the ammo we can get right now." He looked to Lacy. "Tell them what you got."

"Friday's agenda." She held out her cell phone. "Michelle sent this to me and an encrypted file embedded along with it. Aaron, I need your help in opening that file."

Aaron retrieved his laptop and set it up on the table. "Give me your phone." As she handed it to him, he wasted no time opening the file and began to work on the encryption. "She risked a lot sending this to you."

"Seems like everyone's risking a lot these days." Lacy sat down on the bed next to him. "I assume it's details on the other speakers."

"Just give me another second here." He continued to type. "Okay. Here it is." He turned the screen and the others huddled around.

"So, according to the primary agenda, I'm supposed to speak from 10:15 to 10:20. The CEO of Nova Investments is due to speak before me and introduce the other family members of the victims and a few other survivors."

"What about Turner? Is he on the agenda?" Will asked.

"No, I don't see him on here. That must be a mistake," Lacy said.

"Take a look at the encrypted file," Aaron began. "According to the regular agenda, no one from State is listed. However, if you look at the encrypted file she sent, this list includes the president and secretary of state." He turned to Lacy. "They probably don't want anyone to know they're going to be there."

"They must have reason to believe it's too dangerous to make it publicly known," Will replied. "But I don't see Turner on either list."

"Damn it," Lacy began. "Well, this changes nothing. We have the agenda. We know who's speaking. Now all we need to do is get our plan into place."

"Are you sure you want to do it this way, Lacy?" Will asked.

"We have no other choice—not if we want Axell freed."

CHAPTER
TWENTY-FOUR

THE SHADOWS on the ceiling faded as light entered the small room where Lacy slept. Except she hadn't slept at all. Too many thoughts played on her mind. Terrible thoughts of knowing that were they unable to succeed, Trevor would remain imprisoned for the rest of his life and they would likely not survive. While she'd tried hard to stay strong, she was fighting a battle that exhausted her and this morning she would do the only thing that would get her through these next seventy-two hours. She would see her children and pray it would not be for the last time.

Lacy pulled herself from the bed and crept into the bathroom for a shower while the others remained sleeping, or at least were pretending to sleep. She doubted any of them had found rest. Thoughts and actions seemed to impel her at a painstakingly slow pace. Knowing what they intended to do, what she intended to do, made her hesitate, but she had to push past it. It was the only solution now.

With her hair wrapped in a towel and a t-shirt over her damp skin, Lacy emerged from the bathroom. "Will?" His appearance before her was startling. "Sorry. I didn't mean to wake you. Just wanted to get cleaned up."

"You didn't. I was already awake and I heard you get up."

"I need to see my kids and I need to do it before I do anything else."

"Okay, but I'm going with you."

She was about to argue against it, but what was the point? Neither intended to return to Headquarters now. Knowing what part Turner could be playing in all of this, she couldn't underestimate him and that meant staying out of sight. And there was still Lei Jian. "Fine. We'll leave in fifteen minutes."

As he approached her still standing in the doorway, he stopped. "They'll know what you did was for them and the truth."

"Maybe. But will they think it was worth it? Will anyone think it was worth it?" She brushed past him and, upon return to the tight hotel-room sleeping quarters, Aaron had begun to show signs of life. They needed him back at Langley because they had no one else on the inside, able to access systems that could still provide them with valuable information. And, in the end, it was probably safer for him there.

"I need to head out soon." Aaron eyed her. "You'll be okay?"

"Yeah. Will and I are going to take a trip to see the kids. I won't be back until late tonight, possibly tomorrow morning."

"You're going to New York? Now?"

"I have to, Aaron. I have to see them and know for myself that they're going to be okay. That they *are* okay."

"I'll make sure she's safe." Will returned from the restroom, running his fingers through the waves of his sandy-blonde hair.

"You'll keep in touch? When you arrive and when you're on your way back?" he continued.

"Of course. Don't worry. We'll be fine. This is just something I have to do."

Aaron nodded. "If I get any hits on a location for Jian or new intel on Turner, I'll let you and Delgado know."

"What about Agent Fraser? Will, you said he was our eyes and ears?"

"I haven't heard from him yet. I'll reach out for an update. You should go, Aaron. Don't want to be late."

"Right." A final glance to Lacy. "I'll see you later. Be safe."

———

The early start out of D.C. was slowed by traffic but only until they made it farther north. Flying wasn't an option, as they couldn't be sure who was watching the airports. And it was only a five-hour drive. By noon or so, they'd arrive.

What Lacy hadn't worked out yet was whether she would meet with Megan first or go to the school and stay in the background, hoping for a glimpse of them. "I'm not sure they'll want to see me."

"Of course they will. You're their mother." Will kept his eyes on the road.

"I don't feel like much of one and I haven't been for the last six months or so. I've put them through so much already. They lost Jay, then I sent Celeste away, and now they're living with cousins and an aunt and uncle they barely knew. I've let them down in so many ways, Will."

"I've never known anyone to be so hard on themselves as you are, Lacy. You shoulder the blame for this entire thing. Right from the beginning, I saw that about you. You didn't make them blow up the mall. You didn't cause Jay's death and you certainly aren't responsible for what's happening in our own government." He looked at her. "And you aren't responsible for Keith Colburn's death."

"I could've stopped. I could've stopped all of this just like you suggested months ago, but I didn't. I kept at it and kept at it and now you've changed your life. Aaron's changed his and Trevor? He's in prison, or about to be."

"You can say what you want, Lacy. But I won't let you sink into this pit of despair. You won't get out of this if you do."

"Nothing in this life matters without my kids." She turned away, not wanting him to see her emotions rise to the surface. "You'd understand if you had children." She could feel his stare and regretted the words the moment they left her lips. But her heart ached and she couldn't bring herself to apologize.

Several minutes passed when her phone alerted her to an incoming call. "It's Aaron." She answered. "Hey, is everything okay?"

"I found Lei Jian. He arrived in D.C. the day before Sajwani was killed."

"Why didn't we know about this sooner?"

"He was issued a new passport by his government. It was essentially a clean slate and so it wasn't even in the system at all. I ran a check this morning and it finally popped up."

"Do you know where he is, exactly?"

"No, but I informed Agent Delgado and he's going to meet with Fraser. Hopefully, he'll know something from that meeting Turner had last night. Maybe they talked about Jian. Where are you guys?"

"About an hour outside of the city."

"Are you coming back tonight?"

"In light of this news, I think we'd better." She looked to Will. "I'll see what Will thinks and let you know."

"Okay. Listen, I got to go. I'm outside on the burner, but who the hell knows if they're listening? Let me know when you arrive, just so I know you're safe."

"You be careful, Aaron. Please. I'll be in touch. Thanks for the update. Goodbye." She ended the call and looked at Will. "He found Jian."

"I gathered. Sounds like he's in D.C.?"

"Yes. He said Delgado and Fraser would be meeting up soon. Should know something after that."

"Good. I have faith that they'll find him. Don't worry. They'll be all right. I had my doubts about both those guys, Delgado and Fraser, but I think they've got our backs."

"I hope you're right. If Delgado is playing us, Aaron will be dead before we return."

"If he was, we'd all be dead. You think I would've left Aaron there if I thought he was in that type of immediate danger?"

"I don't know what I think anymore. I guess that's the real problem. We've been deceived at every turn."

"You know you can trust me, or are you questioning that now too?"

"No, I'm not. Maybe you're right. I'm sliding down this slippery slope of lies and deceit and it's starting to feel like everyone around me is part of it."

"I think once you see your kids, you'll find the strength to continue. That's what you need right now."

———

Agents Delgado and Fraser waited in their car outside the hotel where Deputy Secretary Turner was holed up.

"You don't think he's caught on to you?" Delgado said.

"Not a chance. This guy is fairly oblivious to the dangers that he's found himself in. He has no idea the lengths to which Lei Jian is willing to go to get what he wants. The dangerous part is that he believes he's the one in control."

"Let's just hope his arrogance continues, because we need to find Jian and I have no doubt Turner will lead us to him."

"The meeting last night only included a man by the name of Dunn. He works with Turner in some capacity. I'd hoped to get something of use, but I guess Turner doesn't trust me well enough to reveal much. If we find Jian, where do we go from there?"

"I could take him into custody because he's not supposed to be in this country at all, but I think that would be a mistake. Somehow, he got in and the tricky part is finding out who helped him. And we need to see him with Turner. Know, without a doubt, the two are colluding. So our only chance at resolution is to keep a tail on him—for now." Delgado peered through the windshield. "Hang on. Is that him? Is that Jian?"

The two watched a man in a dark suit, medium build, and black hair step out of a Mercedes at the lobby of the hotel.

"Can't tell from here. Call Hunter on his landline and have him get into their CCTV and see if he can get images for confirmation."

He made the call. "Hunter, it's Delgado. I need you to get into the security cameras at the Hotel International. We think Jian's just arrived."

"That's going to take some time."

"You don't have it. Just do what you can now!" Delgado waited on the line while Aaron processed the request.

Jian was still inside the lobby.

"I think he's waiting for Turner to come down," Fraser said. "What's he doing? He needs to get that footage now."

"He's working on it," Delgado replied. "Hunter, we're running out of time. I need confirmation on Jian's identity."

"I'm in. Just running it through facial recognition. Give me one minute." He typed furiously on the other end of the line. "Got it! It's him!"

"Good. We'll take it from here." Delgado ended the call. "I'll go in. You stay here in case they leave. Follow them. Don't wait for me. I'll catch up. We can't afford to lose him."

Delgado stepped out of the car and walked from the opposite side of the street toward the hotel. So far, Jian still waited alone in the lobby.

He approached the entrance and slipped in, walking alongside a couple opposite Jian. Staying out of sight, Delgado waited until he finally spotted Turner approaching. He retrieved his cell phone and began to take pictures of the two together. After only a few minutes, they both walked toward the elevators and disappeared inside.

Delgado hurried back out and approached the car where Fraser still waited. "I got them together." He slipped into the driver's seat.

"What now?"

"We wait to see where they go, or if Jian goes alone. And we follow him. He's planning something."

———

Will pulled the car alongside the curb and stopped. "What do you want to do?"

Lacy turned to him. "What I want to do is go inside that school and get my children and bring them home with me. That's what I *want to* do. What I'm going to do is sit here and stare at the playground until they come out for lunch." She glanced at her watch. "Which should be any time now. And then I'm going to ask the front desk if I can go back and see them."

"Are you sure that's a good idea?"

"Isn't that why we're here? Why we drove for the past five hours? Did you think I was just going to look at them from afar?"

"I'm sorry. I didn't know what you wanted to do."

"Damn it. I shouldn't be snapping at you. I don't know what I should do. Hang back, or talk to my sister-in-law. I guess I'm just flying by the seat of my pants right now and I'm taking it out on you."

"You're right about what you said before, about me not having kids. While I try to empathize, I can't. Not really. You're a mother who's had to make some extremely difficult choices. I wouldn't wish that on anyone. I'll stay here. You go on in and see if they'll let you back."

"They'll probably have to call Megan. That'll be a shock to her, but I know she'll say yes." Lacy opened the door. "I won't be long."

"Take as much time as you need. I'll be right here when you get back."

Lacy smiled and stepped out into the brisk afternoon air. The grey clouds appeared weighty and the winds blustery. She pulled her coat around her waist and walked toward the main entrance of the school, which was secured by a gate across the entire perimeter.

Inside, Lacy approached one of the administrators sitting behind the counter. "Excuse me? My name is Lacy Merrick. My children go to this school. Olivia and Jackson Merrick?"

"Yes. How can I help, ma'am?"

"I'd like to request permission to sit with them at their lunch recess, which I believe is coming up."

"Are you on the list?"

"No. I'm not. But if you can call my sister-in-law, Megan Butler, she's their guardian, and she'll verify my identity."

The woman regarded her with some concern. "I'll just be a moment, then, ma'am. Please have a seat."

Lacy sat down and waited, having no idea if Megan would

give permission, but she thought she would. Megan was a good person and while Lacy's arrival might cause some confusion, she doubted her sister-in-law would deny the request.

"Mrs. Merrick?" The woman peered over her desk. "If you'll just allow me to copy your identification, you have permission for a visit. I'll have the children brought here and you may then sit with them for a few minutes, if that will be acceptable?"

"Yes. Yes, very acceptable. Thank you." Her heart soared at the news. She would at least get a few minutes with them and that would make all the difference. Lacy stared at the door, waiting for them, and, for a moment, she forgot everything else.

Her eyes welled when they were escorted inside. Lacy placed her hand over her mouth in disbelief. It had been only ten days, but they were the longest ten days of her entire life. "Oh my goodness." She opened her arms wide.

"Mommy!" Jackson ran toward her, almost knocking her over with the force of his embrace. "I can't believe you're here! I've missed you so much!" He pulled back. "Does this mean we're going home now?"

She looked into his eyes. They lit up with such a sparkle she could hardly believe it. But before she answered, Lacy looked upon her daughter, who stayed several steps away. "Liv." She stood and walked toward her. "Oh, sweetheart." Lacy wrapped her arms around her, but Olivia didn't return the embrace.

"What are you doing here?"

"I—I came to see you."

"We're going home! We're going home!" Jackson shouted.

"Oh no, baby. Not yet. Not just yet, but soon. Very soon."

"What?" The boy stepped back in disbelief.

"See? I knew it. Why did you bother coming at all?" Olivia asked.

"I wanted to see you." She looked at the woman. "May I take them out into the hall for a moment?"

The woman nodded, noting the exchange.

Lacy ushered them into the hall where a bench was nearby. "Come here. Sit down for a minute."

The children sat on the bench, while she crouched down to meet them eye to eye. "I just needed to see you. I didn't mean to upset you, either of you. My heart has ached every single day we've been apart."

"Why aren't we going home?" Jackson asked.

"I still have some things to work out. But I promise you, it won't be long now. How are things with Aunt Megan and Uncle Eric?"

"Fine," Olivia replied. "They're nice."

"I'm so glad to hear that. I knew you'd like them."

"But, Mommy, I don't get why we can't come home yet," Jackson said.

"I know you don't, baby, and I wish I could explain it to you, but it's just not yet the right time. I wish it wasn't this way, but it is. And I had to see you both just to tell you how much I missed you and how much I love you."

"Well, you shouldn't have bothered. Me and Jack are doing just fine without you. Come on Jack, it's time to have lunch. Aunt Megan packed us a good lunch."

Lacy stood and watched as Olivia pulled Jack down the hall. He turned back and waved to her. Tears spilled down her cheeks as she waved back. "Goodbye, babies. I love you."

CHAPTER
TWENTY-FIVE

THE WIND BLEW Lacy's hair against her face, but it could not conceal her pained expression and reddened eyes. Will's heart sank as he watched her approach the car, the outcome of the reunion having manifested clearly in her expression. She stepped inside and closed the door, saying nothing.

"Did you want to drive back or stay here for the night?" he asked.

"I want to go back. Just get this the hell over with." She peered through the passenger window as she spoke.

Will started the engine and headed back onto the highway, back to D.C. where they would face powerful enemies.

Almost an hour into the drive had passed before Lacy pulled her sights away from the window and toward Will. She placed her hand over his, which rested on the gearshift. "Thank you for coming with me. Thank you for taking me to see my kids. God only knows if it'll be for the last time."

"It won't be, Lacy. You will see them again."

A final squeeze of his hand and she released it, returning her attention to the landscape as it sailed past the window in a colorful haze.

It wasn't until Lacy's phone rang with an incoming text that the silence in the car had finally broken. "It's from Agent Fraser," she continued. "Oh my God. It's a picture of Lei Jian with Deputy Turner. They are working together. And here's the proof. This gives us some ammunition." She peered at the phone again. "He says he and Delgado have been tailing Jian since this morning. They've got a location on him now."

"Finally, some good news. Let him know we're on our way back and should be there by dark."

———

Inside the cramped workspace surrounded by glass partitions, Aaron focused on the job he'd been hired to do. His mind never drifted from the idea that at any moment, the people upstairs would discover what he'd accessed for Delgado earlier. Unauthorized access to a private hotel security video from their servers would be easily traceable back to him. And they'd called him on his landline, knowing full well they monitored all calls. It was a brash move he hadn't thoroughly vetted out of the simple fact that the agents needed the information quickly. And it appeared his time had just run out.

Several senior staff had already begun their approach. A momentary lapse of judgment would have him running like hell, but there was no escaping this. So, the only option was to offer an explanation and hope that they would accept it. If not, then Agent Axell wouldn't be the only one in jail.

"Mr. Hunter? Could we see you for a moment?" A woman in grey dress pants and a white blouse approached. This was not his supervisor and appeared to be a department head or someone else with far more authority than Renee Childs.

"Sure." He began to follow them as they headed to an area of the building he hadn't the clearance to visit. This was bad and, in moments, he would find out just how bad.

"Please, come in and take a seat." The woman showed him in while the others filed inside afterward. Upon closing the door, she sat down and retrieved a tablet. "Mr. Hunter, it has come to our attention that at 10:55 am, you accessed the cloud server of a hotel located in Washington D.C. and reviewed their closed circuit video. Is that correct?"

"Yes, ma'am."

"And were you authorized to view that private information? Did someone give you a directive to do so?"

"No, ma'am."

"I see. Can you tell me who this man is?" She turned the tablet toward Aaron.

"I believe that is the former Chinese ambassador Lei Jian."

"Yes, it is. Did you know he was here in the US? Why were you attempting to locate him via the passport database and facial recognition? Do you have reason to be concerned about Mr. Jian?"

"I suggest you tell us the truth, Mr. Hunter." The man beside her spoke. "I'm sure you're aware of the tragedy concerning a high-ranking CIA official and the fact that one of our own is being held in custody for his murder. A man who I believe you also know—quite well, in fact."

"I am aware, sir." Sweat had begun to form at his hairline.

"Then, by all means, tell us why you are so concerned with the former ambassador. Are you privy to information we are not?"

Of course he was, but he dared not say. "I don't believe so, sir. I was just—well I wanted to try to help Agent Axell, sir. I believe he has been wrongly accused."

The woman, to whom Aaron had yet to be formally introduced, continued to stare at him, as though she was attempting some sort of mind-game interrogation technique. "Mr. Hunter, we have a problem here, you understand that?"

"Yes, ma'am. I do."

"Good. Then I must inform you that pending further investigation, you are hereby dismissed and will be stripped of your credentials."

"I understand." Aaron began to feel relief sweep through him. However, no one had yet given him permission to leave and the idea that he was going to be put in jail right at this moment remained at the forefront of his thoughts. "I'm very sorry for any trouble I have caused."

"I'd like to speak with Mr. Hunter alone for a moment if you all wouldn't mind?"

The three other men in the room appeared somewhat surprised but dismissed themselves at her request.

"Thank you." When they departed, she finally began, "I'm Elizabeth Ward, Station Chief at the D.C. office. I believe you and I are after the same thing."

———

The protracted journey had come to an end when Will pulled into the parking lot of the Sandy Point Motel. A shadow stretched across the pavement as the sun fell behind the neglected building. And the only thing Lacy brought back with her was a sense of conflicted feelings. Rejected by her children, whose only wish was to return home with their mother, and encouraged by the knowledge that they finally had the upper hand on Lei Jian. They knew where he was, who he was with, and now they needed to know what he intended to do. The result of which could fix the first problem and offer hope that in time, her kids would forgive her.

Will opened the door to the dimly lit room. "Where's Hunter? He should be here by now."

Lacy entered behind him and switched on another light. "I haven't heard from him. Will, he has no one protecting him now. He could be in trouble."

"I don't want to jump to conclusions just yet. Let's touch base with Delgado. He might've heard from Aaron already."

"Yeah, okay." She sat down on the edge of the bed. "It's been a long day and I'm exhausted. I'm sure Aaron's fine."

"I'll call Delgado now." Will retrieved his phone and the line rang. "It's Caison. Where are you?"

"We're holed up at the hotel where Jian is staying. We're sitting tight until you and Lacy return."

"Any word from Hunter?"

She looked to Will with anticipation.

"No. Not since he got us the surveillance video earlier this morning. Why? He's not there yet?"

"I'm sure he's just caught up with something else. I'll reach out to him again, see what I can find out. What's your plan?"

"Fraser has to take off. Turner put a call into him earlier. He's hoping to find out why he met with Jian. So far, it doesn't seem like he knows Fraser's been talking to us on the side."

"Right."

"I'll stay here and keep watch. You two should stay at the motel. No point in coming out here. I got this."

"Okay. We'll track down Hunter and get back to you. Keep us updated and I'll do the same." Will ended the call.

"He doesn't know where Aaron is, does he?"

Will shook his head. "We'll find him."

"I'll try him again now." Lacy dialed his number and waited. Still no answer. "Where the hell are you?"

The door handle jiggled and Will drew his weapon. He raised his index finger to his lips as he turned to Lacy. The handle continued to rattle until a voice emerged.

"Lacy? It's me. This key isn't working. Let me in."

Her heart dropped into her stomach, relieved at the voice she immediately recognized. "Oh, thank God." She brushed past Will and opened the door. "Where the hell have you been?"

Aaron stood in the shadows of the corridor, his eyes reflecting her fear. "I'm sorry, I was told not to call you. That they probably already have my number." He began to walk inside.

"Who's they and who told you?" Will asked.

"I nearly shit my pants when they took me away. I thought I was going to jail right then and there."

"Who took you away? Aaron, what the hell happened?" Lacy grabbed him by the arm and led him to one of the beds. "Sit down. You want some water?"

"No. I'm fine. Just shaken up is all. I thought we were all going up the creek." He pushed his hands through his hair. "So after I got that hotel footage over to Delgado and Fraser, I got busted. They said I wasn't authorized and, of course, they were right. So, anyway, they take me to this room, a conference room, I guess, and start grilling me. Jesus, Lacy. I swear I never been so damn scared in my life. And that's saying something."

"What did they do, Aaron?" she pressed on.

"They said I was fired and a formal inquiry would be initiated and I was lucky I wasn't going into holding right then and there. But then these guys left and there was this woman. She didn't introduce herself at first, just kept asking me questions and I figured she was one of the department heads or something. But after they left, she told me that we were on the same team."

"Who was this person?"

"The Washington station chief, Elizabeth Ward. She gave Axell the go-ahead to bug Meeks' house. We know how that turned out. Anyway, she said that one of her team was already dead."

"Agent Colburn."

"Yeah, and she knew something smelled bad when they took Axell away. So she wants to help us."

"How can she do that?" Will asked.

"She knows about the groundbreaking ceremony. In fact, there's a joint effort between her office and the FBI's Washington Field Office. Looking out for any unusual activity and stuff. I kind of mentioned what we were thinking of doing. I figured she was already sticking her neck out just by talking to me."

"That's where Fraser works, the WFO," Will added.

"She knows that it was Jian we were looking for and has now put her people on finding out who he's talking to through her overseas contacts. She said he wouldn't be able to do much without help from the MSS. Apparently, he still needs them and vice versa."

"That's not the way it seems right now," Lacy began. "It seems like he's out there on his own, building his own little army here to come after us."

"Right now, she's not in the loop with everything we've discovered. She plans to visit Axell and get the download. She's the only one authorized to see him."

"Then she can get word to him," Lacy said. "We can update her on our progress."

"Yeah. If she hadn't been there to diffuse this shit I got into today, I wouldn't be here right now. With Axell gone, we need her."

Delgado knew the Washington station chief well enough to know she was on the right side of this. After getting the call from Agent Caison, he'd begun to understand that perhaps they weren't out there alone and help was within reach. But even she didn't know about his arrangement with Meeks. It had been the man himself who'd put Delgado in place at FBI headquarters, a risky move that Delgado had played to a tee until it all turned to shit when Axell went off on his own and bugged Meeks' house. If only he'd known, he could've put a stop to it and Axell wouldn't be under suspicion of killing a top CIA official. And a friend.

Maybe it was his fault for not coming forward on his first meeting with Lacy Merrick shortly after the attack. He knew then she didn't trust him, but to involve her at that point would have only put her in greater danger. That was the complete opposite of what he was trying to do, which was to find the truth behind the attack and keep her and her friends out of it, a task in which he had failed.

Now, here he sat, watching out for one of the most dangerous men this country had ever known, only second to perhaps the premier himself. And the Dalian company was simply a puppet. Shen Yang was doing exactly as Beijing had asked. And so far, it had served him well. Dalian company stock had risen sharply since the decline of Liwa Properties and Nova Investments, their subsidiary. It was exactly how the plan was supposed to play out. Except no one had counted on Lacy Merrick. Not Lei Jian and certainly not Delgado himself. However, the dangers ahead of her and everyone she loved were still very much alive and kicking.

Delgado rubbed his eyes as the hour approached midnight. He was glad the others were back at the motel and safe, for now, although his night was merely beginning. The time had come for him to do what he was really there to do. Lei Jian couldn't be allowed to live. Yang was helping him and he believed Yang was behind Meeks' murder. Take out Jian, then destroy Dalian. That was the plan—his plan. And while he knew Deputy Turner was also involved, well, he couldn't get away with snuffing him out too, no matter how much he might want to. Instead, he would settle his grievances with Jian himself.

CHAPTER
TWENTY-SIX

THE FRONT DESK was manned by only two staff members, both of whom appeared young and were probably low on the totem pole, bearing in mind that they'd been assigned the night shift. Delgado eyed them and ascertained which one was most likely to provide him with information. Still youthful and handsome, by only a hair's breadth, he could attract a sideways glance from the so-called fairer sex, although he was wise enough not to refer to women in such terms. However, this offered a path of least resistance. "Evening, or is it morning?" A smile flashed brightly on his face.

"Good evening, sir. How may I help you?"

Right away, he knew he'd made the right choice. Her eyes gleamed just enough to spot the lightning bolt of instant mild attraction. "I'm supposed to be picking up a gentleman and driving him to the airport for a red-eye flight. And, well, I'm afraid he's not answering his phone and I have a sinking feeling he might have overslept."

"Oh, what's the gentleman's name? I can call his room for you if you'd like."

"Actually, I think I'll take up some coffee for him. Help him wake up." He leaned over the counter. "Could you tell me his room number, though? He didn't mention it since we were supposed to meet down here."

With a shifty gaze, the woman eyed her colleague to confirm her inattention. "Well, I guess so. I'm not really supposed to give that out, but you got a job to do and I would hate it if our guest missed his flight." She typed on her keyboard. "What's his name?"

"Lei Jian."

"I see it here." She peered up at him. "Room 1510. Up at the top. He must be very important."

"Well, he thinks he is." Delgado flashed his smile once again and rapped his knuckles on the desk. "Thank you for your help, miss. You have a good night." He continued toward the elevators.

The doors parted and Delgado stepped into the corridor. A sign on the wall ahead pointed to rooms on the left and rooms on the right. 1510 was on the right, at the end of the hall. That figured. His swift departure once the deed was done would be slowed by the football-field-length number of steps he'd have to take to make it out of there.

Given the late hour, he assumed most of the guests were asleep, which presented its own set of problems and he'd begun to consider the only way out would be through the stairwell, which was very near where Jian's room was located. Finally, he had something going for him on this mission.

He'd accepted certain guidelines during his tenure as an inter-agency spy, one being that there was no one else on which to count. He alone was responsible for his success or failure and if it was to be a failure, then he would willingly pay the price. But Delgado didn't believe in failure.

The room was just ahead. He slowed his approach and flicked the latch from his holstered weapon, ready to draw. He placed his ear to the door and heard nothing; however, he remained confident Jian was inside as he'd monitored the lobby for the better part of the day and into the night, having followed him from Turner's hotel only blocks away. There wasn't a chance Jian had left without Delgado noticing unless he'd been smart enough to leave through the emergency exit from the stairs. An idea that had only just occurred as he considered using that very exit. Still, that would mean Jian was onto him and he didn't believe that was the case.

He peered down at the security lock and smiled. Yet one more thing that was going right. The credit-card style lock was well known to have an easy hack, one which Delgado had his people create for him some time ago, and had kept at the ready for just such an occasion.

From his jacket, he pulled the device, which was similar to a small motherboard with an auxiliary cord attached to the end of it. At the bottom of the door lock was a data port, which was used when a battery was to be changed or software updated. He plugged in the cord that allowed the device to retrieve the code embedded in the magnetic strip of the keycard, and within moments, the door opened. It still amazed him how so many hotel chains continued to use this type of lock. But it was lucky for him they hadn't upgraded because that would have created a bit more of a problem that would've meant charming the young woman downstairs enough to get her to give him a key. He was good, but he wasn't under the impression that his prowess was that on-point.

Delgado drew his weapon and pushed inside. The room was dark, so dark he couldn't see his hand in front of his face. He had no idea what he was walking into and a tingling sensation crawled up his spine. Something wasn't right and he began to get the feeling that Jian wasn't alone inside.

Movement sounded ahead. Someone was coming toward him.

Delgado found a switch and flipped on the light, blinding the man who was approaching and himself. The man before him appeared to be a bodyguard and Jian was nowhere to be seen. Delgado fired his weapon.

A bullet whizzed by him at the same time, but when he heard the thud, he knew he'd hit the other man, although he would not escape without injury. With only seconds to spare before security and/or police would arrive, he continued inside the room in hopes of finding Jian.

Delgado made his way to the bathroom door. "Jian, I know you're in there. Come out so we can talk."

No answer.

"We might be able to help one another out if you're willing. Yang is a mutual friend." When there was again silence, he had but one option. He reached for the handle, standing to the side, and slowly pushed it open. A nightlight burned above the basin and illuminated a reflection in the mirror. It was then Delgado knew he'd screwed up. He thought Jian had been alone, but he wasn't. Not in the room and not in there. The man he saw in the mirror aimed his weapon at the door and fired. The bullet tore through the hollow core door and into Delgado's side.

Delgado darted back through the room and out into the hall. Footsteps followed closely as he pulled open the stairwell door and began to run down the fifteen floors as quickly as he could. His side burned with pain. Blood spilled down his leg, but he continued to run. There was no choice. He had to get to the bottom and exit through the rear door. From there, he stood a half-decent chance of making it to his car.

The stairwell door he'd just passed through slammed shut and the man who'd fired back was gaining ground. Delgado looked over his shoulder and dashed toward the left of the staircase, zigzagging down so as not to be caught in the man's crosshairs. He'd begun to feel weak-kneed from the loss of blood and his head was growing dizzy. "Keep going, damn it."

By the time he'd reached the fourth floor, his pace was slowing. Still under pursuit, it became clear that Delgado was about to lose this race and if that happened, Lacy and her friends would be on their own.

———

A sliver of light sliced through the closed curtains, landing in Lacy's eyes. She was already awake, though, because today marked just over twenty-four hours before she would speak at the ground-breaking. Today, they would meet with the station chief at the grounds where they would make their final attempt to end this once and for all. "Aaron?"

He lay in the bed next to her, above the covers, never presuming to get too close. His eyes fluttered open. "What time is it?"

"Time to get up." Will was already sitting up in his bed.

"Have you heard from Delgado or Fraser?" Lacy pulled herself up and smoothed her hair back with her fingers.

"No. Better get in touch with Delgado first and see how last night went." Will pushed off the bed and walked toward the bathroom.

"I assume he would've told us if Jian had left." Lacy pulled on a t-shirt over the camisole she wore to bed, while Aaron pulled on his jeans. Any sense of modesty had evaporated days ago when she began sharing a space with these guys. It was as though the normal things in life, like attraction, didn't exist in this world where people were out to kill them. And that was fine by Lacy. She was neither interested in nor cared to revisit that part of her life any time soon.

Will returned dressed and fresh-faced, as though he'd just

splashed ice water on himself. Perhaps he had. Either that, or he had a boundless energy she did not possess. He was, though, a man who lived by the seat of his pants. No wife and no children, he came and went as he pleased and his time in Afghanistan surely made him care little for the spoils of suburbanites. He'd seen too much, in all likelihood, to care about anything else except the task at hand. "I'm going to step outside for some air. I'll try Delgado and let him know where to meet us."

Lacy watched as he walked out of the room and turned to Aaron. "You think he's all right?"

"Yeah. Looks fine to me."

She peered at the door, which was now closed. "I don't know. Seems off to me."

"I'm sure he's tired, just like the rest of us. This entire thing has been like some kind of damn nightmare."

Lacy walked toward Aaron and wrapped her arms around his waist, pulling him close and resting her head on his chest. "It has been a damn nightmare." She chuckled. "Like I still can't believe it's actually happening, you know?"

Aaron kissed the top of her head. "Yeah. I know."

Will walked back inside and noted their embrace.

Lacy spotted the shift in his expression and broke away. "What did Delgado say?"

"Nothing. He didn't answer. We should drive to the hotel before meeting with Fraser and Ward. I'm hoping he just fell asleep."

"A guy like that? Doesn't sound like something he would do," Lacy replied.

"No, it doesn't. Come on. We need to go." Will grabbed his keys and pulled open the door again. Only steps ahead was his car and he slipped into the driver's seat.

Lacy sat next to him while Aaron stepped into the back. "You okay?"

"Fine. Why?" Will keyed the ignition.

"You seem preoccupied. That's all."

"Aren't we all?" He pulled out of the parking lot and drove toward Lei Jian's hotel, which was back toward D.C.

"You want me to try Delgado again?" Lacy asked.

"No. I can't be sure we wouldn't be causing a bigger problem if he's in trouble."

Perhaps there was a problem. He hadn't heard from Delgado all night and now this morning, he wasn't answering his phone. They'd all become guarded against losing anyone else. Good people had come to their aid and, for their efforts, had been rewarded with imprisonment and death.

Lacy spotted the luxury hotel ahead. "You know where he was parked?"

"Just over there, on the opposite side of the street." Will pointed toward the location. "Looks like he's there."

She noted a slight elevation in his tone that sounded an awful lot like relief.

He began to drive by the car and peered inside. "I don't see him." And now that look was replaced with panic.

"We'll find him. He must have gone inside. Just park and we'll go in."

"Shit." Will shook his head. "I'll go in. You two wait here." He thrust the gearshift into Park and stepped out, diverting toward the side of the building to avoid detection.

Under the porte-cochere were two Metro P.D. patrol cars and Will knew that was a bad sign. He considered returning to the car, but he had to know what happened to Delgado or find him if he was lucky. He approached one of the officers in the lobby and held out his badge. "Excuse me, I'm FBI Special Agent Caison. Can you tell me what's going on?"

"Didn't know they called you guys out." The officer began to size him up and displayed an obvious displeasure at his arrival.

"No, sorry. They didn't. I'm here on other business and wanted to know if there was anything I could do to help."

"Oh, right. Yeah, well, there were reports of gunfire at about two a.m. this morning. But oddly enough, no one appears to have seen anything. And no reports of injuries. So, we're still taking statements, but looks like whatever happened was hushed up real quick. I've got a couple men walking around with the manager checking rooms. Nothing's turned up yet."

"I see. Thank you, Officer. I'll get out of your hair." Will moved on and made his way toward the stairwell, darting inside when he was confident no one would notice his departure. He would have to walk the place to see for himself because this sounded like Jian's work. Which also meant he had help in covering it up. This brought him greater concern for Delgado's well-being.

Will continued to ascend the stairs, and floor by floor, he saw nothing out of the ordinary. No one was around and, in fact, it seemed unusually empty. They must've cleared it out as best they could. "Damn it." He grew concerned that the manager and the cops opening up the rooms would find something and then all hell would break loose. He had to find Delgado and prayed he wasn't lying dead in one of those rooms.

———

A man thumped on Lacy's passenger window. She jumped as both she and Aaron were startled by the sound. But once the fear passed and she realized who it was, Lacy immediately opened the door. "Delgado! Are you okay? What the hell happened?" She began to examine him. "You've been shot. Will's inside the hotel looking for you."

"He needs to get out of there now. Get him out now!"

Lacy stepped out of the car. "Sit down. You're hurt. Aaron, call Will. Get him out of that hotel." She lifted the flap of his jacket. "Oh my God. We have to get you to a hospital."

"No. The bullet went clean through. I've been hiding for the past few hours and managed to find a first aid kit. This was the best I could do with what I had."

"He's coming back now. I told him we have Delgado," Aaron said.

A moment later, they spotted Will jogging toward them. He jumped into the driver's seat, noticing Delgado was now in the passenger seat with Lacy and Aaron in the back.

"What the hell happened? I didn't see anything inside. Is Jian still in there?"

"I doubt it. I tried to take him out, but he had help." Delgado pressed hard on his wound. "I managed to stay hidden."

"Why didn't you call us for help? Why did you try to kill him?" Will's temper heated quickly.

"He killed my boss and I knew he wouldn't stop until he killed all of you too. I did what I thought I had to do."

"And you almost got yourself killed in the process. For God's sake, you may have just jeopardized everything."

CHAPTER
TWENTY-SEVEN

THE MORNING SUN became obscured by clouds as the hour moved closer to noon. They returned to the shabby hotel and helped Delgado back inside.

"We don't have much time before we're due to meet with the station chief and Agent Fraser at the site. We've pushed it back long enough." Lacy opened the door and held it while Will and Aaron helped Delgado. "Look, I know we started off on the wrong foot, but why didn't you call us when you were hiding? We would've come to help you."

They placed him on the bed. "I couldn't take the chance. I had no idea if Jian and his people were still looking for me and there was no way I was getting you all caught up in the crossfire. I fucked up. I know that. I should've taken him out, but I wasn't expecting him to have help. I figured Yang was offering lip service. My informant relayed to me that Jian was on his own and that was the way it was supposed to be. Instead, he had hired guns."

Lacy walked into the bathroom and gathered a few towels. "Here, let's change your gauze." They'd stopped to pick up supplies to help him. "You should be in a hospital. I'm no doctor and I have no idea how bad off you really are."

"I'll be fine."

Lacy regarded Will with concern. "We have to go to the site, but I don't want to leave him here alone."

"I told you, I'll be fine. I'm coming with you."

She laughed. "I don't think so. You're in no condition."

"She's right," Will began. "You'll only drag us down. Sorry, man, but it's the truth."

"Fine. At least let me ride with you. I'll stay in the car. I can't stay here and do nothing."

"You do see all the blood, right?" Lacy asked.

"Just stitch me up. I saw a sewing kit in the bathroom. It'll do for now. Besides, the bleeding is slowing."

She marched into the bathroom and retrieved the tiny kit. "This?" She raised it high. "You expect me to sew you up with this?"

"Yeah. Is there a problem?"

"You're crazy, you know that?" She pulled away the towels and began to wipe the blood from the wound.

"You sure you can do this?" Will asked.

"No. But do you want to give it a try?"

He shook his head and slowly backed away.

"I didn't think so." Lacy went to work stitching a wound with fabric thread and a tiny needle that was supposed to be used to sew on buttons, not sew skin back together.

Will noted a call coming in on his cell. "It's Fraser." Into the phone, he began, "Caison here." He watched Lacy cringe every time she pulled the needle through and swallowed down his rising bile. There were far worse things he'd seen in his day, but it was her reaction that made him queasy. "Yeah, we got delayed. Delgado had a run-in with Jian. He's fine. Well, he will be soon.

Just stay there. Keep her there. We need to do this. There won't be time tomorrow." He listened as Delgado moaned. "We'll be there as soon as possible." He returned the phone to his pocket. "Lacy, you got to hurry. Fraser is already down there and he doesn't want Turner to know. The station chief is there too."

"This is the best I can do." She pulled upright and examined her work. "I don't know if it'll hold."

"It'll hold for now. Thank you." Delgado sat up again. "Let's go."

———

Arriving at the site, once again forced Lacy to work harder than ever to control her feelings. No matter how hard she tried, images of burning buildings, burning and screaming people; they always flashed through her mind and she had no control over them. She doubted it would ever get easier standing at the place where her husband's visit to a jewelry store ultimately cost him his life.

"Lacy?" Will approached her. "You all right?"

"No. But I will be soon enough."

"We need to move." Will started ahead toward the spot where the ceremonial groundbreaking would take place in less than a day. "I know this isn't easy, but we risk too much if we aren't all on the same page."

"I understand." Lacy looked back to Aaron, who was helping Delgado.

"I got him. You go on ahead," he replied without her saying a word. "So much for you staying in the car, huh?"

"I see her up ahead." Will continued toward the far end of the area, which had already been cordoned off for the attendees.

Lacy hadn't met this woman but admired her already, despite knowing she admitted to what Axell had done with the illegal surveillance. She looked back again and confirmed Aaron and Delgado were still okay, but continued ahead to catch up to Will. "I see her too."

On approach, Elizabeth Ward smiled warmly. "You must be Lacy Merrick." She offered her hand.

"Yes. And you helped my friend, Aaron Hunter. Thank you for that."

"I should've done more for Agent Axell, but I haven't given up on him. I'm Elizabeth Ward. Keith Colburn was one of mine. I've had enough skin in this game without knowing the players. Now that I do, I'm here to help."

"Thank you. What's going to happen here tomorrow will change everything. And Axell will be released," Lacy replied. "So what we need to do now is organize."

Agent Fraser soon arrived. "I apologize, but I was checking the perimeter. Did I miss anything?"

"No. We're just getting started," Will began. "As you know, we had eyes on Jian, but unfortunately, after a run-in with Delgado, we lost him." As he spoke of him, Delgado and Aaron finally caught up.

"You look like you lost the fight," Ward said.

"You should see the other guy. SSA Delgado. FBI Head-quarters."

"You must've been the one to have the run-in with Mr. Jian?"

"Pleasure to meet you, ma'am. Yes, I attempted to resolve our problem once and for all, but unfortunately, it backfired on me. So, you better believe I'm ready to make this happen. He won't get the drop on me again."

"That brings me to another point," Lacy said. "How do we get Jian here? This place will be swarming with FBI, CIA, police, and everyone in between."

"Yes, but he knows you will be here and he'll want to revel in his own handiwork. That will be a big enough draw for him," Fraser said. "Turner has the agenda and I know for a fact he relayed the information to Jian in their meeting at the hotel yesterday. His assistant, Dunn, was there. I had an opportunity to slip a recording device inside the liner of his jacket when the three of us met the other night. So he's been listening for us. And it just so happens that Turner cleared his schedule and will be here, alongside the secretary of state. Good news for us."

"I can almost guarantee this has Yang's fingerprints all over it." Delgado tried to put his weight on his own two feet. "He doesn't want Jian to screw this up for him and because he agreed to provide additional security, the payback is that Jian has to step away from his plans, at least during the event. Afterwards is another story. Yang has far too much to lose to let Jian screw this up."

"Speaking of Yang and the Dalian Company," Ward began. "I had an opportunity to do some research on the Chinese corporation. And what I found is that they have ties to not only Lei Jian and the MSS but to those inside the Uyghur Separatist Movement."

"I'm sorry, but who are they?" Aaron asked.

"In a nutshell," Will began, "a hodge-podge of terrorist groups that have carried out numerous attacks in the Xinjiang region of China. Most of these groups want an independent state that aligns with ethnic groups in Central Asia. Which brings a whole other element to our problem. One that we cannot afford to let fester should Dalian succeed."

"I agree. It makes what we're doing all the more important," Ward replied.

"How much help are we going to get tomorrow? We need protection. Merrick and Caison most of all," Delgado asked Ward and Fraser point blank.

"Let's talk about what really needs to happen," Will began. "Yes, we need security. But I think tomorrow's our best chance at getting Jian into custody. Fraser, you have audio and have been present at meetings with Turner. We also have the Kendrick letter and pictures of the deputy secretary with Jian. Lacy, after your speech, as we discussed prior, you'll present that evidence to the secretary of state, who will be alongside the president, I assume."

"Right, but we hadn't figured out precisely how to execute that plan."

"They'll both likely be shaking hands with the victim's family members, including you. That's when you'll want to address the secretary and inform him that you have this information. You'll have to be discreet. And so will he, but I don't think that will be a problem. Any hint of an issue tomorrow will be addressed swiftly and quietly," Will replied.

"And while you're doing that, I'll have operatives in place to keep an eye on Jian. We won't let him slip out," Ward said. "Fraser, I know you'll have people here too."

"Hunter, you can offer backup for Lacy because questions will be hurled in her direction and both of us will have to be there to field them," Will said. "They'll ask about you and Axell and your involvement."

"Yeah, got it."

"What we'll all need to remember is that we will have very little time to pull this off," Delgado added.

Ward began to walk around. "Let's line out where we'll all be and time everything out. We have to be precise. The secretary and president won't stay one minute longer than their schedules allow."

"What about Director Mobley?" Lacy asked. "Do we let him in on this? He knows we're working on something. He could offer support."

"My concern with that is when this hits the fan, I don't want him to go down with the ship."

"Maybe you're right, but he better step up when this does come to an end. We're going to need his support, Will. The time for political maneuvering is over."

"I couldn't agree more. But the fewer people who know about this, the better we'll all be. The MSS could have people in places we have no idea about. Including the FBI."

———

The deputy secretary tossed back the last of his drink and set his glass on the kitchen counter of his hotel suite. "Your men couldn't find the body? So we have no idea if the man who came after you is dead or alive, or who the hell he is?"

"I can only assume he is associated with the FBI agent and the woman. I've been forced to leave my hotel and lost a man—one who didn't belong to me—and I'll have a price to pay for that alone." Jian clasped his hands behind his back and paced the room. "But I don't see that you've offered any additional help, so I feel as though I am on my own in this venture."

"You're not on your own, I assure you. Everything will work itself out tomorrow at the groundbreaking ceremony. You just need to trust me."

"Then perhaps you should seek to have me placed under your protection. How can I continue to fear for my safety in such a manner?"

"As Yang is still indebted to you and now me, he will make the necessary arrangements should he wish to continue to reap the spoils of our new arrangement."

"What is in this for you, Deputy Secretary?" Jian eyed him. "You were not part of our initial plan and, in fact, the undersecretary worked exceedingly hard at ensuring your exclusion. So why are you offering to help now? What do you stand to gain?"

"You forget that I protected you and Yang by ensuring your dirty little secret didn't reach the upper echelons of my government. That goddamn letter Kendrick wrote. If the secretary had been made aware, you would not be standing here right now and would have suffered a worse fate than the plush surroundings your government provided for the past six months."

"You have not answered my question. Apart from the fact that your political career and aspirations would certainly be slaughtered were the truth to be revealed, if our plan succeeds, as I suspect it will, what do you have to gain?"

"As you're aware, the same administration was re-elected by the American people earlier this month. And as such, my job is secure for the next four years. However, when my time comes to an end here, I do not wish to run for higher office, and would certainly not be a hold-over were a new political party to take control, so where does that leave me?" He poured himself another drink. "I'll tell you. It leaves me to garner speaking engagements, write a book, and perhaps eke out enough money to allow for a mediocre retirement. I, however, wish for more." Turner smiled. "After the attack, after Kendrick's retirement, the writing on the wall was quite clear. I purchased a large quantity of Dalian stock in the immediate aftermath before it began reaping the benefits."

"And you stand to earn a great deal of money if this remains a secret. Their stock continues to grow."

"Now you're understanding what it is that I am about, Mr. Jian." He raised his glass and downed another shot.

CHAPTER
TWENTY-EIGHT

THE TIME HAD COME and today would be a day that would define the rest of Lacy Merrick's life if she was lucky enough to survive it. She was running on pure adrenaline now. Sleep hadn't come in any form during the night and now the sun spilled over the horizon and shone through the pinholes of the worn-out curtains in the worn-out motel. Her heart and mind stayed firmly on her children. This was for them as much as it was for her. Someday, they would know what she tried to do for their father and the country. Whether she succeeded was already written in the stars, yet Lacy wasn't lucky enough to be privy to that information. None of them were and she could not know if these people who surrounded her now would do so after the day was done.

"You ready to go?" Aaron appeared from the bathroom and sat down next to Lacy. "Did you eat anything at all?" He looked at the bag that sat on the small table. "You should eat a bagel. It'll help settle your nerves."

"I had a little bit of one and some coffee." She turned to him. "Didn't help much. I still feel like I want to throw up."

"Me too." He smiled. "We'll get through this. We have help. Good people who know what they're doing."

"I know. I miss Trevor. I wish he was here. What if we can't help him?"

"Lacy, what you're about to do today will put an end to this. Axell will be exonerated." He patted her knee. "Try to eat a little more. We'll have to leave soon."

"He's right." Will pulled on his shoes. "Try to get something in your stomach. Believe me, it will help." He checked the time. "Delgado, we need to leave in ten minutes. How are you coming along?"

Agent Delgado wrapped the fresh bandage around his wound. "Fine. Just finishing patching myself up."

"Good. We need to get this show on the road." Will stood and pulled on his jacket.

Lacy plunked a few more scraps of bagel into her mouth and washed it down with coffee. "Okay. I'm ready."

Within minutes, they were on the road, heading back to the mall where Lacy lost her husband, along with so many other families who lost loved ones. And that was where it would end. One way or another, it would end today. On the drive, all Lacy could think about was not her speech, not those she knew would be in attendance, not the plan that they'd plotted out so judiciously. But it was, as always, her children. They'd be getting ready for school now and their aunt would drive them. A task that had, in the past, become banal in its meaning, but now was the only thing she wished she could do at this moment. It was what she should do as their mother. But another was caring for them—Jay's sister, who had lost her brother at that mall and had worked so hard to overcome the pain, just as his parents had.

She'd told them about the ceremony, or rather, got a message to them, but also said it would be best if they weren't there. They stopped asking questions about why a long time ago. They knew what she was trying to do, if only in abstract terms, and if they needed to stay away, then they would and she would explain in time her reason.

Lacy turned to Will, whose eyes were on the road and whose thoughts she could not presume to know. He'd turned out to be a good friend, one that Jay would've liked too. He'd completely changed the course of his career just to help her and who wouldn't admire that? However, she felt that any form of repayment would never be sufficient.

She turned to the backseat where Aaron and Agent Delgado sat, peering through their respective windows, both appearing to gather their strength to see this through. Aaron, a man who never wanted to be anything more than one who walked the line between right and wrong, but who'd most definitely teetered on the edge of wrong for the past six months, even if it was to do right in the end. A friend whom she knew had garnered some feelings for her in recent months, but could not see it in her heart to return those feelings—not now. Perhaps not ever. Her heart still belonged to her husband and it would remain that way for the foreseeable future.

Finally, she turned to Agent Delgado, a man she had written off as being on the wrong side of this battle since the day they met. But one who, in his own covert way, was on the right side after all. Still, he'd nearly lost his life yesterday and, by default, had more than proven his loyalty to the cause. He'd lost a friend and who knew what lay ahead for him when this was all over.

The only one in this team of co-conspirators she did not yet possess a level of comfort for was Station Chief Ward. Axell had trusted her, but could she have done something to prevent his detainment? Lacy couldn't be sure, but she had helped Aaron, keeping the truth of his actions from her colleagues. That had to count for something. However, her part in all this was minimal, a backup team that Lacy hoped would prevent Lei Jian from leaving the ceremony today a free man.

"Lacy?" Will turned to her. "We're here. You okay?" It seemed he noted her distant gaze.

"Yeah. Fine. I'm ready." She tugged on her jacket as if to reinforce her words.

He pulled into the parking lot where, as of now, only a few cars were parked. The ceremony wasn't to start for another hour, but they needed to be there early and ensure everyone was in place and Lacy was at the designated speaker location in plenty of time.

"Okay. Let's get this done." He stepped out of the car and helped Delgado from the backseat. "You sure you're okay to do this?"

"Don't think I'm going to let you take all the glory, Caison." Delgado smiled. "Let's find Fraser and make sure we know when Turner is here."

Aaron stepped out last and joined Lacy. A false sense of assuredness appeared on his face.

"It'll be okay. It'll be over in a matter of hours now. All we've worked toward, it's about to come to a head."

"No matter what, Lacy, I want you to know that I would and will do anything for you and the kids. Jay was my friend and I know he'd be proud of what you're doing."

"He'd be pissed is what he'd be." Lacy smiled. "But I know he'll watch out for us today." She began to walk toward the staging area and the final touches on the stage were being installed. "You see the others?" she asked Will.

"Not yet. Don't worry. They'll be here."

She continued and the stage came into full view. The American flag placed prominently as a backdrop. A podium for the guest speakers and several chairs that lined either side of the stage. Rows of guest chairs were being placed for an audience that was to include the family members only. And at the very back, a place for the media, who, in Lacy's opinion, had failed enormously to properly question the death of Undersecretary Kendrick. Perhaps none of this would have been necessary if they were not so partisan in their treatment of the administration and would have discovered the story of a lifetime right under their collective noses. Still, Lacy would give them fodder today—and a great deal of it.

"I see Fraser up ahead." Will picked up his pace and, upon reaching him, extended his hand. "Everything all set?"

"Yes. Turner will be here in about thirty minutes."

"And what about Lei Jian?" Lacy caught up to them and asked the only question that mattered in her mind.

"Dunn all but confirmed Jian's attendance as well. Seems the two had a lengthy dinner last night and Jian stayed in the deputy's suite."

"For fear I'd find him." Agent Delgado, with the help of Aaron, was the last to arrive.

"No doubt." Will turned to Lacy. "Why don't we get you to your section and let you prepare."

She turned to the others a final time before they were about to change the world. "I just want to say thank you to all of you. You've risked your lives for me, for this country, and I would not be standing here were it not for all of you. Good luck."

"Good luck to you, Merrick." Delgado made the final statement, encompassing what they were all thinking. "Godspeed."

Will placed a hand on her shoulder and smiled. "See you soon."

While the others departed, Aaron waited with her. "I don't

know what's going to happen, Lacy, but I love you. You know that, right?"

"Of course I do. I love you too." She kissed his cheek. "Now's the time for us to make Jay proud." Lacy turned and headed toward the back of the stage to prepare.

Several police officers, firefighters, and other first responders began to arrive and Lacy knew the time was drawing near. The courage it would take for her to follow through with her plan hadn't yet been fully summoned. She feared that all of these people who had risked their lives during the attack would learn a horrible truth and wondered just how much it would change things. And then the family members began to arrive. Just like her, they'd lost loved ones in the mistaken belief that they were victims of Islamic terrorism, a phrase that had been ingrained in the American psyche and, in fact, the entire world.

"Just calm down," she told herself in a whisper, but when it caught the attention of another, she grew fearful.

"It's okay. Just share your story. That's why we're all here," the woman said.

"I lost my husband."

"I lost my daughter." The woman took hold of Lacy's hand. "Just speak from your heart. It's all any of us can do."

"Thank you." Out of the corner of her eye, Lacy spotted the deputy secretary. She feared making direct eye contact because she knew the truth about him and her eyes might not keep that truth hidden.

More and more people arrived and began taking the stage, taking their seats, and the media was in full force with their microphones and cameras. But Lacy hadn't seen the secretary of state or the president yet. Not even Director Mobley, whom she knew was due to take the stage as well.

"Mrs. Merrick?" A man approached her from behind.

"Director Mobley? I—I knew you were coming; just hadn't seen you yet."

"I had some things to take care of. Are you ready?"

His tone conveyed the double meaning hidden in his words. While he wasn't made fully aware of the plan, she knew Will had kept SSA Kelly informed and that he had passed along certain information. But she couldn't confide in him. He wasn't a part of this yet and she would do her best to keep him out of the loop. Because what she was about to do would cast eyes in his direction too. And she hoped he would not be made a scapegoat in all this. But then, that would be up to her to make completely clear. Those who had a hand in this would pay—and pay dearly.

The music began and a choir began to sing. The lump in her throat was far too big to swallow down now and her hands trembled. She was glad to have eaten something and was grateful Aaron had insisted upon it.

First up was the president and it was the first time Lacy had ever seen him up close. She wondered what he'd known—if anything—about the people in his charge. Had he known what they'd done to the country? The enormous deception? She couldn't know for sure but didn't think he did. However in the press conference, when she thought all of this was going to come to light, he said nothing and in fact offered a vague apology. But that was her grief talking. Perhaps he knew nothing and she wouldn't condemn him without cause.

She stood near the left of the stage and eyed Director Mobley. He must've felt her stare because he turned to her and nodded as though he was giving his permission. Lacy closed her eyes and inhaled a calming breath. Never before could she recall being so nervous. Her heart pounded in her chest and if it weren't so cold, her brow would be drenched in sweat.

Several minutes passed while she watched the families in the audience wiping their tears as others spoke. She, too, would have been overcome with emotions if left unchecked, but she couldn't—not now. Not when she needed every ounce of strength she could muster to get through this. More than once in the past few minutes did the idea cross her mind to scrap the whole thing.

As she peered again at the families, she searched for Lei Jian. Had he been there? If so, where? In the far distance was Elizabeth Ward and this offered some comfort.

"Mrs. Merrick?" One of the organizers approached. "It's time. Please, follow me." The man led the way toward the stage and began to ascend the first of three steps.

Lacy halted.

"Ma'am?" He offered his hand. "It's okay." He helped her onto the steps, then onto the stage. "Director Mobley will introduce you."

Lacy was shown to the podium and stood to the left of Mobley while he spoke of Lacy as "one of their own" and how she'd been instrumental in the investigation, fighting through her grief and pain; and that she was a woman to be admired. But that wasn't how she felt at this moment.

All eyes fell upon her and they wanted to hear her speak. They wanted to be inspired by her story; her courage. But that was not what she was here to do. In fact, the real reason she was here was to stand at this podium and do what she should have done months ago. She would not wait to see the secretary and reveal her knowledge. She would not wait to speak to the president to tell him the horrific tale. Instead, she would take the truth to the people. Unfiltered, unedited. The truth as she knew it.

"Mrs. Lacy Merrick." Mobley stepped aside and placed his hand on her back.

Lacy approached the podium and smiled at him before lowering the microphone. "Thank you, Director Mobley. It has been my honor to serve under your guidance and the rest of the Bureau for these past several years." She peered out into the crowd and spotted Will and Aaron. Both stood near the back but smiled when they caught her eye. Lacy drew another breath and continued. "I lost my husband, Jay Merrick and, like many of you, wondered how such a thing could've happened so close to home. I felt especially responsible because it was my job to know. My job to listen and be wary of information that crossed my computer screen on a daily basis. I am but one of so many who felt the same. With each occurrence, each attack, we felt responsible. Only this time, this one, it cost my husband his life." Lacy looked again at the families.

"And I went back to work and I did what I knew I did best. I listened. I learned. And I discovered, with the help of extremely bright and talented people on my side. Inside the Bureau and out. I learned—we learned the truth." Her eyes again landed on her friends, whose faces already appeared uncertain.

Aaron turned to Will. "This wasn't what she had written down."

Will eyed the station chief, whose team was closely monitoring Lei Jian. She returned a confused look.

"I learned that more than one group of people seek to change our way of life. Who seek to take from us the rewards of our hard work, our savings, our lifestyles, everything we have. They, too, are terrorists. But of a different nature." She began to notice the uncomfortable shift of Deputy Turner in his seat as he beamed his gaze to her. In the audience, murmurs began. The media began to snap pictures of her. Ward's team shifted into place around Lei Jian. She must've sensed what Lacy was about to say.

"However, they have one advantage over those whom we call Radical Islamic Terrorists. While they seek to destroy our nation from the outside, this new enemy seeks to destroy it from within. An enemy we see in our daily lives, in the faces of those whom we elect to protect us from these atrocities. Not all. But some who hold the highest power." Lacy looked at Deputy Turner.

The president had already been escorted off the stage by Secret Service, but not Turner and not the secretary of state. Not yet. Lacy knew she had but only a few sentences left before they would accost her. The truth had to come out and it had to be now.

"To the families of the victims and survivors of this horrific attack, you should know that people in our government knew of this attack. They knew it was coming and chose to keep their mouths shut for their own political gains. Isn't that right, Deputy Secretary?"

The crowds began to turn. The media was pressing their way forward and Lei Jian tried to make a run for it. But Ward's people held firm. Will and Aaron and even Agent Delgado had nothing short of shocked expressions. Will began to shake his head at her, but she would not be silenced. Not anymore.

"The deputy secretary would have you believe that this was all the work of an Islamic attack. But no. Far from it. His undersecretary took part in a plan with the Chinese government to pull off the attack and lay blame elsewhere. And they did. I have proof of this involvement." Her voice began to rise in response to the growing dissonance. "I have proof that the Chinese government planned the attack and that that man," she pointed to Jian, "was the mastermind behind it. He wanted to ensure China could continue to acquire American companies, own their employees, and control our economy. They are responsible for your loved ones' deaths. And for my husband's."

The Secret Service overtook the stage and ripped Lacy from the podium, carrying her down the steps and around the rear to the line of black SUVs.

"Wait! You have to stop Turner and Jian! You have to get them!" she began to yell.

None of her team could be seen from back there. She was on her own and had no idea if they'd secured Jian. But she'd done it. She'd spoken the truth. But she wondered as she stood, arms clasped on both sides by secret service, would anyone believe her?

CHAPTER
TWENTY-NINE

PEOPLE HAD BEGUN to swarm the SUV where Lacy waited to be whisked away to someplace she had no idea where. But it was done. She was free of the horrendous truth she'd been keeping and now all hell had broken free.

"Please, I need to get my kids. Can you please send someone to get them?" she begged the driver, who appeared to wait for instruction.

"You're going to have to sit tight, ma'am. You just kicked one hell of a big hornet's nest."

Lacy had no idea what had happened to Will or Aaron or if they managed to keep Jian in place. The entire world had just been turned upside down and she needed answers. "Please! Tell me what's going on!"

The driver didn't respond until his radio sounded with a voice on the other end. "Ten-four. We're on our way." He keyed the ignition and revved the engine to try to disperse the crowd.

Other Secret Service agents were attempting to control them until the police took over and began to pull everyone back.

The SUV started forward slowly. Lacy didn't think they could see her inside, which was a good thing. Most appeared angry, wanting answers. And that was entirely her doing. But would they get answers from this president who'd won re-election and had nothing to fear, unless he had been involved? This was still something to which Lacy had no real idea but hoped her faith in the office of president hadn't been shaken.

As she looked behind her, Lacy spotted the other SUVs following, but still no sign of her team. "Please, can you just tell me if they captured Lei Jian?"

"Not only do I not know who that is, ma'am, I couldn't tell you even if I knew. Now just sit tight and we'll be there soon."

"Can you at least tell me where we're going?"

He peered at her through the rear-view mirror with a look that expressed a resounding "no."

––––––––

Will pulled Aaron through the crowd, attempting to find Delgado and the others. The police were dispersing people all around them, and the media kept shouting out for answers that would not come.

"What the fuck just happened?" Delgado hobbled toward Will. "I've been looking for you two."

"Where's Ward?" Will asked him.

"I don't know. Can't find her."

"Please tell me her people got Jian?" Aaron asked.

"Man, I have no idea what's happened to anyone. I don't know shit right now, same as you. This is crazy. Where the hell is Lacy?"

"I don't know. Secret Service took her away. We have to get to her." Will stopped. "Wait, what about Mobley? He's got to know something. If we find him, we'll find Lacy."

"Good luck, man. He's gone along with the rest of the VIPs.

Hold up, I see Ward. Over here." Delgado headed toward her. "Please tell me you got Jian."

"We had him. They took him away."

"They?" Will caught up with Aaron still in tow.

"Secret Service. They rounded up everyone right after they took Lacy away. What the hell happened? We had a plan. You guys know she was going to do this?"

"No." Will looked at Aaron.

"Don't look at me. I had no idea. But I sure as hell don't blame her."

"Maybe not, but that wasn't the goddam plan," Delgado started. "If she was going to pull this shit, she should've told us."

"Why? So you could try and talk her out of it?" Aaron asked. "She did what was right and what we should've done months ago."

"Doesn't matter now. What's done is done. We need to find Lacy." Will retrieved his cell and pressed a button. "Director Mobley. I'm so glad you answered." He looked to his team while they waited for news. "No, sir. I didn't know, but can you tell me, sir? Where are they taking her?" He looked to Aaron this time, who appeared afraid for Lacy. "Thank you, sir. We'll be there as soon as we can get out of here. Goodbye, sir." He dropped the phone back into his pocket. "Mobley says they're taking her to Headquarters."

"Did he say if they had Jian?" Elizabeth asked.

"I'm sorry. I should've asked. He wasn't supposed to answer his line and just asked about Lacy. He did say to get to Headquarters now. You should come too. We need your help to get Axell released."

———

While she wasn't in handcuffs, Lacy felt very much the prisoner as she sat in the conference room in the high-security wing of FBI Headquarters. But she wasn't alone. Two field agents flanked her. She didn't know them and it seemed they weren't up for chatting, so she remained silent.

It was the arrival of Director Mobley that brought some relief and animation to the two agents.

"Give us the room?" Mobley asked.

The agents left them alone and the director sat down. "Well, I knew you all were planning on something. Didn't think it was going to be this."

"Sir, Agent Caison and the others—they had no idea what I was going to say. They were just there to make sure we captured Lei Jian."

"We did, by the way," Mobley began. "Capture Jian? Secret Service has him and will turn him over to us for questioning soon." He held her gaze. "I know why you did what you did. I can sympathize because it's something I would've done if I were in your position."

"With respect, sir, you *were* in my position."

"Maybe so. But it's much more complicated than you think, Lacy. This whole thing is a great big Charlie Foxtrot."

While this was no laughing matter, Mobley's use of the very term she and Jay employed around the kids made her smile. "I couldn't agree more. So what happens now? Am I going to jail?"

"Jail? No. I assume the deputy secretary is, but then again, that depends on what you can provide. You said you had proof. And I'm hoping it's the kind of proof that will end this once and for all."

"We gave you proof before, Director, and it still wasn't enough. Why would it be now?"

"Because you made your case in front of God and the rest of the world. In front of the victims' families. In front of the press.

You got the president's attention. Now you just need to come through with something we can use."

"And it's not an election year."

Mobley nodded.

"Before I say anything more, I need to know my children are safe. If Jian makes contact with any of his people, he'll find them and go after them."

"He won't. He can't and we're informing the current ambassador now, along with the Chinese president. There's no telling if the premier is involved. That'll be up to their president to decipher. But that doesn't mean we can't get your children and ensure their safety."

"Thank you, sir. They're staying with my sister-in-law in Long Island. If I can just see them."

"You give me the contact information and I'll send a helicopter. But right now, I need you to tell me what proof you have of Turner's participation with Lei Jian."

"First of all, I'm confident he ordered the murder of the CIA officer, Camden Meeks, and pointed the finger at Agent Trevor Axell. Agent Axell was helping us."

"And you have proof?"

"Of that? Not entirely, but I know all you have to do is search his phone records and talk to his assistant, Bryce Dunn."

"Let's talk about what proof you do have, then."

"Several days ago, Turner discovered a letter written by Kendrick in which he confessed to his cover-up of the attack and his entanglements with Lei Jian. Apparently, it was Kendrick's form of insurance in the event of his death, the letter would come to light, and it did. Turner was attempting to keep that quiet in order to, I assume, keep his position. But it was at that point, I believe, that Turner got involved, at least, more directly involved.

"We also have evidence that he expedited a visa for one of Lei

Jian's people, a man by the name of Ahsan Sajwani. While I can't be sure, I believe it was payment for his appointment to the position some months prior to the attack. So, we can't be one hundred percent sure that was Turner's only involvement or who he was doing the favor for.

"Through a coordinated effort, Agent Fraser, with the WFO, gathered proof that Turner was working with Jian to take out me, Agent Caison, and pretty much everyone I know. There's a lot more here, sir, but I realize this is a lot to take in. The scope of this was much larger than any one of us believed."

The door opened and the president entered. Mobley immediately stood. "Mr. President."

"Director Mobley. You've had a word with Mrs. Merrick?"

"Yes, sir."

"And is what she said at the ceremony true?"

"I believe so, sir—yes. Although this will require opening a formal investigation."

"I'm sure. Then we need to do everything in our power to make sure this brave young woman is safe."

"And my children, sir—Mr. President."

"And her children."

"Mrs. Merrick was also working with a few others. They're on their way down here now."

"Good. I think it's time I understood what it was my State Department was involved in." He turned to Lacy. "Mrs. Merrick, based on what you know now, do you believe the secretary is also involved? I have intentionally kept him away at this time until you can tell me more."

"I—I don't believe so, sir. But I can't rule it out. That's why I think it would be a good idea to order a full-scale investigation into the entire State Department."

"Oh, you do, do you?"

"Yes, sir."

The president turned to Mobley. "Perhaps we ought to look into Mrs. Merrick's request, but in the meantime, I'd like to be briefed on the situation. So when her colleagues arrive, we should sit down and figure out what the hell happened today."

"Yes, sir. Once all the parties arrive, I'll arrange a briefing with the chief of staff."

"That won't be necessary. Arrange it with me directly." The president began to leave but stopped and turned to Lacy again. "Mrs. Merrick, while I hope what you've said is true, and especially for your sake; in my heart, I pray that it isn't."

———

Elizabeth Ward stood in the hall and was speaking to Director Mobley when Will and Aaron arrived, under the guard of other agents.

"Secret Service still has Lei Jian in custody. He was carrying a weapon," Ward began.

"How long do you think they can keep him?" Mobley asked.

"A few hours—at best—until we can get direction from the president. The Chinese ambassador will order his return. He didn't exactly do anything wrong this time except enter the US when he was not legally allowed to do so."

Mobley spotted Will approaching. "Agent Caison, you finally decided to join the party."

"I apologize, sir; we were held for questioning by the Secret Service until just minutes ago. Where is Lacy Merrick?"

Mobley tossed his head in the direction of the conference room. "In there. We should go in and try to figure out what the hell is going on. I have to brief the president as soon as possible."

They entered the room where Lacy still sat alone. "Oh thank

God. You're okay." She smiled at the sight of her closest friends. "Where's Agent Delgado?"

"Meeting with CIA Director Handley. He's making the case for Axell's release based on what he and Ward knew."

Lacy looked to Director Mobley. "What happens now?"

"Now you tell me what it was you and Agent Caison were doing this morning."

"Look, I know you had an agreement with Agent Caison, and I just want you to know that he had no knowledge of what I was planning. As far as he knew, the arrangement was for me to hand the information we received on Deputy Turner over to the secretary and the president. It would then be up to them to handle it. But the problem I had with that was that I feared the same thing would happen as before." She looked to Caison and then to Mobley again. "I couldn't chance it being buried again. I just couldn't. Not after we lost another friend and Axell was put in holding. I wasn't going to let him take the fall for helping me."

Mobley looked at Will. "Is this true? You had no knowledge of what Mrs. Merrick had planned?"

"It is true, but I stand by her decision. When we first came to you, Director, we thought it would be over. That justice would be served. Instead, it was covered up."

"I understand that was a blow, but I thought we were working together toward a solution, one that would work within the system."

"I tried to work within the system," Lacy interrupted. "And it seemed the deeper we got, the more corrupt it became, and soon I realized there would be no easy solution after Agent Colburn was murdered. That was the beginning of the end."

"Still, one of you should've come to me. I could've offered more protection, more resources," Mobley continued. "I should've been in the loop on this once you changed directions."

"I didn't want to risk your further involvement, sir," Lacy said. "Not until I had what I needed and now I do. And the world knows it." She pulled the flash drive from her coat pocket and slid it across the table. "You'll find on here a letter from Undersecretary Kendrick. He confessed to his participation in covering up the mall attack and who was ultimately responsible for it. It was discovered on a computer in his office by a member of Turner's staff. It was a file that had been deleted, but of course, they never really are deleted. I believe he knew it would be discovered and there would be little anyone could do to stop the truth from being exposed after that."

"And you can prove this came from Kendrick himself?" Mobley asked.

"When Turner's assistant discovered it and brought it to Turner's attention, that's when I believe, he decided his only solution was to work with Jian to end any further inquiry. It was only a matter of time before the WFO would've gotten hold of it." Lacy turned to Will. "We also have photos of Turner with Jian at his hotel yesterday. And there's one other thing, sir. We're confident that the Dalian Company and its CEO, Shen Yang, were responsible for the murder of Agent Colburn and for the attack at the restaurant that almost killed Agent Caison and me. But Agent Delgado knows more about them than I do."

Mobley sighed and took to his feet. "You've given me a lot to chew on, Mrs. Merrick. I'll take this to the president. In the meantime, you'll have to stay here, and so will Agent Caison and Mr. Hunter."

"What about my children? Please, can you bring them home?"

Mobley nodded and left the conference room.

"Why didn't you tell us?" Aaron began. "Did you think we wouldn't be behind you on it? I thought we were all in this together."

"I thought you'd try to get me to change my mind. Convince me that the way we had it planned was the best for all involved." She looked at both of them. "I'm sorry. When I looked out into the faces of the families, I just couldn't lie to them. They'd been lied to for long enough." She turned to Will. "What do you think the president will do?"

"Everything will change now, Lacy. Nothing will be the same. I wish I could tell you what the president will do. I just don't know. I don't know what's going to happen to any of us."

———

The cameras were fixed on the president as he sat at his desk in the Oval Office, preparing to speak to the American people. The cameraman began his countdown and soon held up three fingers, then two, then one, and the president began.

"Good evening. The events of the past twenty-four hours have opened my eyes to the corruption inside my own administration. And not only that, but they have opened my eyes to the bravery of certain individuals who risked everything to expose that corruption. As you know, evidence has been presented that concludes the attack on the Fairfax mall was planned and carried out by parties associated with the Chinese government. I am not here to condemn that government, but only those who sought to harm the American people. However, as a result, until those people are dealt with, economic sanctions will be put into place and from this point forward, all companies with majority ownership in the Asia-Pacific region are barred from conducting business with the United States. The fallout for the American worker will be substantial, but this is a necessary step to show our resolve for the atrocities committed on *our* soil, against *our* people."

Lacy sat on the edge of her sofa, watching the broadcast, waiting for the shoe to drop, for yet another politician to cover something up, but so far, that was not what was happening.

"I think you did it, Lacy," Aaron began. "You made this happen and the entire world is sitting up and taking notice."

"We did this. All of us." She looked to Will, who was sitting on the side chair. "You all risked your lives and we brought the truth to the people. But what will happen in the fallout? What if I destroyed everything?"

"Sometimes you have to tear something down in order to rebuild it and make it stronger," Will began. "No matter what happens now, Lacy, things will be different and it will be hard, but I believe this was what had to happen. No matter how hard I tried to work within the system."

A knock sounded on her door. Lacy made her way to open it and peered through the security lens, smiling while tears immediately streamed down her cheeks. Upon opening the door, there stood her children. "Oh my God! My babies." She opened her arms.

Jackson lunged toward her, falling into her arms while Olivia hung back, still hesitant. "Mommy! I missed you so much! Are we home for good now? I don't have to go away anymore?"

"No, baby, you don't have to go away ever again." She held him tightly and turned her sights to Olivia.

"They said you did a brave thing."

Lacy pulled back from the embrace and held Olivia's gaze. "I did what I thought was right, what I thought your daddy would've wanted me to do."

Olivia began to tear up. "I'm sorry, Mommy." She fell into Lacy's arms and the two held one another closely.

Will and Aaron entered the foyer and spotted Delgado standing with Lacy's children. Behind him, another approached.

Lacy finally stood. "Agent Delgado, thank you for bringing them home." She spotted the woman in the distance and began to cry once again. "Celeste." She pulled her close. The woman who had helped her so much through all of this. "Thank you for coming home. Thank you."

"That's what this place is. It's my home and I'm so very glad to be back." She pushed Lacy gently away. "Is it finally over?"

"Yes. It's over."

Lacy turned back to Delgado. "What about Agent Axell? Any news on his release?" But before he could answer, she saw him. "Trevor!"

"Boy, I can't get a word in edgewise over here." Delgado stepped aside yet again for Axell.

"Lacy." He pulled her close and hugged her almost as tightly as she had her children. "You did it."

She began shaking her head. "We did it. You risked everything for the truth and you lost a friend."

"Can I go see my room? I want to see my room!" Jackson began charging up the stairs.

"I'm going to see my room too!" Olivia followed him.

"I'll visit with them while you all figure this out." Celeste headed toward the steps. "I missed them so much."

"The president's speaking now," Lacy said.

"I heard. He's not going to say anything we don't already know," Delgado replied. "They took Turner into custody and Lei Jian is on a transport back to Beijing. But this time, they won't be releasing him. In fact, if he survives the night, I'd be surprised."

"What's going to happen to Turner?" Aaron asked.

"Federal prison. I don't know how long. And so will his assistant, Dunn. Kid should've got out while he stood a chance."

And what will happen when they do rid themselves of Jian?" she pressed on.

"The Chinese premier will want their president to see that they understand the severity of the charge and will want to have the sanctions lifted as quickly as possible."

"But how can we let them back in?" Lacy continued. "They tried to undermine our entire economic system. Surely they'll pay for what they did."

"Money's money, Lacy," Will began. "It'll only be a matter of time before they're allowed to trade with us again."

"Listen, I'd love to hang around, but I've got to go clean out my office," Delgado began. "No more FBI for me. Heading back to Langley for a new assignment."

"Thank you, Agent Delgado—Martin, for everything. I know we started on a rocky path, but I also know what you've done for me," Lacy said.

He smiled and tipped his head. "I hope to have the pleasure of working with you all again in the future, but if I don't, you take care of yourselves, and Axell, better watch yourself at the office. I owe you a hard left hook."

"Any time—after I've had a few drinks. Take care, Delgado," Axell replied. "What else is the president saying?" He started into the living room.

"Looks like he's finished. I'm sure it won't be the last time he'll have to account for his people. I wonder if the country will forgive him," Will replied.

"So I guess we're back where we started," Axell sat down. "Caison, will you be returning to Louisville?"

Will turned his attention to Lacy and back to Axell. "I don't think so. There's a lot of work to be done here and Kelly has asked me to stay on. And, you know, I've moved all my stuff here now, so there's that."

"And what about you, Hunter?" Axell continued. "What are your plans?"

"Well, I guess I'm not returning to Langley, which I'm kind of happy about. I mean, I'm not cut out for all that espionage stuff. I'll probably just go back to consulting for mom-and-pop companies. Help them fight the war on cyber security."

"Well, there is a reason why I came here today, apart from giving thanks to Lacy for making sure they got me released. I owe you a lot, Lacy."

She didn't know what to say because he'd given up so much to help her too.

"So, I guess I'll just say it." He looked at the three of them. "A new joint task force is being formed at the president's request. And he's asked that I head it up. Director Mobley will be a part of it as well."

"What's it for?" Lacy said.

"It'll involve coordination between the FBI and the CIA and will involve monitoring foreign companies' activities in the US and abroad, on a more specialized level. More scrutiny than before. After what happened, the president believes we need to get a better handle on the new war."

"A new war?" Aaron asked.

"The economic war. One that will use, as we've already seen, all available tactics necessary to achieve global trade dominance."

Lacy began to see where Axell was headed. "And who else will be on this new task force?"

"All of you in this room. We all have a special skill set that will be useful. And, we've proven we can work together effectively."

Lacy glanced up the stairs and began to think of her children. "I won't put my children in harm's way again, Trevor. I can't do that to them."

"I'm not asking you to. No one is. We'll operate under

complete anonymity. Publicly our jobs won't have changed. Privately we'll report directly to Mobley and CIA Director Handley. They'll both, in turn, brief the president on any and all activity we deem to be a concern."

She looked at her friends surrounding her now. "I'm in if you all are."

"I'm in," Aaron replied.

"Me too." Will placed his hand on Lacy's shoulder.

"Good. Then we'll start as soon as possible." His cell phone buzzed with an incoming message. Axell retrieved it and read the message before returning his attention to the newly formed task force. "Jian's just been executed by his government."

"Oh my God," Lacy began. "It's finally over."

"Except for one thing," Axell said. "Our first target is the Dalian Company. Based on what we know right now, Shen Yang has covered his ass pretty well. It'll be tough to get proof of his cooperation with Jian and Turner. And, to top it all off, they just sold a majority share to a stockholder here in the US to avoid the sanctions."

"Why am I not surprised? The Dalian Company. Where it all began," Lacy said. "Good."

THE END

ABOUT THE AUTHOR

Robin Mahle has published more than 40 crime fiction novels, many of which topped the Amazon charts in the US, Canada, and the UK. Most recently, she has delved into the world of psychological thrillers published by Joffe Books.

Also a screenwriter, she has adapted some of her works into teleplays, which have gone on to place in film festivals nationwide.

From detectives to federal agents, and from killers to corruption, her page-turning tales grab hold and refuse to let go. Throw in tense action and thrilling twists, and it becomes clear why her readers come back for more. Robin lives in Coastal Virginia with her husband and two children.

ALSO BY ROBIN MAHLE

www.ingramcontent.com/pod-product-compliance
Lightning Source LLC
Chambersburg PA
CBHW061944170626
46813CB00006B/2531